Confess

Poppy Dolan lives in Berkshire with her husband, where she is a keen baker and crafter as well as a prolific author of many laugh-out-loud romantic comedies, including the bestselling *The Bad Boyfriends Bootcamp*.

You can get in touch with Poppy on Twitter @poppydwriter and on Facebook at PoppyDolanBooks. She doesn't bite. Unless you are a dark chocolate digestive.

Also by Poppy Dolan

There's More To Life Than Cupcakes
The Bad Boyfriends Bootcamp
The Bluebell Bunting Society
The Woolly Hat Knitting Club
Confessions of a First-Time Mum

Confessions OF A First-Time Mum

POPPY DOLAN

CANELO

First published in the United Kingdom in 2023 by Canelo

This edition published in the United Kingdom in 2018 by

Canelo
Unit 9, 5th Floor
Cargo Works, 1-2 Hatfields
London SE1 9PG
United Kingdom

A CIP catalogue record for this book is available from the British Library.

Print ISBN 978 1 80436 453 6
Ebook ISBN 978 1 78863 054 2

Cover design by Emily Courdelle

Look for more great books at www.canelo.co

Printed and bound in Great Britain by Clays Ltd, Elcograf S.p.A.

1

For Chicken and Tiny.

In years to come, you might think it's unfair that I've used so much of your experiences as babies for the inspiration to this book.

But in the years to come beyond that, when you might just become parents yourself, you'll totally see that I deserved some payback. Some serious payback.

I love you both, and it's been the best joy of my life to have you.

Confessions of a First-Time Mum

Blog post 2.13am 12/02/2018

I hate Humpty Dumpty.

There, I said it. Hate the guy. Glad he fell. He had it coming, sitting up high on a brick wall when his innards are only protected by a thin shell. Idiot.

And what a waste of resources – all those hours of valuable time for the king's horses and the king's men, trying to reassemble his broken bits of shell and sticky egg gloop. They could have been rounding up high-waymen or eating apples. They probably didn't even get overtime FFS.

And what about Humpty's poor parents? Did he think about them when he was doing his risky parkour nonsense? Imagine their trembling, pale eggy faces as they get that call: 'Your son is gone. He fell off a wall. We tried everything we could… He was just sitting up there, apparently. Who knows why.'

Or maybe this burning, raging hatred I feel comes from the fact that I have sung this rhyme for the eleventy-millionth time to-night and I. Just. Can't. Take. It. Any. More.

It's the only thing that soothes Big Baby in the middle of one of her screech sessions.

Humpty Dumpty, sung on a whispery loop right into her tiny ear, until she finally runs out of steam and falls asleep, her eyes puffy from an hour of screaming, her adorable snuffles a small repayment for all the jiggling and rocking and singing and pleading and bargaining and weeping I've done to get her there. And before you say, 'Download it on your phone and just set the song to repeat, idiot!' please know that this idiot has tried that shortcut and all I got was an infant looking at me with red-faced fury, as if she'd bought VIP tickets for Streisand and I was fobbing her off with a Britney bootleg CD. It has to be me, it has to be live, it has to be just loud enough to be heard but not too loud or she starts wriggling and crying and raging again. I've said before that she's not an easy baby, right?!

Other Half suggested I record myself singing and he could play it, take over a few of the ear-splitting duties maybe, but she wasn't falling for that, either. Big Baby's Mum Only Please policy is round the clock: it applies to who feeds her porridge, who changes her nappy, who pulls her clothes on, and off again, who does her bath and who does the 11pm, the 2am and the 4.30am sing and jiggle and sing and jiggle. And it's me, just me. So here we are.

And here I am, baby finally conked out in my arms, her face as round and red as a bowl of jam, a cuddly dead weight in my arms as

I sit up against the unfriendly wooden head-board of the bed. The totally angelic look on her face as she slumbers almost – almost – blocks out the memory of the wrangling to get her to sleep. This face may terrorise me when it's in full scream but it's also the face I love the MOST in the world. I could drink it in all night. Even if the weight of her head is starting to cut off circulation to my arms.

Luckily my phone was in grabbing distance, so you're now treated to this angsty, hormonal, bad-tempered, sleep-deprived post that I've tapped out with one thumb. You're welcome.

You're most likely yelling, 'Sleep when the baby sleeps!' I know you are. And you're right. But knowing I'll probably be up again in two hours or so and that trying to slide her into her cot without waking her is a Rubik's Cube of a puzzle my knackered brain can't handle, I'm choosing to blog instead. To speak to you. Because you understand, right? You get it. That's why you're awake at whatever ungodly hour you're reading this. Because you've already read everything else on the internet. Because you haven't slept for more than three hours straight since you became a parent.

Good night or, if you're like me, good sitting-up-nap.

First-Time Mum x

Chapter 1

Undressing in public.

At 9.15 on a Wednesday morning.

I'll be honest, it's not exactly what I had in mind when I pictured my maternity leave.

But at least the leggings hitting the floor this morning are Cherry's and not mine. At six and a quarter months, she doesn't really have a problem with being naked in a room full of strangers; in fact, by the way her legs are bicycling in the air I'd say she's getting quite the kick out of it today. And if she's gurgling and gurning, rather than puce-red and screaming at the top of her lungs, then who cares how it happened. Let's just drink it in. Because this girl is LOUD when she wants to be.

That's another thing I never imagined about being at home with a new baby: having to sprint out of coffee shops and sensory classes and the library (God, especially the library) because your bundle of joy sounds more like a bundle of cats screaming into a megaphone. In our first few months together I didn't make it through one class or one coffee morning without having to give in to the white-hot, clammy shame and running home. There are only so many winces and grimaces and even tuts from fellow mums you can take before you break and take shelter on the sofa with *Homes Under the Hammer*. She'd still yell at home, of course, but at least I was the only one there to see it. But that feeling of shame always lingered, even after half a packet of chocolate digestives. So it's just easier for everyone if we leave the baby classes and the library well alone.

The baby weigh-ins at the local community hall are the one space that I don't feel embarrassed to the point of spontaneous combustion. Run by a team of veteran health visitors, they quickly reassured me on my first visit that they'd seen it all, not to worry, and have a Penguin biscuit and a cup of tea. I actually wept with relief over that first Penguin. And something about these smiling ladies and their collective smell of lemon hand-sanitizer seems to chill Cherry out too. As a result, I've been back every week since, rain or shine, scream or gurgle. It's our one regular outing.

I had this fuzzy, Insta-filtered film of maternity leave that used to play on a loop while I was pregnant: I'd make a whole tribe of mum mates and we'd swap sweet potato purée recipes while sipping cappuccinos in a stylish little cafe with mismatched cushions. These days the closest I get to that is scalding myself on a McDonalds hot chocolate when I've run out of options to get Cherry to nap and I've chauffeured her around town in the car, taking refuge in a drive-thru when she finally drops off. The thirty minutes of precious nap time that follow I usually spend on Twitter or Instagram, feeling even more rubbish about all the bright and breezy things I'm not doing as a mum.

But the weigh-ins I can manage. The weigh-ins I have nailed by now, mostly because I know no one will judge me for a weepy outburst (mine or Cherry's) and it's only a ten-minute walk home should a nuclear meltdown occur (usually Cherry's, but I can't pretend I've not lost it many times in the last few months). It goes like this: you wheel in your buggy and take a ticket from the raffle book by the door, leaving your baby's red medical book in the tray. You then plonk yourself down on a plastic seat and wait your turn. In this waiting moment, I try and catch the eye of any other mums in the room. Not easy when I'm usually the very first in and all the other mums are there with newborns and are squinty and half-asleep due to extreme sleep deprivation. Don't get me wrong, Cherry's no sleeping angel but, six months in, I've just gradually accepted that I will never sleep for more than four hours together ever again. Those newborn mums haven't had that sad realisation yet. They're still in the shock and grief stage of mourning their old sleep patterns. And lie-ins. Oh, sweet Jesus, lie-ins…

The few times I have caught the eye of a mum or two, I've totally blown it. Simple questions like, 'Gorgeous baby! What's her name?' Or, 'Oh, she loves her Sophie giraffe, doesn't she? So cute' leave me spluttering and stumbling over my words, like a teenage boy from a single-sex school when faced with a hundred real girls. I usually go red, mumble something lame into my change bag and dash up to the front when my number is called. Another potential mum mate slips through the net, all because I've forgotten how to talk to humans. I'll go home and role-play it over the washing-up: 'Thanks!' I coo brightly, to the Brillo pad, 'her name is Cherry, after my gran. Her name was Cheryl but everyone called her Cherry. And, 'She really does! She's chewed off most of the pattern!' Cue tinkling laugh. 'Did you know they've sold fifty million Sophies worldwide? Amazing!' But somehow I can only talk this easily over crusty lasagne dishes. Not great for anyone, but especially awful when you consider

I was a brilliant PR executive before I went on leave. But that feels like a million years ago now. That feels like another person altogether. Something about those early weeks with Cherry, where she cried and cried and I cried and cried and Ted just stared at us both, open-mouthed in panic, have stripped away who I was, how I used to feel, and now I'm this incoherent blob left behind. I used to be the absolute queen of small-talk. Now I just feel small, full stop.

Now I'm brilliant at nappy changes, bouncing an angry baby to sleep on my gym ball and whipping Cherry's clothes off in under three minutes so she can be weighed before the cold air on her nethers starts a huge wee all over the table. It's happened. It's happened a fair few times.

This is my life now.

I keep one hand on Cherry's portly tum as I crouch down and fish her leggings off the floor.

'That's it!' the West Indian health visitor sitting in front of me beams in approval. 'Keep baby nice and safe. We never know when they might choose to roll over for the first time!'

The glow of a job well done, even one this tiny, spreads through me as I unpop her vest, wriggle it up over her head and then unfasten her nappy.

'We're ready for you!' the Scottish health visitor with the all-white bobbed hair beckons me over. I really should have thought to ask their names when I first started coming religiously – yet another social skill that's deserted me – and now it's far too late. So in my head they get tagged by accent or hair colour. Not really fitting for the people who've kept me sane, but it's the best I can do.

She presses a few buttons on the electronic scales and I gently lower Cherry in.

'Lovely, lovely.' Her Scottish burr is always reassuring, and Cherry swings her fists about in her general direction, which is one of her signs of affection. The health visitor notes down a number in our red book, closes it and hands it back. 'All spot on, right on track. A good weight.' The ember of the approval buzz comes back to life in me again. 'Anything you want to talk about, any worries?'

'Well, actually I was think—'

'Be quiet! Be quiet!' A shrill voice fills the room.

'Nice girls! Nice girls!' Now the same voice is echoing back, overlapping itself, bouncing from wall to wall. I scoop a naked Cherry up into my arms on instinct.

Through the open door of the room I'm in, I see two toddlers, each with a cap of thick black curls, bound into the waiting area. They continue their loud yabbering as they run up and down the rows of chairs, bumping into the knees of the few other mothers there and shoving a buggy out of their path. A tall, olive-skinned man with matching dark hair leaps into the room seconds later.

'Esme, Olive!' he hisses through clamped teeth, 'be quiet, please! Nice girl behaviour for Dad, please!' Even with his face pulled into stress wrinkles he is gorgeous – like, David Gandy gorgeous. Like, *whoah*. Cheek bones you could hurt yourself on.

Old hormones I'd forgotten about suddenly sit up and beg. *Woof*, very *woof*.

A warmth spreads around my ribcage, maybe embarrassment for having such impure thoughts in front of infants. But then the warmth splashes the tops of my trainers.

'Oh, Cherry!' The wet patch on my T-shirt is growing, making my baggy white tee suddenly very clingy and see-through. I plonk her back on the changing mat and scramble on a new nappy and her clothes. Of course I have two sets of spare clothes in my bag for her, but none for me. Of course! My cheeks burn with shame. What did I think would happen if I held a naked baby on my hip?! And it would have to happen in front of Britain's Next Top Dad. He's still chasing his girls at breakneck speed around the room, so with a bit of luck he won't see – or smell – what's going on over here.

I grimace at the health visitors in apology and wheel us quickly out of the room and towards the bathrooms, where I can be safely alone with my mortification.

–

After five minutes of redressing Cherry while I shiver in my wet T-shirt, ten minutes of blotting at it with rough paper towels, another ten of crouching under the hand dryer while Cherry screamed her head off (she's not keen on the noise) and five minutes of looking in the mirror muttering, 'Idiot, idiot, idiot,' to myself, I finally realised I could just take off my white T-shirt and zip my jacket right up to save my decency.

Better to feel like a secret flasher than having a cold, wee-stained top stuck to your skin.

I'm just pushing the pram out towards the front doors, when the same two toddlers tornado-whirl out in front of me, and beat me to it.

Their tiny hands slap against the glass. 'Out! Out! Ooooooout, Dad!'

Here comes the model again, striding towards them with a scowl amidst his designer stubble.

'Would you like a hand?' I hear myself squeak, pointing towards the door. He doesn't seem to have a buggy with him, so opening those heavy doors with twins around your feet and not have them immediately run into the car park is going to be a struggle.

With a sigh, he turns sky-blue eyes to me, flicking them up and down over my outfit. I feel like those piercing peepers can see through my old nylon running jacket and to the bobbled grey maternity bra underneath.

I cross my arms over my chest.

'With your girls?' I prompt, in case he hasn't heard me properly.

'I can *manage!*' he spits, rolling his eyes to the ceiling.

The health visitors file out of the room behind me, locking up with boxes of hand gel and biros under their arms.

I will not cry in front of them today. In fact, I will not cry today, full stop. Mean man or no mean man, today will be a good day.

Blinking rapidly, I grip the plastic handle of my buggy and tap my feet as I wait for the grouchy sod to depart. Holding the door open for my health visitor buds, I think: *These are manners, mate. They don't cost anything, you know.* I think it in a really ballsy, pithy way. The way the old Stevie would have just said out loud, if someone had pushed in front of her to the bar or if a client had been throwing their toys around for no good reason. But mum Stevie just thinks them and keeps her lip buttoned.

Alone in the car park, I take a deep breath. I've tried to appreciate the small things in the last few weeks, put things in perspective when I feel low. OK, my social life is coated in dust, I get no sleep and all my rare conversations with my husband revolve around Cherry's first taste of mango or some new hanging baskets outside the GP surgery. But I have a lot to be grateful for. A healthy baby, a husband, all my body parts in working order. Spring sunshine falling on my face, the rustle of blossom in the trees as a breeze picks up, peace and quiet.

'Shit, am I in the right place?' Someone is rattling the locked doors to the centre, just behind me.

'We're closed for today, dear!' the Scottish health visitor calls out, from the open window of her car as she starts her engine. 'Clinic hours are nine-fifteen to ten.'

The woman, now slightly slumped against the doors with a tiny baby in a sling at her front, looks at her watch. 'It's ten-oh-seven! Could you just nip back in? I won't take a mo to get him naked, honest.'

Scottish lady smiles the patient, uncrackable smile of someone who has heard every wheedling trick in the book, but she's far too busy for that kind of nonsense. 'That's nine-fifteen next week – we look forward to seeing you!' Her little red Fiat crunches away on the gravel.

'Stuff it. I'll put him on the digital kitchen scales at home.' The woman shrugs and peers down into the sling, readjusting its stretchy folds slightly. 'Did you miss it, too?'

I've been such a silent observer in this little exchange, it takes a moment for me to clock she's talking to me. She's got a pixie crop of thick, honey-blonde hair, sticking up at all angles, and ruddy cheeks from walking at speed with her little bundle.

'Um. No. First one here, actually.'

Her eyes widen. Oh good, I sound like a swot.

'Well, I've got to do something now I'm here. If I've made it out of the front door I should capitalise on that. Fancy a walk around the park?' She nods in the direction of the scrubby play park opposite, next to the local football grounds.

'Yes!' I could jump for actual joy. A potential mum mate! *Don't mess this up, Stevie. Stay cool.*

But I'm so studiously staying cool, I'm not saying a word as we amble around the grass. What can I ask her? What can I say? 'Oh... er ...'

'I'm Nelle.' She turns to me. 'And this is Joe. My third, god help me.'

'I'm Stevie, and this is Cherry.' I chuck Cherry's cheek proudly and come away with a dried-on bit of baby porridge. 'My one and only.'

Nelle smiles. 'A right couple of rock chicks, you two! Are you named after Stevie Nicks?'

And so begins the conversation I've had roughly 4,000 times in my life.

'Yup. My mum was living in the States when I was born and she owned a record store there. Big into music. But Cherry's not so much rock and roll – it's after my gran, Cheryl. Though everyone called her Cherry, back in the day. And she's grown to fit the name now – red and round.'

'I like it! And there I was, thinking you'd be a mum-mum, being first one in at the clinic and everything.'

We reach a faded park bench and both flop down wearily. 'Mum-mum?'

'Oh, you know, those women who take mum duties that bit too far. *Mum*-mums. They grow their own organic quinoa and still have time for a blow-dry every other day. Wouldn't be seen dead in their pyjama bottoms at the park.' She waves down at the checked flannel trousers she's wearing.

Oh, please, oh, please let me make her my mum mate.

'I'm lucky if I make it out of the house and I've remembered trousers at all,' I chip in, my voice slightly wobbly with nervous energy.

Nelle laughs and I feel my shoulders drop with relief.

'So how old are your other two? I think you are amazing to have more than one.'

Nelle chews the inside of her lip. 'Not amazing. Foolish? Poor memory, maybe? My others are thirteen and eleven. And this one' – she looks down at the little fuzzy head nestled in between her cleavage – 'let's just say he wasn't exactly on the menu. A *surprise* fortieth birthday present, if you catch my drift. But he's lovely. Six weeks tomorrow.'

Despite knowing better about the realities of newborns and all their mysterious, maddening complexities, I feel a rush of maternity mush as I catch a glimpse of a tiny little ear, like a pasta shell. Sweet!

Nelle shuts her eyes. 'I could just fall asleep here, do you know what I mean?'

'Oh, yes.'

'Maybe if I did just nod off, all day, someone else would magically feed the baby. And sign for the grocery delivery. And pick the others up from school. And make sure the PE kits get washed. And answer all the business emails for bookings. Then make some magical tea that everyone will eat happily. Ugh.'

'So… three is pretty hard, then?'

She smiles weakly. 'Yes. And no. It's not that any particular bit is difficult. It's just that… it's just that it *never ends.*'

'Shit.'

'Exactly.'

Nelle opens her eyes and scans the park. 'Still, could have been worse. Could have been twins!' She juts her chin in the direction of the swings, where Mr Hot But Mean is trying to push one squalling toddler while the other is trying to climb out of the seat, head first. I don't think the 'nice girls' message has hit home.

Nelle blows out a big, exasperated breath. 'He's not having a good day.'

'Neither was I, when he was massively rude to me earlier.'

She frowns at me. My heart leaps into my throat. Did that sound too bitchy? Have I gone too far? *Idiot, idiot, idiot!*

Pushing down on her thighs, Nelle eases herself up. 'Well, we can't have this. Come on.' She starts striding in his direction. My cheeks are on fire as I trot after her. Never mind three kids, with a tone so commanding, she could marshal three hundred of them.

'Hello there!' Nelle calls cheerfully. The Mean Man briefly flicks his eyes to us but then looks back to his swinging tots. He's got them both securely in now and is pushing in tandem. 'Thought we'd introduce ourselves, as fellow local parents!' she chirps on.

His chiselled face barely flickers with interest.

'How's your day going?'

In an instant, he spins on the spot to face us. 'Look, I don't need help. I don't need guidance. I'm a dad, not a stand-in mum. I'm not "babysitting"' – he actually does the air quotes but angrily, like he wants to give the air a strong pinch – 'I'm not clueless. I'm just a dad. *Not* in search of pity or a helping hand. Yep?' Out of steam, he goes back to his duties.

'Oh, boy,' Nelle replies calmly. 'I really think we all need some caffeine. I'm Nelle, this is Stevie. Like the rocker. Coffee at The Jolly Good?'

'The… pub?' I fall over my words.

She looks at me as if I've got my shoes on the wrong feet. 'Yes. But the first tequila shot is on me. Actually, they do a really decent coffee and the garden has no sharp objects.'

'Will,' the Mean Man mutters.

'Sorry?'

'I'm Will.'

Chapter 2

The Jolly Good does, in fact, do a decent coffee and a big plate of toast. Nelle seems to know the barman, too. He plonks the buttery pile down in front of us at the bench we've decamped to in the beer garden with a wink.

'Lifesaver.' She beams at him.

But even the excitement of caffeine, toast and new mates cannot dull the nervous twitch that I shouldn't be in a pub on a weekday mid-morning. With a baby. With a bunch of babies, for that matter. What if someone sees? What if it's one of the health visitors and I go on a Bad Mums Watchlist?

Will clears his throat. 'This is all on me, by the way. To say sorry for my outburst. I... my girls are...' He looks over to where they are dancing madly in front of the pram for Cherry's amusement, hopping from foot to foot and singing what sounds like a version of a Lady Gaga tune. She's cooing like no tomorrow, so I'm considering asking him whether they have an hourly karaoke rate. 'Well, they're full of energy. And a right handful, if I'm honest. It's bad enough that when you're the dad in the toddler group everyone expects you to do a half-arsed job, but when you have a pair of turbo-charged two year olds to wrangle, the very best you can do is half-arsed. And I hate reinforcing that stereotype. I feel everyone's watching me, waiting for me to give them a can of Coke each while I read the paper.' He rubs his hands down over his face and growls in exasperation. 'But none of that is your fault. So I'm very sorry. And thank you for coming to talk to me. You've no idea how you've rescued my day.'

'Or mine,' I brave.

'Pleasure!' Nelle raises her coffee cup in a toast. 'I know I'm no wallflower. Sometimes you'll have to remind me to put a lid on it. But all my original mum mates are well out of the baby stage now. In fact, some of them are in the GCSE prep stage.'

'It can be… well, I've found it's pretty… tricky to make mum mates. Sometimes.' My voice cracks just a smidge.

Will nods in agreement. 'For me, it's hard not to come across as some sort of creep. I worry the mums I meet might think I'm chatting them up.'

Nelle laughs. 'I think you'll find most of the mums round here would *love* that!'

I try not to blush and out myself as one of those mums. 'I always have to abandon potential social things when Cherry kicks off. Hard to get to know new people when your baby has just vomited on their pristine pram hood and is now screeching like it's a yodelling competition. She has reflux. Silent reflux. It's a pain in the arse, if I'm honest.'

Just as Will gives an 'Oh' of sympathetic understanding, Nelle replies with an 'Eh?'

I rush to explain myself, so I don't sound totally ungrateful for the gorgeous baby currently smiling madly in her pram. 'I mean, all babies can be sick sometimes. But Cherry is particularly partial to bringing up her milk and food. And then, most of the time, reswallowing it.' Nelle can barely hide the grimace she makes. 'So the stomach acid irritates her throat on the way up, and then on the way down again. Hence being in a foul mood so often. I give her this really mild antacid each morning, but I'm not always convinced it's helping.' I fiddle with my watch strap.

'The girls had it, too,' Will says. 'Up until about three months. Very common in twins, because they're often born early, before their throat muscle have time to fully develop and so keep everything nicely held in. It is such a—' His voice drops and he mouths the next word, '*bastard* and you never know when they'll grow out of it. But they do,' he finishes, encouragingly.

'God, I hope so. I hate to think of her having horrible heartburn all the time. In the grand scheme of things we're lucky; some babies have it so badly they can't keep anything down, and they lose weight, they develop food aversion later in life...' A shudder moves through my shoulders as I remember all the late-night Dr Google sessions that have shown me these terrifying scenarios. 'I shouldn't begrudge her a cry of annoyance but when she does get the serious grumps with it, people look at her like she's this demon baby, and me like I'm not even trying to help her.'

Nelle gives a snort of derision. 'It's plain to anyone with half a brain that you take excellent care of that girl – she's plump and happy. And if she cries sometimes, then she cries. They can stuff it. We were all babies once. We all irritated someone's ears without meaning to. Hey, don't suppose you guys fancy trying Tinkle Tots tomorrow? Stupid name, I know, but it's a new music class and they're doing a free taster session. If Cherry gets upset we can form a protective human shield around you from any mardy mums, Stevie. It's got to be better than staring at the laundry pile, right?'

I feed Cherry dinner, clean up the resulting carnage, watch a bit of *Twirlywoos* – a children's TV godsend – bath her, dress her, give her the last milk feed of the day, spend twenty minutes jiggling her through her nightly screama-thon until she conks out, and all the while I am wrapped in a cloud of fluffy white joy. Mum mates! Well, parent mates. But two of them! This is the most meaningful social interaction I've had in six months – so much better than chatting to the postman.

As I trail around the house, picking up errant muslins, building blocks and four half-drunk mugs of stone-cold tea, I'm lost in a vision of the three of us heatedly discussing international politics or the destruction of the green belt. Or gender roles in *Peppa Pig*. Or car parking charges in town. I would happily talk through the For Sale ads in the local paper if it meant I had adult company.

'Steve?' Ted's voice cuts though my imagination, just as I was wittily analysing a leather sofa for sale outside Marlow.

'Sorry, sorry. Hiya. You're back early.'

'Well, it's *seven-fifteen*.' He looks at his watch and sighs, as if I was making a dig. I really wasn't. It was an innocent enough comment, seeing as he usually drags himself home at around eight. His work is full on, and he's good at it. Add in the commute out of the City, and I can count on one hand the times Ted has made it home for bath time in the last month. I shouldn't grumble – he's a great dad. When he's here. And he works really hard to support us. But, sometimes, it feels like our different kinds of work – his, which involves digital asset management; and mine, which involves angry-child-into-car-seat management – exist in wholly separate universes.

Ted slings his laptop bag down by the foot of the stairs and I have to bite my lip from criticising. I'll just move it myself, in a minute. I'm no neat freak but I appreciate not having something to trip on just there when I bring Cherry down in the pitch black. She's such a loud complainer when she wakes up in the night that often I bring her down to the dark living room to feed her and then try and bounce her to sleep, softly singing in her ear all the time. I try to keep the noise away from Ted, so he can sleep ahead of a long business day, but I have to admit I don't feel very benevolent about it when he's upstairs in the land of nod and I'm staring at a blank wall, exhausted and bored rigid, my round bum bouncing on my yoga ball while my ears are full of baby cries. And to think I imagined I could deflate that ball, once I'd used it in labour! Pah! I've barely been off the damn lime-green thing since. And to add insult to injury it really, really doesn't go with my fancy grey and sulphur-yellow colour scheme.

But even pangs of sleep envy won't deflate my good mood tonight. Nope. I've got something to actually *talk* to my other half about! Not just how Cherry is progressing in her attempts to turn over to a sort of sideways plank: up on her side, with one arm trapped underneath, she does a lot of grunting and wiggling and then flops onto her back again, usually depositing a mouthful of sick onto her onesie in annoyance. I keep taking videos of these odd breakdancing attempts of hers and messaging them to Ted but he only ever says 'Ah!' in reply, so maybe it's only me that finds them hilarious and totally absorbing.

Tonight, though, I can talk about Nelle and Will and our pub chat and the class tomorrow and how I might cultivate them into the mum mates I've always dreamed of... Well, I won't say that last bit. I haven't exactly been honest with Ted about my disaster of a social life. To say it out loud would be to make it real, I suppose, and to admit to the fact that the effervescent, bold woman he met four years ago has gone. Maybe it was a mix-up in the maternity ward, but instead of the wrong baby, Ted brought home the wrong mum. This one's shy and timid and... dull. I know life's not exactly a laugh a minute for him: work all day, hear your wife drone on about the newsagent not stocking her favourite pick and mix any more, get woken several times in the night by the World's Angriest Baby, rinse and repeat, rinse and repeat. I suppose I don't want him to have any more proof that I've turned into a friendless frump.

Ted throws his suit jacket onto the sofa. Again, I don't make a peep. I'll hang it up in a second. He stretches his six foot four frame up, his hands almost reaching the ceiling in our little cottage. Back in our London flat, it was all airy industrial rafters and tall white walls. But then again, I'd take a lower ceiling for breathable air and a garden of our own out here in the burbs. He makes a kind of frustrated grunt as his shoulders drop down again.

'Ha! You sound like the baby when she can't roll over!' *Oh, why did I say that? This was going to be a non-baby conversation.*

'Hmm?' His head has dipped down, his back slightly hunched. Which means he's checking his emails. Again. And not listening. Again.

I head to the kitchen to start making dinner, pulling out whatever from the vegetable drawer and chopping wildly, with more energy than my body really has. 'Stir fry OK?' I call out.

'Hmm,' he replies. Fine. 'Actually...' Oh, I really hope he's going to suggest a takeaway. I'd kill for a Thai red curry today. And to not have to cook something myself, more importantly.

'Tomorrow night I won't be in for dinner. Client event. And do you know if my really fancy suit is clean?' He's rifling through his laptop bag now, leafing through memos and printouts, not really looking at me, because he knows the answer. I won't kick up a fuss that he's out late and I'll dig out his suit and smarten it up. Of course I will. What else would I be doing? Just keeping his firstborn child alive. Just keeping his house ticking over, on my tod. Just struggling to remember who I really am. A finder of lost suits. A milk machine. A speed-eater of digestives.

Think positive, I remind myself, as I chuck strips of onion and pepper into the wok. *Be mindful. You are now also A Mum with Friends. You are borderline Instagrammable! Tomorrow is going to be brilliant fun, with real-life adults. The kids will muck about with tambourines. You won't even watch one* Homes Under the Hammer. *That's progress.*

'I'm trying a new class tomorrow, with Cherry. And Nelle and Will – some friends.'

Ted sets down his printouts on the kitchen table. 'Right. Will... as in a man?'

'Yup, he's a stay-at-home dad now, but he used to work as a buyer for Selfridges. He's got twin toddlers. They are... live wires. And Nelle is locally born and bred, and runs a party-planning business with her family. She has a sweet little six week old. Just some mum mates of mine. Mum–and–dad mates.' I could expand and say that Will moved here with his husband, but I'm enjoying the idea that Ted might feel just a teeny bit of jealousy at the idea of me hanging out with another man. It's silly, but then so is being so ridiculously happy at meeting two fellow flesh-and-blood parents: I'm keeping my voice level, when all I really want to do is whoop and air-punch.

'OK.' Ted is rubbing his chin. 'Right. We should all hang out one weekend, or something.' As I open my mouth to chirrup that that would be a lovely thing to do, he keeps talking: 'While you're cooking, I just need to answer a few emails upstairs, yup?'

His great big thumping steps going up the stairs answer his own question. And because our house is such a true, old, rickety cottage, each step makes the floorboards shift and complain, finished off by the metallic twang of the baby gate as he closes it behind him a little too forcefully.

I hold my breath.

'Waahhhhhgggggggghhhhhhhhh!' That noise is nothing to do with the wonky beams or the tilted floors. That is a noise of our own creation. Specifically, *our* DNA... but Ted's stupid gallumphing about.

'Baby's awake!' he yells down from the landing.

No shit, Dad of the Year, I think darkly, taking the stir fry off the hob. And now the jiggling and singing and rocking to sleep will begin all over again and I can wave goodbye to forty-five precious minutes of my child-free evening.

If someone had told me motherhood would be so much like *Groundhog Day* but without any sort of laughter or pathos, I might have had a rethink.

—

The promise of matey bonding time has me springing out of bed this morning. The 2am feed, the 6am feed: I almost whistled through them both. Breakfast is doled out with the merry patience of Mary Poppins on pay day. Cherry smacks the plastic top of her high chair, sending a few lumps of wet baby cereal arcing through the air like she's manning a catapult. Well, it's probably been three minutes since I wiped the floor. It could do with a clean. Spit spot, and off we go.

'Now, Cherry Pie, what on earth are we going to wear to this new baby class, hmm?'

If this was an Eighties movie, there'd be an upbeat synth pop tune blaring out as I dig through my wardrobe and hold up various outfits to the mirror. This long checked shirt or *this* long checked shirt? The Dorothy Perkins jeggings or the New Look jeggings? Perhaps the music would change to something more ominous now: a lone cello and some kettle drums as I flick through hanger after hanger of brilliant clothes I can no longer fit into. A weird fact about pregnancy that no one really tells you till it's too late is that your hips and rib cage spread out to fit the baby in as it grows. And they take their sweet time moving back in again. Combine that with a paunch of fat around my tum from all those 4am digestives, and a saggy double chin, and I'm not exactly runway-ready. Not that I aspire to be stick thin or any madness of that kind; I'd just really like to get back into my favourite slate grey, fancy jeans and the sky-blue silk shirt that was my lucky charm in pitches and dates alike, back in the day. But neither of them can take in my post-baby body, and I've not exactly helped by shunning all exercise in favour of cheese on toast on the hour.

Cherry is watching me from her position on my bed: lying on top of two giant muslins (to absorb any sick) and encircled by a range of cushions, should she decide to commando-roll while my back is turned and thump onto the floor. You never know. Now and then she lets out a grizzle that confirms this process isn't much fun for either of us, so I break into a gaudy song and dance routine of Incy Wincy. With mad leaps and jazz hands – the lot. That buys me three minutes at a go. How do those glam mums on Insta do it? How do they perfectly coordinate a crisp white peasant blouse with jangling yet tasteful bracelets and a big, bouncy blow-dry while children crawl around their feet? I don't even know where my hairdryer is. I don't think I've used it since I was six months' pregnant and I lost the ability to bend over.

'Sod it,' I whisper to myself as I reach for my trusty striped Breton top. The mum staple. But it's from Joules so it feels classy and the three quarter-length sleeves are super-flattering. I spin around to Cherry. 'What do you think, missus?'

A mouthful of white throw-up leaves her lips.

'Everyone's a critic. Watch it, or I'll put you in the pink tutu nightmare Auntie Phyllis sent.'

My lovely Aunt Phyllis really does try, bless her. I think she feels that with my mum living in the States again, she should step up and be a surrogate mother figure. This shows itself when she sends a range of outfits for Cherry that I can only describe as pageant-worthy: scratchy tulle, sequinned ra-ra skirts, 'Daddy's Little Princess' stamped over nylon onesies. It comes from a good place, but it's so very, very bad.

I wipe up the sick with a corner of a muslin and heft Cherry up, walking her to her room. She's got a ridiculous mini-wardrobe which I couldn't resist buying when I was three months' pregnant and totally clueless about the reality of babies. They don't need hanging space – you need stuffing space! I crouch down and rummage one hand around in the pile of clothes in the bottom. Cherry also has a Breton-striped all-in-one but I worry that would ring mum-mum alarm bells with Nelle. I think I'll play it safe: a grey marl vest with tiny robots printed on it, and purple dotty leggings. There's some sort of balance there.

Twenty minutes later, after cleaning up a thunderous poo from Cherry that made her sound like a backfiring van, we are ready to hit the streets. I'm washed, I'm dressed, I'm coherent: this is going to be a good day! I might rehearse some conversational topics on the way there, but nothing too controversial for starters. Something flickers in the back of my mind — ask questions. That's what I did when I was meeting new people as a PR and I'd forgotten their names and backgrounds but I wanted them to feel included. I'll ask questions. People love talking about themselves.

My trainers are bouncing along the pavement as I happily head to the community hall. Cherry likes a running commentary to keep her amused so I prattle on: 'There's Mr Tilbury's cat. Hello, cat! And people have put their bins out today. But not the recycling, oh, no, no, no — that's on a Tuesday. *Recycle, recycle, recycle!*' I start singing a little ear worm from a *Peppa Pig* episode.

And then my pram wheels collide with something. Speeding out of the public footpath that starts at the bottom of our street and takes a back route to the park is a luminous green scooter.

'Move!' shouts its owner to me, dark eyes glowering up from a curtain of sandy, straight hair. He can't be more than four, but he's got the weary aggression of someone who's been stuck in rush-hour traffic all his life.

Annoyingly, on impulse, I do move back and he scoots off down the pavement, just as I am thinking of mature but cutting things to say to him. My mouth twitches and my lips curl, but I've missed my moment.

Where are the flipping parents?!

A flick of shiny, golden-blonde tresses precedes a woman dressed all in expensive grey tones. She must have seen our mini-collision and heard his tart little shout. I wonder if her apology will be just as smooth as her hair.

But nothing comes. Her glossy lips stay closed but her eyes flick up and down, over my slightly stained jeans and maybe just a hint of muffin top. I inch further behind the handles of the pram.

I now totally get what Nelle means by a mum-mum.

Confessions of a First-Time Mum

Blog post 3.12am

Baby Groups: Not for the Faint-Hearted. Or the Wet-Haired.

Baby groups: a soft, cosy haven for the new mum, right? A place to meet likeminded mum friends, take a load off for forty-five minutes, bond with your baby and come away with a new affinity for parental life and strengthened mum skills. Yes?

Um.

No.

Maybe I've just been to the wrong groups. Maybe I was so mental from lack of sleep that I wandered into Aggressive Negotiating for Women 101 and that explains all the blank stares I get in return for my nervous grin. No one moves a bag from a chair for me, and the little cliques in corners move closer together, whispering and nodding. Their whispers make me very self-conscious about my wet hair, baggy leggings and Big Baby's general whiff of curdled milk.

So I always end up with the chair right next to the person taking the class, further distancing me from the others as Super Swot and putting me right in the line of sight when everyone starts singing and clapping, and I am completely lost mid-verse of 'Three White Mice'. (I swear, once a class leader turned to me, interrupting the song, and snapped: 'We don't say 'blind' any more! It's offensive!' as if I was scrawling graffiti on the RNIB building.) Big Baby does not dig the tunes and quickly builds up a head of steam into a major meltdown. The class leader will take this as a moment to cheerfully demonstrate some distraction techniques for When Baby is Crying: flying her around like a plane, pretending to drop her down with a lunge, blowing raspberries in her face. And Big Baby demonstrates that she is a baby that will not fall for that crap, thank you very much, her face getting redder and sweatier with each failed method.

The eye rolls spread round the room like a grumpy Mexican wave. No one else's baby is this angry. No one else's baby is ruining it. No one else came dressed like they were going to service a boiler.

The shame and the noise get too much. There's only so much polite smiling I can do when underneath my face my head is awash with tears and panic and despair. And so each time we bolt, the sound of Big Baby's shouts trailing me out of the community centre, behind the high street and back to the car park.

So, all in all, a great day out and totally worth £6.50 a time!

Is it just me? Have you been to a class that hasn't been a minefield of social codes and ear-drum splits? Actually, don't tell me if you have because that would just confirm that it's ME who's the incompetent one here.

Stay strong, stay well fed.

Love,

First-Time Mum x

Chapter 3

'I can't believe I'm doing this shit all over again,' Nelle mutters out of the side of her mouth, in my direction. We are bicycling the babies' legs very gently, to the tinny tune of a boppy backing track. Tinkle Tots is the kind of operation where the class leader is given a playlist, a boxful of props, some anti-bac wipes and is then free to set up camp in a village hall and play such *original* songs as: 'This is the way we bring up wind, bring up wind, bring up wind.' I'm gingerly rotating Cherry's more than plump legs as she lies on her back, staring up at me in boredom. Yes, I'd love an effective way to bring up her wind but she's also the most volatile vomiter on the planet. I've gone eight days without her puking on something in a public space and that's a personal best, so I want to keep it up. Will didn't have much luck, either, in getting his girls to do the toddler version of pretending to climb up an invisible ladder, hopping from leg to leg. They chose instead to climb up the very real stage and race back and forth, in and out of the heavy velvet curtains. So he politely made his excuses after this madness and said he'd meet us at the pub in a few days. I think quite a few of the mums were sad to see him go but happy to watch him leave. On the poster Tinkle Tots says it caters up to three years, but I doubt they've encountered a burst of two-year-old energy quite like the girls, let alone when it's double strength.

Joe seems happy enough, a bubble of spit at his lips as his mum tenderly moves his limbs about to the tune. But it's clearly not giving Nelle the same feels.

'Ten years on, and they're still playing the same bloody songs.' This earns her a glare from the mum on her other side. My cheeks colour at the awkwardness but Nelle seems unfazed.

'And now it's time for a trip to Tummy Time Town!' comes the chirpy voice of the class leader. 'Little ones on their fronts, so we're working on strengthening the neck and preparing for the crawling milestone. We have mirrors and fairy lights for them to look at so they're engaged and to improve spatial awareness.'

Nelle turns her head my way and crosses her eyes. I bite back a giggle. As much as I want Cherry to hit her milestones and be able to shift her plump self around on all fours, I do wish someone could phrase it simply and sensibly. And not like we've all suffered major head injuries.

'I don't know about you,' Nelle mutters, 'but I need a trip to Tequila Town after this.'

Somehow we get through the remaining twenty minutes without my new friend's head exploding, Cherry freaking out or me letting the laughter spurt out of my clenched lips.

Pushing the prams up the hill towards home is a sobering blast of reality. I'm trying to keep up my end of the conversation, desperate as I am not to let this chance of a solid mum mate pass me by, but I'm only managing about four words at a time before the wheezing beats me. Maybe it's time to take the cellophane off that post-baby Pilates DVD my mum oh-so-sweetly posted me straight after Cherry's birth?

Nelle seems pretty happy to steer the chat anyway; I love how unapologetically forthright she is. I haven't met anyone like that in ages, probably not since I was sitting around a highly polished boardroom table. In fact, I used to be like that. Once upon a time, in a galaxy far, far away...

When we reach the end of my road, we pause for a quick goodbye, the prams side by side. Cherry waves a chubby arm in Joe's direction, dangerously close to getting a handful of his tiny foot. She must be getting hungry. At their current size ratio, she could probably finish Joe off in two mouthfuls.

'Same time next week?' I ask, my voice reedy with hope.

'Nah.' Nelle's lips form a flat line.

'Oh, right.'

She must see my eyes crinkle in a disappointed wince. 'Not that I don't want to. We've got this mother and baby show to get ready for. Hoping to get some more party bookings that way – christenings, baptisms, super-duper posh first birthdays. God knows we need them.' She chews the inside of her mouth. 'The glamorous life of a family business, eh? You get no say in it, but you're stringing crêpe paper garlands up for the next forty years. Still, I shouldn't complain. It keeps us in chicken nuggets and nappies.' She rolls her eyes with a smile. 'I've never asked you what you do! Give me the Stevie CV.'

I scuff my already well-scuffed trainers against my pram wheels. 'Oh, yes. Um, PR? Public relations? I was a PR exec at a firm in London.'

Nelle's lips form a perfect doughnut shape. 'PR! You sly fox! A professional schmoozer in my midst and you never said a word. Don't like to toot your own horn, eh?'

I feel my cheeks burning. If only she knew. If only I could say, '*These says I couldn't schmooze a garden hedge. I can't toot about my skills.*' What skills?! I couldn't toot a party blower, most likely.

'Yeah, um, well…' I just want the conversation to move on. I don't like to admit the real state of my head to myself, let alone a new friend.

Nelle is suddenly scrutinising my face, her eyes narrowed. 'You are just what I need.'

'Sorry?'

'We've paid all this money to have a stand at the Mother and Baby Fair at Heather Academy, to drive some sales. It's got to pay off because it was *not* cheap. Because of netball and rugby practice, I'm going to be there all day with my mini assistant' – she points at Joe – 'while my other half does the dropping off. Besides, he couldn't sell a ball of wool to a kitten, as much as I love him. You should come! And, Cherry! Come and be my secret weapon. Come and work your professional magic for me. Please?'

She's got one hand gripping the handle of my pram now.

I put a hand to my red-hot face. 'Oh… the thing is, Cherry will most likely scream the place down after five minutes. That wouldn't make for a great experience for anyone. So, um…'

'Nonsense! It's a baby show – they're not going to mind a bit of a wail. And there'll be freebies: toys, snacks, kiddy music. She'll love it! It'll be like a baby Glasto for her. We could take a playpen and loads of stuff to keep them entertained. Give Mummy a chance to put her work head back on, right?'

Nelle's smile is so completely huge and sure of itself that I uselessly work my jaw, with no protest forthcoming. No reasonable doubts could take down her conviction. And the truth is too pathetic to admit: I don't want to come because I'm scared of talking to people.

'Uh… sure?'

The hug that follows is brief but so strong it nearly knocks me off my feet.

'Excellent! Oh, this is going to be a million times more fun with someone interesting along for the ride. And we'll have cake on tap and gossip! This might just be the most fun I've had in months.' She winks at me and the glow of acceptance runs over me like a hot shower, washing my nerves into the drain. Maybe it *will* be OK, if I'm there with Nelle. She's got a personality big enough for the both of us, she's never going to let things go awkward or quiet. I'll hide behind her, if I need to, or fake a poo-splosion in Cherry that I have to run off and deal with.

'I'll ping the details over later, yup?' Nelle's eyes light up all over again. 'And we can ask Will! Even more fun, and total arm candy to send all the mums running in our direction. They don't need to know he's gay. Well, now I'm buzzing! Ha! Better stop waffling and get back for the school run prep. See you soon, yes?'

I wave Nelle off and we turn down our narrow street. I think I have about three layers of emotional sweat on my forehead: nerves from wanting to make a good impression hanging out with my new mates today; utter terror at the idea of having to dig up my old work skills again and *talk* to people in some sort of convincing way; and then a sheen of relief that Nelle must like me or why would she invite me?

'That's what we'll focus on,' I say down to Cherry, as she works on getting her buggy book deep into her drooly mouth. 'That Mummy has made friends, and people DO like her. That's the important bit. The rest… we can deal with later. And something a bit more interesting to tell Daddy later, hmm? Rather than a problem with the lint tray again. If Daddy puts his phone down long enough to listen, of course.' Cherry's faint eyebrows wrinkle. 'Not that Daddy isn't wonderful! Because he is!' A stab of guilt hits me. I really shouldn't bitch about Ted to his actual child. I might inadvertently turn her against him and raise some crazy child assassin by mistake. 'Daddy is hardworking and gentle and kind. And he used to buy me really nice Jigsaw jumpers for Christmas, when we first met. And he knows to screen Granny's calls sometimes when she's being particularly mad. And… he makes a good cup of tea.' I stick up a thumb to indicate that this really is a crucial skill in a life partner. Cherry can't hear this too soon.

Of course, this is exactly when this morning's mum-mum swishes my way again, bouncing down a garden path and out onto the pavement in front of me. No crazed scooter terror ahead of her now, but the same impossibly perfect hairdo and pristine outfit. She holds something up in her hand and I wonder if she's about to wave? Maybe she was just having a bad start earlier, and wants to make amends? Maybe all mum-mums aren't so bad?

I raise my hand in a casual wave to return the gesture, when the squeaky beep of a 4X4 unlocking goes off in my ear, sending me a good few inches in the air. She was unlocking her car. She was not waving.

As she strides past Cherry and I, effortlessly swinging the car door open and folding her gazelle legs inside, I want to rip my hand off and throw it in a privet hedge.

Nope, mum-mums really are that bad.

I've been so jumpy about this whole Mother and Baby Fair for the last week that I snapped Ted's head off for putting the fabric conditioner back in the wrong spot on the shelf this morning, which then led to him muttering, 'No need to thank me for putting on a few loads, then.' But as he settled down to watch some rugby match or other on his smartphone, I knew he wasn't seriously miffed. He was getting a silent Saturday all to himself, after all. Sod. Why didn't I insist he keep Cherry and I go alone? Like all good ideas, this one has come too late. Besides, I don't want Ted to get an inkling that I'm secretly bricking it. I may have bigged up how much Nelle begged and pleaded for me to be there, for my professional expertise to rescue her family from the gutter. As far as he's concerned, I'm Alan Sugar in jade-green jeggings right now. And the one thing Sir Alan does not do is back down.

A horn beeps from the end of the drive and I flinch. 'Nelle is here! Bye then!' I wave at his downturned face, the green glint of the screen bouncing off his cheeks.

'Bye. Laters. Oooooh.' He draws his breath in, a long gasp.

'What? What?' I dash back into the living room.

'Murphy fumbled that. What a balls up.'

Visions of devastating news bulletins or texts to say someone has fallen down the stairs or off a boat or down a gangplank and then off a boat now start to fade. Since having Cherry and that triggering all those hyper-sensitive parent hormones, I am at a constant threat level of Wets-Knickers-at-Doorbell.

You would think my husband would remember that and not make such cliff-hanger noises.

I stuff my feet in my boots and pick up Cherry, clipped tightly into her car seat. Nelle said parking was really restricted at the venue so we could both go in her car. The idea of Cherry in the back with Joe – Baby's First Buddy Road Trip! – appealed in principle, but swinging her hefty weight by the rigid plastic handle of the seat, and the pull at my arm socket, is not such a fun reality. I have packed her several sets of clothes, two boxes of baby biscuits, three different rattles and my iPad for emergency *In the Night Garden* episodes. I'm ready for puking, wailing and any meltdown she might choose to have today. If I can distract her enough to stay quiet and content, I might be able to think in a straight line for thirty seconds and have a half-decent adult conversation. Maybe. And, besides, she really can be a peach when she's in a good mood and for once I'd love someone to compliment me on my lovely baby. Even if I have to shove two gingerbread men in her gob to get her to smile.

As I yank open the back door to Nelle's little red Metro, my terror alert peaks at What-The-Fucking-Christ and I jump backwards, immediately sheltering Cherry behind me. There, in the driver's seat, is a clown. A fucking clown.

'Hiya!' The scarlet, over-painted mouth talks.

Nelle?

'Wha… what are you doing?'

'Oh, this?' She gestures casually to her red nose and rainbow wig. 'I do the clowning at kids' parties. Thought I might as well show off the goods! Give people a free demo on site.' Her black semi-circular eyebrows drop – hard to do under so much face paint. 'Sorry, does it bother you? Oh, shit, do you have a phobia?'

Breathing deeply in through my nose, out through my mouth, I take a moment to find myself. 'No, not really. Just… out of context it… it's a bit alarming.' My hands tremble just a little as I manoeuvre Cherry into the car and look for the little metal bits to lock the seat into. *Chill out, Stevie*, I remind myself, *you're still on a friendship probationary period — she mustn't know how weird you are inside.*

'Let's do this thing!' Clown Nelle grabs the steering wheel as I hop into the passenger's seat.

'Yeah!' I muster an air-punch, praying we don't break down. Waiting for roadside assistance like this would be just too trippy. Luckily, the radio starts playing some Katy Perry and our energetic singing soon drowns out the little anxious voice inside my head.

Nelle's get-up attracts lots of double-takes on the way to the event, but maybe it isn't the exact kind of attention-grabbing she's after. At the traffic lights, a few mothers with small children in tow clasp their little ones' hands closer to them and scurry off. The security guard is totally white as he waves us through the entrance.

As we drive into the car park of Heather Academy, I forget all about Nelle's polka dot harem pants, gasping at the sheer scale of the Hogwarts towers before me. I'd heard that this was *the* best, fanciest private school in the whole county but seeing it up close is something else. Gothic arches, stained-glass windows, manicured lawns. Pretty different from my Watford comprehensive.

'Wow,' I breathe.

'Oh, I know, right? Just don't ask about the fees, you'll pass out cold. Still, we should get a good, aspirational crowd who have the cash to hire party planners. I think we'll make a really good team, chick.' Nelle winks before she starts to clamber out of the car, the curly multi-coloured wig being squashed against the doorframe as she does so.

When I open the back door to retrieve Cherry I can't believe it – she's asleep. Perfectly asleep. Not even the movement of being wriggled out of the car and the noise of the door clicking shut wakes her. Wow. This never happens. Usually the merest bump of the pram against a kerb wrenches her from sleep. But hey, let's not overthink it. I'm just going to enjoy this adult time and do Nelle a favour while my head is clear.

We hoof the children inside, through eight-foot-high carved oak doors and into the lobby where the Mother and Baby Fair will be taking place. There's already a photographer setting up shop, a very fancy range of prams on display and an aromatherapy table sending over some lovely wafts of lavender and citrus.

'Here we go.' Nelle plonks Joe behind our table and I follow suit with Cherry. It's not much to look at right now – a plain trestle table and two brown plastic chairs – and I'm about to suggest we ask the school if we can borrow a tablecloth or something when Nelle puts her hands on her hips and says, 'Right, you watch the tiddlers and I'll grab the props from the boot.'

I very much hope these are props for the stall and not a second Coco outfit for me. I don't think my frame could take clown shoes. Or my sanity.

When Nelle marches back five minutes later, she has an IKEA bag full of tricks: a lovely red and white gingham table covering; very cute and traditional bunting in lots of pastel colours and prints; some poster boards with blown-up photos of past events, I'm guessing – bouncy castles, petting zoos, a happy child blowing out candles on a giant cake; plus handfuls of flyers and business cards and logoed balloons to hand out. As both babies are still spark out, Nelle and I get busy with setting up a lovely, welcoming table. The whole thing shouts English Countryside Idyll and the rusty, professional part of my brain starts to loosen up, appraising it as a really strong and well-delivered message. But then everything I've come to see in Nelle in just a week or so has led me to believe she's one smart cookie.

She stands back from our handiwork, hitching up her oversized trousers and tilting her head to one side. 'Does it need something else?'

'Hmm. Hang on, is there a kitchen here, do you know?'

Her eyes light up behind the thick white slap. 'Ooooh, a coffee. That could be just the thing. If memory serves it's beyond the matron's office, down the corridor off to the right.'

'OK. Back in a sec.'

But it's not two coffees I return with, though I will make another trip for those if Cherry's nap stays blissfully long, but a white teapot stuffed with silk flowers.

'I'm not totally mad' – I laugh nervously as I set it down on the trestle table – 'I just thought we had space for one last bit of set dressing and what says quaint English pursuits more than an old teapot? I was actually after two teacups but this is so much better, and Matron won't miss her flowers for just a few hours.'

Nelle flashes me a double thumbs-up. 'Love it. Gorgeous! You *are* my secret weapon. Now we've got half an hour yet before punters are let in, so I might hunt out some biscuits for long-term survival later. If Joe wakes up, just jiggle the carrier with one foot and he'll probably nod off again, bless him.'

With Nelle stalking off in her Technicolor outfit – a slight squeak from one clown shoe that I'm not sure is accidental or not – I'm left gazing at these two snoozing babies. Joe, tiny and wrinkly in a navy striped onesie, his eyes gently closed in two crescents, not a peep coming from his general direction. And Cherry: round, plump, legs like ham hocks next to Joe's, a sheen of sweat on her red cheeks as she snoozes, a hefty snore breaking the silence every now and then. As I watch, she pulls a grimace and wiggles her feet around and I wonder if she's just swallowed some sick in her sleep. You can normally set your watch by her upchuck and she hasn't been sick all morning.

If you strolled past now, you'd see a woman in reasonably clean clothes, minding two peaceful babes and you'd think, 'Well, motherhood looks dreamy.' But Cherry sleeping like this, and being calm in public, is a dream – it is not reality. This is not my day to day, far from it. If she wakes up, there's no jiggling with your foot and falling back asleep like an angel. There is only hellish yelling and fat fists flying. I love my daughter but she is not at her most sunny just after a nap. And this is the first nap to go beyond forty-five minutes that she's had in… maybe ever?! All the books tell you that you should be getting a good three hours of sleep out of them at a time, you know, when you can 'rest', 'take it easy' and practise 'self-care'. Self-care for me is a two-for-one on digestives at the supermarket. That is, if I get all the way through the shop without having to abandon my trolley due to one of Cherry's epic brawls. I bet Joe could get through a trip to Sainsbury's and a car wash and a trip to the chemist without splitting anyone's ear drums. But not our Cherry.

A wet snore escapes her mouth and Joe doesn't even flinch, safe and sound in a deep slumber.

A stone hits the bottom of my stomach: this is how babies are supposed to be, only mine isn't. Probably because I'm getting it all wrong.

My eyes sting suddenly so I try to find something else to look at, some other s for my rattled brain. But on every table, on every wall, are popping up more and more examples of how Cherry and I aren't doing it right: the photographer with his compilation board of tiny babies curled up in pumpkins or on sheepskin rugs, bows perched on their perfect heads. Well, despite the best intentions, we never did get Cherry to that first-week photo shoot. The scarlet forceps marks on her face weren't exactly something I wanted recorded for posterity, and I was so deranged with tiredness and hormones and guilt and worry that I could barely find the camera app on my phone, let alone a photographer's studio.

There's someone here advertising baby massage classes, a black and white blown-up photo of a slim, smiling mother cooing down at her perfect babe. Another class I've failed to take my daughter to. Another chance to bond, to help calm her, to teach us both some life skills, instead, I've hidden away with daytime telly and a daily weep.

And as I clock the companies offering hand and feet moulds, personalised artworks and handcrafted wooden toys, it's like a shopping list of my missed opportunities to be a top-notch mum and give Cherry all the top-notch things in life. I bet that swishy mum-mum on my road has all her children's digits preserved in solid silver.

But I'm not giving into the blues now. Not now. I'm *out* and I haven't had to flee in shame yet and not one mouthful of sick has hit anything. I just need to keep my mind ticking over. So I whip out my phone.

I haven't checked my emails in ages, now I think of it. Reading the tiny text on my phone always feels too much like work at the end of another tired and tiring day, so I usually abandon it in favour of Netflix and red wine. But there's no better way to fake that you're important and popular by checking your phone, after all.

The first one I come to is from Mum. Her monthly check in, no doubt. Living in the States, the time difference makes it tricky to speak on the phone sometimes so we've fallen into an email pattern. She wasn't the most maternal mum when I was growing up. Not that she did a bad job or locked me in the broom cupboard or anything, but I could tell early on that making sandwiches and wiping chins didn't fulfil her. Motherhood wasn't enough. She loved music and the whole Eighties music scene – big hair, tight leather, rocking hard – and although she tried to make it work in the UK after she and Dad split and we moved back to be closer to her family, for years she was just itching for another adventure. So my first day at uni halls was the same day she booked her flight back to San Jose and bought a vintage record store of her very own. I miss her like mad sometimes, but I can't deny she's really happy out there.

Hello chick,

How's my Cherry Pie? Still a lovely porker?!

I've had a postcard for you from your dad. I keep giving him your address but I don't know what he does with it in that shepherd's hut of his. If only he'd wake up and get

44

electricity and a goddamn laptop. Anyway, he said he felt your karmic presence on one of his hikes and he's thinking about you. Whatever that means. So there you go.

The store's ticking over. Grime still seems to be the thing. God, I miss guitars.

When are you going to come out and see me?! I'm forgetting what you look like, you know. Do it quick while Cherry's still free on the flight.

M x

Today's not the day to delve into feelings about Dad living in the Rocky Mountains without a phone, or get angry about Mum eschewing all the trappings of motherhood bar the ability to make me feel guilty in just a handful of words. Today I'm living in the here and now, I'm making friends, my baby is a sleeping angel. I'm living my life.

Well, I'm trying to. Standing here alone, guardian to two freakishly quiet babies, I feel about as isolated as if I'd climbed to the top of the fourth plinth in Trafalgar Square. So maybe a bit more phone staring, to be safe. I'll warm up to actual human interaction slowly. Seems wise when my social muscles are so stiff.

Just as I'm deleting some sale emails from my old favourite places to shop for clothes, pronouncing great deals on the season's sharpest looks (if it's not super-comfy jeggings I'm not interested), a new mail pops into my inbox. It's from Sarah, my best mate from work. God, I haven't thought about her in months. My heart pangs suddenly for our carby lunches with side servings of office gossip and relationship dissection. I suppose I've been rubbish about keeping in touch because she might be able to see through my platitudes and rumble what a rookie beginner I am at all this mum stuff.

From: Sarah Rimmer

To: Steviebutnotabloke@hotmail.co.uk

Subject: SSSSSHHHHHHHHHHH!!!!!

Hey lovely,

How's that gorgeous baby of yours? And how's Ted behaving himself? Spoiling you rotten, I hope, mother of his perfect child.

Look, I know this is super-naughty of me because technically we're not supposed to contact you on leave when it comes to business matters… BUT I thought you'd want to know some super SUPER-shitballs exciting news.

Marcus is leaving. Like, next week. I know, right?! Not a poach, he's just decided he's had enough of modern life and he's going off to be a forester, whatever the fuck that is. Like a security guard for trees?! Bit different from PR but, hey, it takes all sorts.

So that leaves the lead accounts management role open… Now, I haven't heard anything about who they're considering (but if you're not on the list they are CRAZY) but in an emergency meeting where we had to divvy up Marcus's clients, Marion said she would personally handle Fierce Beauty cosmetics…

Until YOU get back! She wants you to have it long term!!!!

So are you ready for a mega-bucks client?! Fashion week, celeb endorsements, freebies galore and a monthly budget bigger than my mortgage. If I didn't love you so much I'd be a jealous bitch right now.

Well, maybe I'm still a bit jealous. But I was just bursting to tell you. How amazing?! But when Marion tells you in due course just fake surprise, yeah?

Look, you've got to come into town with that beautiful girl of yours and we'll celebrate this properly over a lunch. I even promise not to swear in front of Cherry.

S xxxxxxxxxx

My fingers shake as I close down my email app. Fierce Beauty. Me. One of the hottest American cosmetics brands of the last few years. And me. A PR job that all my colleagues would kill for: glam parties, new product launches people actually care about, vloggers biting your hand off for the new nude lip-stain. And me: the woman who's forgotten how to talk, how to sort her eyebrows out, how to wear clothes that don't come with an elasticated waist.

My hand is now full-on wobbling as I slip my phone back in my handbag.

I blink in the hard strip lighting. It bounces up off the old parquet floor and makes me wince.

And now my eyes start to swim and my head feels a bit woozy, like when I was pregnant. And I'm not sure if the floor is slippery or maybe my legs are weird? I clutch the table top through the cloth, holding on for some stability. Must be because I still haven't had my morning caffeine. That's it. Yup.

A huge beach ball wrapped in striped jersey nudges its way into my eye line. It's attached to a woman. Oh, right. She's actually pregnant. My eyes struggle back into focus.

'Hello!' Her smile is bright, no eye bags or grey tinge to her skin. *First baby, then,* I hear myself thinking bitterly. 'Do you do naming days? Not christenings, you know, but a Humanist ceremony? With a celebrant? That's what I'm thinking of.' She rubs a hand down and around her ginormous bump.

'OK,' I force out, not really knowing if Nelle does such a thing.

'What kind of price would that be? And would it include food – could you lay that on? I'm thinking for about seventy-five people.'

Her words echo about in my ears and I realise I am grimacing in my attempt to compute what's been said. The pregnant lady's smile is also starting to fade.

'Uh…um.'

She's shuffling her feet now, frowning. I know I should be saying something. Fast. I know I should be talking.

'Erm. Ah…'

Nelle needs this business. She needs this deal. This could be a big gig. Quick. Quick!

My jaw just grinds shut, teeth against teeth.

Why aren't you saying anything?! Anything at all! Just at least keep her here till Nelle gets back. Just some chatter! What kind of idiot can't talk polite nonsense for five minutes?!

The pregnant woman is now looking at her watch, and then over her shoulder. She's going, any moment now.

A flaming idiot who can't make small-talk. Well, this would just be perfect in front of the Fierce Beauty clients. Get up in front of them in a boardroom and grunt. See how well that goes. See what's left of your career then.

Now it's not just my jaw that feels clamped shut. It feels like someone's squeezing my windpipe too. It's closing shut. I can't. I'm not sure I... *Here's that dizzy feeling again.*

'Hello!' A familiar, smooth voice calls. The woman instantly brightens and pulls her shoulders back.

'Will. Oh, thank you.' Relief makes my lips unlock and I realise I have left little claw marks in the tablecloth from where I was holding on so tight.

He strides in our direction, unbelievably good looking in just black jeans and a grey marl sweatshirt.

Will's here to help out. Will can smooth this out. He can help me talk to this woman.

Yes, Will will see you don't even know how to talk to a fellow human. He'll see that you're a pathetic mess. Say goodbye to your new mum mates, idiot!

'What's the deal, then?' he asks, with a chirpy smile. Being out and about with no toddlers in tow must feel like a two-week holiday, I imagine.

He looks between me and this very pregnant lady, who has switched her entire attention to Will.

If I had the choice between a mute fool and a model-like hunk I think I know who I'd be training my eyes on.

The silence lengthens and fills the space all around us. I feel it winding around my arms and legs, heavily weighing me down; I feel it building a wall between Will and this lady and me. And I'm not doing anything about it. I'm just standing here, dumbly, as everyone in the room figures out I am a broken excuse for a person.

'Loo,' I blurt and run down the first corridor I can see.

Chapter 4

'Stevie, sweetie?' I can see two red clown feet through the crack under the toilet door. Oh god, she found me.

'Fine,' I wheeze, my hand on my chest as it flutters up and down.

'Are you having an asthma attack? Can you let me in? Love, we're worried about you. Will's here. He said you didn't look well when you rushed off.'

I squeeze my eyes shut but tears escape down my cheeks anyway. This is not how today was supposed to go. This is not how my life is supposed to go. This is not how I'm supposed to be.

A horrifying thought pops into my head and I leap towards the lock on the door, then yank the whole thing open. 'The babies!'

Nelle smiles, her gigantic red mouth turning up. 'The babysitting firm said they'd keep an eye on them for five minutes. Proper professionals. But they're still asleep. Good as gold.'

Well, chalk that up on today's list of abject failures: too busy having a bonkers meltdown to think about my baby. The small, helpless child I am supposed to love and care for and protect. Great. So that's a failure at my day job AND a failure at motherhood. Smashing it.

I hang my head and more tears plop down onto my jeans.

'Hey, hey.' Will's long arms wrap around me as he pulls me in for a hug, the soft grey jersey material of his jumper absorbing all my snot and running mascara. 'What's happened, Stevie? Something at home?'

Nelle rubs my shoulder. 'You can tell us anything, love. There's a strict code of ethics about bathroom confessions: nothing goes beyond these four walls and the hand dryer. Promise.'

Tell them anything, OK. Where do I start? Um, I've become the world's most boring wife, my husband would rather make eyes at his iPhone than at me, I'm a crap mum as evidenced by a baby that's permanently angry or puking or both at the same time, I have no friends to speak of, I'm only friendly with the health visitors in the baby clinic, and I've lost all the skills that used to make me excellent at my job. And just at a time when I'm being offered one of the biggest breaks in my career, when I should be jumping for joy about this new client, the thought of having to schmooze and present and confidently charm makes me feel like a ten-tonne lorry is driving over my chest.

So where do I start?

'I'm fucking it all up,' I weep onto Will's chest, and he pulls me that bit tighter.

–

In the end, as all the words came finally flooding out and, sensing this wasn't going to be a five-minute boohoo cured by a chocolate Hob Nob, Will gently untangled himself from my floppy limbs and held me at arm's length so he could look me squarely in the eye. 'You're not fucking anything up. I know that for a fact. What you need right now is to talk this all through, preferably not this close to a toilet. So here's the plan. I'm going to go back and man the table. I can fluff it for a few hours and just give out Nelle's email for follow-ups. And, hey, I am the *master* of handling two babies at once. If they cry, I'll call you ASAP. Now – go.'

Someone so handsome and stern really must be obeyed and in my post-hysterical-sobbing mood I was pretty powerless to put up a resistance that *No, I should be with Cherry* and *What if she wakes up and I'm not there?* But I let Nelle lead me out of the back doors of the school and towards its playground: all rustic wooden structures and woven rope swings. No graffiti on a wobbly-springed hippo for these guys.

We huddle under the triangular roof of a slide, taking a seat opposite each other on the benches built within it.

Nelle takes a deep breath. 'I'm not going to preach at you, love. I'm not going to give you some inspirational poster line about new dawns and clear skies and that kind of crap. But what I will say, having once been a first-time mum myself, is that all these things – with your other half and how you feel about work and how you feel you're doing as a mum – they're not actually a mountainload of different issues. They're set off by the same thing – having a little kid has stripped you of your confidence. It hasn't actually changed who you are or what you can do, but the broken sleep and the hours of being cried at and the constant work of feeding and changing and washing, all that has tricked you into thinking this way. You've had no time, no energy, to put into feeling good about yourself. Am I right?'

I nod.

'You know, if you think about it, having a baby is a lot like being locked up in Guantanamo Bay.' She points a finger at me as if that is totally self-explanatory. 'They wake you up with loud noises and bright lights at all hours, they play distressing, heart-wrenching noises at you, you're forced into hunched-over stress positions like when you're breastfeeding, you can't choose when you eat or wash or rest. Someone has taken that control from you and it really, really sucks.' Nelle shrugs her shoulders and rolls her eyes to the scrubbed-pine roof above us.

I never thought I'd hear the sagest breakdown of motherhood from a fully painted clown sitting under a slide.

'But,' she moves over to sit next to me, 'it gets better. The real you comes back: she really, really does. And you will realise that you will be fantastic at your job again and that Cherry is only so… full of vim and vigour because you keep her healthy and hearty. And happy. I know you say she never stops crying but she's just got the one noise and she's using it. But that's not a reflection on the job you're doing as her mum. I know I'm going on – I could be an Olympic long-distance talker – and you probably hear all of this from your Ted.'

Biting my lip seems to be the best way to avoid commenting on this or crying all over again.

'What does he say about your work worries?'

'Ah. Well.'

'Well?'

'He doesn't really know. I haven't told him.'

Even when I was in full, ugly sob mode back in the bathroom, Nelle didn't look as concerned as she does now. She swivels on one hip in the tight space to look at me head-on, creases forming in the white paint on her forehead. 'How can you not have told him? Doesn't he wonder why you're not yourself?'

I pick at my thumbnail. 'I sort of... don't let on. And he works so hard, travels so much, that the last thing I want to do when he finally gets home and switches off his laptop is whinge and moan and weep.' I look out at the perfectly mowed, stripy lawns of the school's cricket pitch, wishing that life could be so orderly, so manicured, so free of lumps and bumps. And with a place where everyone knew just where to stand and where to run to and who was on your team. 'The thing is, this is so not *me*. This is not the woman he married. I was bold, confident... *gobby* at times. A force of nature, he called me in his wedding speech. And as much as he loved me for that, I loved it in me, too. If I... if I say, "Oh, hey, I have no friends and I'm worried I'm a crap mother and I'm not sure I'll ever earn another penny again", not only am I admitting that to him and possibly burning the last romantic bridge in our marriage but—' I take a big sticky swallow, and Nelle cuts in.

'—you're admitting it to yourself? Love, I think you just have.'

I wipe my nose on the heel of my hand. 'Oh. Yeah. And it feels just as crappy as I'd thought it would.'

She loops an arm around my shoulders. 'It's that bloody confidence trick again! These feelings aren't real. For one: you are a great mum. Fact. You're first in line at the weigh-in, for god's sake!'

I say after a groan: 'Oh, please don't remind me! What a nerd.'

She bustles on, 'Two: whether you work again, and at what, is up to you, and it's a decision you don't have to take just now. If they're holding a big client for you, let them. They can stall while you take the time you need to sort out your next step. That will come as you work through this crisis of confidence. And three – and I can't believe I am having to spell this out to you when I am here, hugging you, telling you you're great – you HAVE friends. Unless Will and I are chopped liver—?'

'I haven't heard anyone use that expression since I last spoke to my Aunt Phyllis.'

'She's a wise woman. It's a great phrase. But seriously, we're here. We want to hang out with you. And that work friend of yours, who emailed, she loves you enough to break serious HR rules to tell you something exciting. When those dark little voices get to you, remember her and remember us, just for starters.'

Blowing out a deep breath, I straighten my posture and lean into her hug a little bit more before breaking away. 'OK. I hadn't thought of it like that.'

'You're not the only one with that voice, Stevie. We've all got one. It's just about remembering those voices are complete pillocks.' Nelle stands up and brushes off her crazy pant legs. 'Now, we'd better get back. Will might be locked in some mum-mum's car boot by now, little honeytrap that he is.'

Nelle and Will gently insisted that I take it easy for the rest of the morning, entertaining the wee ones behind the table after their monster naps, and only talking to people if I fancied it. And with red puffy eyes and streaks of wept-out make-up on my sleeves, I can't say that I did just then. Nelle seemed happy with the number of phone numbers she took for quotes and Will seemed adept at convincing parents that they really needed two miniature Shetland ponies for their child's birthday party, as if just one was somehow faintly embarrassing. In his Selfridges days he must have been the king of upselling luxe over necessity.

When the fair wound down and we were packing everything back into Nelle's car, I felt as if the choppy waters in my heart had finally settled. It had been a stormy swell of emotion all right, not something I had really wanted to happen in front of two new friends, but I felt a little looser around my rib cage, a little lighter in my step.

Cherry was all safely clipped into the car and the last blue IKEA bag shoved into the boot. Nelle closes the boot lid with a thunk.

'That was a good morning.' She takes off her foam red nose and throws it into the handbag that was under her arm. 'Now my advice to you, Stevie my love, is to go home and tell Ted all about it. ALL about it, you know what I mean?'

The vice around my ribs cranks up again.

–

Saturday afternoon plays out like so many in our family dynamic. On paper, it looks pretty healthy: a family of three, enjoying quality time at home, toys out, radio on, not a raised voice or angry glare on the scene. But, inside, I'm not feeling all that rosy.

While I'm sitting crossed-legged on our rug, Cherry sitting in front of me like a happy Buddha demolishing all my Duplo towers, Ted is snugly reclining on the sofa, the papers scattered about him like some sort of rustling blanket. He made us both a cup of tea ten minutes ago and somehow I think he feels his contribution is over.

'Here's a green one. And a red one on top. And then another green one,' I sing-song as I build Cherry her twenty-ninth tower of the last twenty minutes. 'And those are the colours of Daddy's rugby team, aren't they,

Daddy?' I'm throwing out the most tenuous line for him to come and join in, to interact, even if Cherry couldn't care less about the Leicester Tigers than she does about particle physics. I would just like to tag team this baby entertaining for a while, not be the sole entertainer plus feeder and bather and soother. It might give me some headspace to figure out how I'm going to talk to him about my hour-long breakdown today. About how there are some things I haven't been totally honest about…

'Isn't that right, Daddy?' I say again, to grab his attention back from the supplements.

'Oh? Yup, yup. That's right.' But he stays on the sofa and turns another glossy page.

'Ted,' I now say a little more sharply, as Cherry grabs out at my arm, indicating that I'm taking too long to get things to a good smashing height. 'Want to come and join in?'

His brown eyes appear over the top of the cookery section pages. 'Hmm? Is she getting whingey? I could take her out in her pram.' He looks at his watch.

'No, we're just—'

He stands up, his legs always surprising me that someone could skilfully control limbs so long. 'Actually, I could take her out now as I need to get down to the pharmacy in town.' My heart soars. He's noticed we're nearly out of baby wipes; he's going to buy them without me having to ask. 'I need to pick up some travel stuff – they're sending me to Hong Kong for all of next week.'

My leap up onto my feet is nowhere near as graceful as his: it takes a hand pushing against my knee and a middle-aged 'Ooof' noise. 'Wait, what?'

'Yeah, it's all last minute. They asked me on Friday and I was so shattered I forgot to say. Leaving crack of dawn Monday.'

'Wha—Monday as in the day after tomorrow Monday? And for how long?' I can barely croak the words out. Cherry is now chewing on the back of my jeans.

'Back next Saturday, about lunchtime, I think.' He says this so casually, like he hasn't just lobbed a grenade into my world.

I can feel heat rise to the tips of my ears. 'HOW can they do this? Did you tell them it's not that easy to waltz off for an entire week when you have a six month old?'

Ted blinks at me like I'm a deranged prisoner behind soundproof glass in one of those little visiting booths, and I haven't worked out how to talk into the phone. 'I'm not waltzing anywhere, Stevie. This is an important project and it's part of my job.'

'But…' My heart is thumping as I look for a reasonable argument. I hate it when he stays calm in these situations and I go straight into near-hysteria. I've already cried crazily this weekend: I won't do it again. Until at least tomorrow. 'Couldn't you just Skype into the meetings? You've got all the tech to do that.'

Cherry begins to yelp and protest on the floor. She hates being left out of anything – she has infant FOMO – so I whip her up into my arms.

Ted rubs a hand over his light stubble. 'It doesn't work that way,' he says gently, and I feel patronised and fill with another blast of rage. 'I have to be there to form relationships… you know how it is.'

I want to smash some building blocks into his face. I want to yell, 'No, I don't know how it is because I haven't had a professional moment in nearly seven months and I never get to escape this domestic drudgery and the only highlight of my week is looking forward to a weekend when that drudgery is shared, is normalised somehow. And now you're going to leave me behind to be totally alone in a mountain of dirty nappies and glued-on porridge dribbles and lose yourself in room service and cold beers and power suits. You absolute arsehole!'

But I don't yell that. I don't say anything. I am so immobilised by the rage I feel, all I do is fall into the hypnotic sway of the hips that comes when you hold a squirming baby, shifting my weight from foot to foot.

Ted holds out his arms towards my baby. 'Shall I take her, then? Give you ten minutes to yourself?'

My hand stays firm on Cherry's meaty bum. 'No. Thanks,' I mutter. 'I'd better get used to being on my own with her, hadn't I? Just the two of us.' I plonk us down on the carpet again, busying my shaking hands with a whole other tower. Sod the green and red, sod the Leicester Tigers.

I keep my back to Ted, but his sigh reaches me over my shoulder. 'Stevie, please. Don't be like this. I have to go. And you'll be fine, you know you'll be fine.'

When I don't move he sighs again. I know I'm hurting him, this man I love, by going into shutdown mode. I know I should be a grown-up and face the problem that's just erupted between us. But I don't want to be the bigger person, not today. I'm the bigger person when I pick up his dumped coat. I'm the bigger person when I wash his socks. I support him and his career and the things that stress him out. But when do I get my turn at that kind of support? Who's there to take the burden off *me*?

A few minutes later I hear the jingle of keys being loaded into his pocket and he shuts the front door behind him.

Confessions of a First-Time Mum

Blog post 3.15pm

'Fine': the real F word.

'Fine' used to be a fun word, when I was younger and before I had a kid.

'How's your food?' a stylish tattooed waiter in a London gastro pub would ask. 'Fine!' I'd chirrup back, tucking into my perfectly cooked rack of lamb served on a slab of tree trunk, getting to eat my food warm and just the way the chef intended, not stone-cold and with solidified fat marbling the meat, because I'd had to rush to change a nappy or awkwardly bring out a boob in front of gawking drinkers.

I might look at myself in a mirror of a changing room with a new, low-cut, slinky top on, turning this way and that, holding in my few extra centimetres of flesh with a deep breath. When I liked what I saw, I might cheekily think, 'Girl, you look fine in this. Buy it and wear it out tonight!' And just like that, I'd bought a new outfit and decided my evening plans without having to consult sleeping and feeding patterns like a star map, for weeks in advance. Without having to worry that even if I did beat the odds and make it out for a night, I might fall asleep next to a speaker in a night club at 10.23pm because I'd been awake 20 hours that day.

When friends would ask, 'So, how are you?' I would say, 'Yeah, I'm fine' and I would really mean that. I would mean everything in my life is good and easy and right. Because I never thought that much about what went into achieving that kind of natural happiness. Because I took it for granted.

And now fine is a totally different word, and laden with so much more meaning than ever before. It's actually a pretty heavy word, now I think about it. 'Fine' means 'acceptable', 'I can live with it' and 'This will do'. It's not pub lunches or new tops or friendly chats. It's pushing a pram around and around in circles even though my legs are so tired I think they might crumple underneath me, and then a sweet old lady at a bus stop will ask about the baby and I'll say with a fake smile: 'Fine.' It's about deciding that a jumper to pull on for the day is 'fine' because there are no major stains on it and it doesn't smell all that bad. It's muttering that the baby onesie is 'Probably fine' because you managed to wipe up the sick sharpish with a baby wipe and the thought of putting the washing machine on yet again today makes you want to scream.

It's the 'Hey, it's fine' you hear down the line when you call to cancel a plan with your pre-baby friends because of a worrying temperature or a night before of only 45-minutes' sleep. And in their tone you can almost hear yourself getting crossed off a mental list of people to socialise with.

It's scraping by.

And when people ask, 'So, how are you?' I still say, 'Yeah, I'm fine.' Because to let it all out, all the resentments and complaints and hardships, sound like ingratitude. For being given a beautiful child. For having a baby. For doing what so many couples desperately want to do, and can't. For having an extended maternity leave when some mums have no choice but to go back to work at three months to pay the bills.

I'm honestly not ungrateful, I swear. Sometimes the impossible perfection of my daughter's round cheeks actually takes my breath away. And she'll look at me with her quick, sharp eyes and pull a face and inside I feel like The Wizard of Oz when it goes Technicolor.

I love her, sweet Jesus, I love her to bits, but that doesn't make everything 'fine'.

So, my OH is going away, at the last minute, on a work trip. And he tells me, 'You'll be fine' and I think that tells me everything I need to know about our different experiences of parenthood. He believes it. But I know the reality.

My thumb is starting to cramp up as I hit 'Publish'. Cherry fell asleep after her mid-afternoon feed, like a warm Doberman on my lap, and I didn't want to risk that by moving her. Besides, the warm heft of her on my lap, the sweet smell of her freshly washed babygro, the slow lift and fall of her chest as she snoozed, was so comforting. A little bubble of sofa love. So I shoved my boob back into my nursing bra and poured all my frustrations with Ted into a blog post.

It was the one thing I didn't spill the beans about to Will and Nelle this morning – mostly because it doesn't feel real, my little blog. I've had about 300 hits in the last month and I'm convinced it's men after porn and, because I say boobs and nipples so much, the metadata wrongly brings them to First-Time Mum. I hope the reality of the mastitis and bloody, oozing nipple cracks I detail are their just desserts. First-Time Mum is not here for anyone's sexual gratification, thank you very much. She's here to say everything I'm too much of a scaredy-cat to say in real life.

But I suppose it's the one thing I expected for my mum life before Cherry's arrival that has actually come true: I had this vision of myself keeping a little blog going, journalising our adventures and milestones, 'keeping my mind occupied' in the time before going back to work. I saw it as flapjack recipes and pics of handprint collages, and baby and I in sunnies on our first beach holiday (which has still yet to happen). But what it turned out to be was an SOS. A catalogue of my shortcomings. A way to say 'this is hard' without saying it to a flesh-and-blood person who might judge me or dislike me or tell everyone I'm a bad parent.

And today it's the space for the things I can't say to Ted.

He's still out — he texted to say he was going to swing by the supermarket and get me in some things for next week. And that's a token effort and all, but I know really he wants to prolong his break out of the house. He has so much more freedom than me that sometimes it feels like I really am the mad prisoner behind the glass and I have to watch him swan off into the great unknown every time he goes to work. To a land where he can pee in private and take lunch just when he pleases and eat food he hasn't microwaved himself. And the idea of that sweet freedom makes my domestic incarceration so much more of a bitter pill to swallow.

He'll have drinks in Hong Kong. Dinners. Cocktail parties. He'll bring back a cuddly toy for Cherry and think balance has been restored. But what kind of balanced relationship can you have when one person is free to hop continents and the other can barely manage a stress-free trip to Sainsbury's?

Ted and I used to think the same about everything: food — you can't have too much butter; travel — the path untrodden is all well and good but where can I get a decent glass of red around here?; domesticity — if you make a mess, you clear it up. Genitalia has nothing to do with it. So how has everything slipped so drastically since we've moved from a two to a three?

I was ready to take on more of the household chores, of course I was. He's earning the money to pay the bills so it's fair enough I push the hoover around more than usual. But all of a sudden I realise I'm doing all the washing. All the cooking. I'm remembering his family's birthdays and organising trips up to Leicester to see them. And he doesn't even seem to notice. It's like it's background noise to him these days. Home life is the brief pause between working weeks and international flights.

When no one else is listening, there's always the internet. I disabled my comments section after a string of spammers, but I also didn't want to log on one day and see a paragraph of badly spelled abuse about what a lazy, ungrateful harpy I was and how I should feel lucky to have a roof over my head and a husband and a healthy baby, especially when I'm such a bitch. I don't need a troll to tell me that: I *am* lucky. Ted might feel like he's on another planet at the moment, but in so many ways he is a great partner and dad – dependable, a provider, calm and steady. We're OK for money and, bar her reflux, Cherry is fighting fit. I lost a pregnancy early on, about six months before we conceived Cherry, so I know what an incredible feat of biology and luck and magic dust it is when the stars align and you get that squirmy bundle to take home from the hospital. I wouldn't have my life without her. Rather, I'd like to keep her, but with more sleep and time and sanity, please?

My phone vibrates on the sofa cushion and Cherry's head wriggles for a moment, letting just a little cool air in on the sweat patch she's leaving on my trousers. Another bout of luck that my miracle hasn't woken up.

It's an invitation to join a WhatsApp group: 'Mums I'd Like to Befriend', from Will.

> Will: Coffee at mine on Monday? I can't bring myself to say 'play date' but you know what I mean. 10.30? I'm off Roger's Lane, no.5 The Annexe.

Nelle pings back before I can think of a snappy reply.

> Nelle: Can't wait! What can I bring?

> Will: Tarpaulins. Hoses. Hazmat suit.
> Anything that will help clean up after a craft
> session with my girls.

> Stevie: Hahahaha! I'll bring my Marigolds
> and sheep dip. X

I might not be heard by my husband these days, but I have found two sets of ears who totally get me.

Chapter 5

It really isn't all that much of a walk to Will's house and, having done so many pram walks around the neighbourhood to trick Cherry into sleep over the months, I know every street and cut-through and back alley like the inside of my nappy bag. Also, from those agonisingly frequent pram walks, I did my fair share of snooping: creeping past at a glaringly obviously slow pace to rubber-neck into every grand living-room window the vicinity has to offer. I was only caught out once by a very well-coiffed OAP who was pulling back her curtains just as I was hazily wondering whether they were Laura Ashley or not. The look she gave indicated I would never have the chance to ask her.

So from my property perving, I know The Annexe is fancy – like tea at Claridge's fancy: only for the elite, not how your average Jo gets his cuppa. I haven't actually walked down it myself because it's a private road and all gravel, so would have played havoc with my pram wheels, but I peeked in enough times to get a measure of each unique property: all relatively new builds but with differing styles and all hidden behind long drives and willowy trees. And I'd rather not park my battered old runaround on a drive like that. I'm not sure Will's neighbours would thank me for that feeling of shame, too.

As we reach the front door – after what felt like a 5k fun run from the gate posts to the house itself – I crouch down to Cherry's level and check her over for any strings of drool or protruding bogeys. Once she managed to grab a fistful of leaves from a passing hedge and I only realised when I stopped at a crossing and saw green smudges around her lips. Digging chewed-up leaves from the mouth of an angry baby is not a skill they teach you at NCT classes.

Cherry is passable enough and her legs are kicking about like billy-oh, excited by a new door and the noises behind it. This kid is nosey and seeing as how I knew the route here without having to Googlemap it, I know just where she gets it from.

'Let's not throw up on anything that looks expensive, OK? Aim for the machine-washable things. And Mummy will be careful of her tea on the sofa. It may well be bespoke. But we'll have fun, OK? You get to see Joe, Esme and Olive again. Making friends is fun!' I use my most gooey, positive tone.

Cherry briefly screws up her eyes and sticks her tongue out, as if to remind me I've sometimes said the very opposite after a disastrous baby group session.

I ring the doorbell and soon after the glossy, cherry-red door swings open. 'Hello, come in. We're already into our third Play-Doh session of the day. *We're having fun!*' Will gives the demented smile of a possessed ventriloquist's dummy.

As I kick off my shoes in the tiled hallway, I admire the crisp light grey walls against the polished navy blue floor tiles. There are scuffmarks at knee height from pushchairs and scooters and toddler boots, sure, but there is still a very well put together air about the place. There's a dado rail about a foot below the ceiling and the space in between is painted a matt gold. And I'm in love with it. There's a dark grey painted hat stand with just one tweed trilby hanging on it. I admire anyone who can keep up that kind of interior accessory with two toddlers in their lives. I nearly trip over one of the girls as I wander through the hall, gazing up at the blue Tiffany lamp suspended from the ceiling. Beautiful. It's a good job I never used to frequent Selfridges in my London days; if I had when Will was stocking the place, I would have been overdrawn faster than you can say vintage radiator.

'Is this' – I stroke my hands along the old-style radiator that runs along the wall, towards the kitchen – 'real vintage?'

'Pfft, no.' Will shakes his head. 'I love the look but I actually want to be *warm* in my house. I know a guy that makes them to look old. I don't go in for many gay stereotypes – Madonna, I can take her or leave her these days – but interior decorating is a pretty big deal to me, and all of my people.' He salutes a rainbow flag postcard that's tucked into the big gilt mirror to my left.

'It's all so lovely,' I breathe. 'If you ever fancy a project I have a bijou cottage in need of an expert eye.'

Will nods. 'I'll be right round once the girls are at university. Come on through, let's get the kettle on. Nelle said she would be a bit late due to some sort of diamond wedding crisis. I do hope one of the couple hasn't...' He pulls his mouth into a wide grimace and draws his finger across his throat.

Olive and Esme are at the kitchen table, which is covered in a big oilcloth with a giant mallard print repeating over it. The Play-Doh scattered in molehills around them is clearly much-loved: it has taken on that

69

murky green sludge colour that mixed-up Play-Doh ultimately becomes. Their heads are bent in mirrored concentration as they smash and roll and chop and rip.

'Ha! I think I'd only reach that many years married if I was heavily medicated for the next few decades.'

Will only raises his eyebrows as he gets out some mugs. 'I'm guessing no big heart-to-heart at the weekend, then?'

After plonking Cherry in a high chair at the kitchen table, I cross my arms over my chest. Sometimes she insists on being held all the time in a new place, while she acclimatises, but with an entertaining duo to stare at, my cuddles are quickly forgotten. 'Nope. He announced he was off to Hong Kong for the week. Left this morning.'

'Ouch.' He mirrors my stance. 'Swine.'

I put my hands gently over Cherry's ears and she wriggles to be free. I sneak a look at the twins but they are still fixated on their creations. 'I would go so far as to say *arsehole*.' I mouth the last word silently.

Will nods. 'I don't know the guy but if it were me I'd absolutely be calling him one of those. Loudly. I would get him a bathrobe with that embroidered on it.'

'Maybe for Christmas.' I take the thick ceramic mug he hands me. I feel like one of those jammy sods who gets to eat dinner with Nigella at her house at the end of her cooking show.

'Christmas?' Two small heads whip up in my direction. 'Santa?'

My new friend closes his eyes ever so slowly. 'No, loves, still a while till Christmas. Though Santa *is* watching you all year, to see if you're being good and following all the rules.' He points at a behaviour chart on the wall that is conspicuously empty of reward stickers.

I feel I should quickly make amends for opening such a can of worms in front of two very smart two year olds, so I aim for distraction. 'So what are you guys making here?' I pull out a scrubbed-pine chair and sit next to Olive.

'This is a pizza shop,' says Olive.

'Tsk,' snaps Esme, 'it's called a pizza *cafe*, Olive.'

The twin dynamic is quickly established.

'Oooh, pizza! I love pizza. Could you make me one, please? And a little one for Cherry, if you have enough dough.'

Esme grabs a handful of green-grey. 'Yes, we do. This is the dough. This' – she grabs another lump – 'is the cheese. And that' – she points at a ball Esme is squidging – 'is the tomato.'

'And, Esme, how much is one of your pizzas?'

Esme looks to Olive who nods. 'Um, two pounds?' Her voice goes up at the end.

'Bargain. Could I have ham and pineapple, please?' The two girls fall into hysterical giggles, as if I were Mr Tumble in the flesh.

Olive rolls her eyes. 'Silly! You don't put pudding on a pizza!'

Will laughs with a low chuckle. 'I wouldn't bother trying to explain it, Stevie. I'm not sure there's any logical way to explain a Hawaiian, actually. But while they're safe with non-toxic substances, let me give you the tour.'

If I was ready to swoon at the hallway, I'm deep into fainting-Edwardian-lady mode as I gawp about the three large bedrooms upstairs. Will and his husband's bedroom is lusciously papered in what must be a hand-painted print of thick green leaves and vines twisting and undulating together, with Victorian-era industrial-looking light fittings to offset the opulence. I never would have had the balls for the maroon velvet curtains but, boy, do they work. They have a guest suite and the walls are a perfect pale, powdery blue. Just the backdrop for lying in bed with the papers and a croissant, as you snuggle down in the thick and crisp sheets on the uber-enormous bed. Lush. The girls' room has a similar subtle but stylish feel – dove grey walls with large, pewter-grey, sparkling stars painted all over in an artfully scattered pattern. The kind of kids' decor that you dream you'll have when you are pregnant and before you realise that most toys come in an undisguisable shade of lime green and that your child will reject the beautiful bespoke handmade caramel blanket your colleagues bought you and instead chooses as a comforter an old nightshirt of yours with the Guinness logo on it.

Just as I'm marvelling and cursing at Will for managing to keep out the tacky, tawdry baby stuff that seems to push the walls of my house further apart, I spot them: stickers. *A-ha!*

Over the heads of the matching toddler beds (navy blue and not a whiff of an IKEA locking nut between them) are matching rows of Peppa Pig stickers. Will spots my eyes lingering on them and I blush.

'Yes,' he deadpans, 'the Peppa family portraits were not my idea. But when the girls moved into beds from their cots – they were escaping head-first otherwise I never would have given them that kind of freedom – I was desperate to give them an incentive to love their "big girl beds". And I let them choose the wall stickers they wanted. Which, of course, was exactly the same choice. But it seemed to do the trick.' He sighs and stuffs his elegant hands in his pockets.

'Well, then,' I say, trying to lighten the gloomy mood that's suddenly crept up on us, 'mission accomplished. Nothing wrong with a bit of Peppa if it gets the job done. God knows I've watched enough of it in a desperate attempt to entertain Cherry while I can eat some cheese on toast without having my hair pulled. And it's not the *worst* animation out there. Could have been sodding Paw Patrol.'

He looks at me and smiles, but not the kind of real smile that makes your eyes wrinkle. A sort of flat smile. 'It's not Peppa per se I object to. It's... Oh, this is going to sound pathetic.'

'More pathetic than crying in the loos because someone asked you to price up a christening?' I raise my eyebrows and his eyes do crease this time.

'That was not pathetic, Stevie. But, well, the thing is,' he rubs his hand over his chin, 'they've both killed off their Mummy Pig.'

I blink. This is some kind of parenting speak that has passed me by. Clearly I haven't been hitting the parenting forums enough in the early hours. 'Pardon?'

Will points to a gap in both the line-ups of wall stickers, between Daddy Pig and George. Identical gaps. 'That's where Mummy Pig used to be. I should know, I spent forty-five minutes making sure they were all on perfectly straight and without air bubbles. And then a few weeks later, all of a sudden, she's gone. The girls have scratched her off. Found two sticky balls under their pillows when I went hunting.' His hand is at his temple now.

'So... they love a male parent then!' I chirrup.

Will shakes his head just a fraction. 'No, that's not it – I don't think. You see Adrian is Daddy, I'm Dad. But, more than that, I'm the one who's at home all the time, I'm the one who makes cakes with them, cleans them down after a baked-bean lunch, mostly I put them to bed and wipe their bums and all that. I'm the...' – his voice drops into a gravelly whisper – 'I'm the mummy, traditionally speaking, and they've removed me. I'm invisible.'

A tiny shudder passes down my back. 'No, no. That can't be right. It must just be... random. They were feeling crafty and Mummy Pig just happened to be closest.'

'But they chose the *same* character, at the *same* time. That must mean something—?' He's turned to look at me now and I can see small grey bags under his eyes that I hadn't noticed before. I am not the only one having sleepless nights, it seems; for some, there are other worries keeping them up at night.

Without thinking, I reach out and squeeze his arm. It's like solid clay under my fingers, only giving a fraction to my touch. I quickly drop my hold as a flash of a memory of Ted hits me – my hands, his arms, a wild, distant look in his eyes: a really rude memory, and one it is not cool for me to be thinking of in the bedroom of two toddlers. Blimey, how long has it been since I touched Ted like that, even incidentally? Even in the kitchen, passing by to grab the milk? Let alone in flagrante. I shudder again and remind myself what the particular topic of anxiety is here. And it's not my sub-zero sex life.

I spot two matching Jelly Cat rabbits on the beds: one grey, one pink. The grey bunny is missing both ears and has what looks like a paint splodge on its stomach; the pink bunny has a leg roughly stitched back on with black thread and is missing nearly all the fur on its face.

I clear my throat. 'It's *The Velveteen Rabbit*,' I say with confidence. 'Look at those bunnies – I bet they are only so... worn because the girls love them. They get taken everywhere and cuddled and squashed and decorated with love, I bet?' Will nods. 'So they didn't peel off Mummy Pig because she's somehow not important or their least favourite. They went for her first because she's *the best*. She's the *most* important and they just wanted her close. That's why they put her under their pillows. To be close.'

Will's eyes flick to the ceiling as he mulls my cod-psychology. 'Hmmm.' It seems to be trickling through. 'Perhaps. Adrian has definitely said I'm making too much of it. But when your whole day is fairy cakes, beans, wipes and the works of Julia Donaldson – and each day is the same day, over and over again – you're desperate for it to mean something. I'm lucky to get this time with them, and I'm happy to be the one at home, really I am. We had the girls through a surrogate and all that organisation and paperwork and waiting was too much to juggle with a full-time job as it was, much less when two squalling babies came along. So I'm happy with my lot in life; I'm so happy we got to have the family we dreamed off, and in one fell swoop. But, even so, the thought that you've been picked off and discarded by the beautiful tyrants you love so much is pretty heart-breaking, you know?'

I nod. I really do know. What I hadn't known was that the draining nature of motherhood is not just a feminist issue. It's the soul-sucking nature of *parenthood*. And it's universal: man, woman or any combination of the two. It's only because we love and worship these little darlings so much that their smallest, most inconsequential movement can cut right into our hearts.

The metallic clang of the door knocker makes us both jump and dislodges my Jerry Springer-style Final Thoughts.

'That'll be Nelle!' Will pulls his shoulders up just a fraction and rubs his hands together. 'Time for cup of tea number two, and to check those girls aren't smearing Play-Doh into the Amazon Echo again.'

–

'So when the brief said "French cuisine, Parisian décor", I thought – great. Fab. Simple, classy and our caterers can do top-of-the-line French food for 125 people. And so we get cracking on planning this diamond wedding – it's the two sons sorting it as a surprise for their parents, which seemed lovely, very Waltons. And I email them both the plans, the estimates. And one brother, Grahame, emails straight back saying we need to leave a big space clear for the dancers to come in and do their thing. Then the other – I forget his name, let's call him Not Grahame – pings in saying "Wot dancers?!'" Nelle leans forward to slurp some tea, well clear of Joe's head in the sling at her front, and then dives straight back into her story, red-faced with the walk here and the pleasure at retelling such a palaver. 'And Grahame says, "The can-can dancers." And again Not Grahame is like "Wot?!?!" – all misspelled and loads of crazy punctuation, the works. So then Grahame starts to explain it's the Moulin Rouge theme they talked about, how his wife Steph has her heart set on it and Not Grahame starts going bonkers, saying how mad that is as a theme for a couple in their eighties and Dad has his dicky heart and Mum won't appreciate either a heart attack or seeing ladies' frilly knickers flashed at her over her quiche. And then Grahame hits back saying he's the only stylish one in the family and they should listen to him and Steph on this. And Not Grahame says he wouldn't trust Steph to choose him a stylish pair of socks, let alone a huge party with all their nearest and dearest. And then all sorts of stuff starts flying, about stag dos and broken Action men and why Mum only ever put Grahame's angel on the top of the Christmas tree. Do you know, I think they completely forgot I was CCed in to the lot of it.' She ruffles a hand through her pixie crop. 'I mean, I was LOVING it, don't get me wrong, but I also had my son's school texting me, saying he was in detention for vaping. Vaping?! And this chap' – she nodded down at Joe – 'going through some bonkers cluster-feeding obsession. So I was boobs out, at the PC, Googling how dangerous it is for a young teen to vape and whether anyone had ever died of angina at a can-can show. Sorry.' She looks in Will's direction.

'It's OK. I know women have boobs. They're not what made me gay. It was frilly knickers, actually.'

Nelle laughs; a big, throaty cackle, and Joe jerks awake with a yelp. 'Oh, Christ, here we go, milk machine time again.' She busies herself unwrapping her stretchy sling and unclicking her feeding bra at her shoulder, underneath her top. 'So that's my day, all seven shades of… silly of it. And you guys?'

I push another rice cake in Cherry's direction. Usually she can get through five or six easily in one sitting, without really being hungry, but she is so transfixed by the Play-Doh version of *Saturday Kitchen* going on in front of her that she doesn't even register me. It's lovely for once not to have to desperately halt a meltdown in a social situation – and every sip of hot tea is utter bliss – but just a split-second image of that Mummy Pig-less scene upstairs comes to me. I start joining in the cookery lesson to shake it off, and to avoid Nelle's question. I have a feeling she'll think I'm a wimp for not telling all to Ted yesterday. But it's hard to get out your rawest emotions when you are sweltering with blind, hot rage.

'So, what's on the menu, ladies?'

Olive purses her lips and thinks. 'Sushi. And Wotsits.'

'Ooooh, sushi! Haven't had that in ages. Could I have some tuna sashimi and a few cucumber maki, please?'

Esme eyes the green lumps in front of them. 'Ummmm, yeah. Here you go.' She plops a tennis-ball-sized blob in front of me.

I haven't played with Play-Doh in decades. This could be a phase later down the line with Cherry that I could totally embrace. I'd love to get rolling and squishing with her, and see what her sharp little mind can concoct. Plus, as activities go, it's halfway mindful. I borrow a plastic rolling pin that neither girl is using and start flattening my lump out into seaweed sheets. As I'm cutting out a square with a funny rotating wheel with spindly edges, Olive lowers her thick dark brows at me. 'What you doing?'

'Well, sushi is held together by seaweed.'

Both girls stick out their tongues and happily shriek, 'Bleurgh!'

Will interjects. 'Not just off the beach, though. Special edible seaweed that's very good for you.'

Esme continues to mime vomiting and Olive nods in approval.

I may have opened another can of stinky worms there, so I push on. 'So you've got your... wrapper. And you put rice on top.' I crumble some Doh all over my wonky rectangle. 'And then the cucumber sticks.' I roll some cigarette-like sticks and lay them inside. 'Then it all gets wrapped up into one big sausage and we chop it up.' I've never managed a Swiss roll but strangely I feel unbelievably proud of my jumbo sushi roll. I chop one piece off the end to demonstrate, then carefully manoeuvre the rest in front of the girls so they have one end each to work on. With matching tongues now stuck out in matching concentration, they begin their work. And Cherry sits, hypnotised, a thin strand of drool running from her chin to her neckerchief. God bless those baby neckerchiefs.

'You're good at that,' Nelle says in a half-whisper, so as not to disturb the sushi chefs and their training.

'Making Play-Doh raw fish? Well, that's certainly a career avenue for me if PR goes belly-up.'

She rolls her eyes. 'No, entertaining kids. And without even a big red nose or comedy shoes.' She winks. 'That's a whole heap harder than entertaining adults, trust me. Because with adults you always have watered-down beer and Prosecco. At our parties, as long as we feed and water the grown-ups, it's a doddle. But kids' parties—? Jeeeeeez.' She pauses to unlatch Joe and bring him to her shoulder for a burp. 'No, with kids you need entertainment, and then back-up entertainment, and music, and games, and party bags.'

Will chimes in. 'And don't forget allergies, intolerances, anti-sugar parents…'

'Bouncy castle, petting zoo, giant cake in the theme of that week's favourite thing…' Nelle ticks off on one hand as the other rubs circles on Joe's back. She really is a pro at this.

I shrug. 'I like big groups of kids. I was an only child and didn't have many cousins, so I was always seeking out where other children were, when I had the chance. Only so many album sleeve notes I could read in my mum's attic. When I was seventeen I went and did one of those American summer camps, as a counsellor, you know? Loved it. Maybe that's why I got into PR – always looking for a chance to chat!' My breath runs out as I'm reminded how far I am from that bubbling twenty-something now, who took a badly paid PR internship just to find a place in London and be let loose on the world. Even when I just had a new brand of cough mixture to push. I loved it.

Nelle smuggles Joe back under her striped top for his next course, on her other boob. 'And talking of talking, how did it go with your husband. Ted, yes? I'm rubbish with names sometimes. I keep referring to these two as Olive and Humous in my head.' She tips her head towards the twins and both Will and Esme look deeply crestfallen. 'Sorry, sorry. I'm an idiot.'

I squidge a tiny ball of Doh under my index finger. 'Well, it didn't go, now you mention it. He dropped the bombshell that he had to go to Hong Kong. For a week. Leaving today.' I turn my wrist so my watch face is showing. 'In fact, by now he's well settled into business class with a G&T and a Vin Diesel movie, if past form is anything to go by. I spent all of Sunday evening just trying not to shove his head in the toaster.'

'Not that violence is ever the answer,' Will says for the benefit of his daughters, while miming a haymaker move well behind them. I smile.

'Blimey!' Nelle's eyebrows disappear into her hairline for a moment. 'Did he ask you if that was OK? Did he even apologise for stuffing up your week and laying all this extra work on you?'

I press my lips together into a hard line, a cold churn of anger starting up again below my stomach. 'Nope. He just said I would be *fine*. Fine. Fine with all the night feeds and early starts and loads of washing and eating toast for dinner alone and talking to the walls. All fine. Totally, absolutely, peachy *fine*.'

Will pulls up a chair to the kitchen table and sits down next to me, suddenly jabbing his finger into the oilcloth, hitting a mallard in the throat. 'That reminds me of this brilliant blog piece I read this morning – I was meaning to forward it to you both. Here.' He whips his phone out from his back pocket and swipes a few times. 'This mummy blogger said the same thing – her husband swanning off with a casual "You'll be fine" and how he just didn't get it at all. And the pressure to look like everything's fine, all the time, when it's not. Even to a little old lady at a bus stop.'

Every single part of me freezes. I feel my phone vibrate in my handbag, at my feet. The link Will has just sent.

It can't be.

But even from the first line of his message I can see an all-too-familiar URL. I can feel my breath becoming a solid block of ice in my lungs. I glug back some tea to try and shift it but end up spluttering desperately.

'Steady on, chick.' Nelle rubs my back gently. She turns to Will. 'It's not one of those online writers who's got cool trainers and pictures of their kids in front of graffiti, is it? Because I don't need another way to feel old and lame in Mothercare, thanks.'

He shakes his head. 'I don't actually know anything about her. "First-Time Mum." She's anonymous; no pictures or anything. It was this other blogger I follow who reposted it on her Facebook page. It's been viewed 12,000 times already, just since last night.'

The details of Will's impossibly perfect cream kitchen start to swim in front of my eyes. Twelve… *thousand*? In one night? No. No, that can't be right.

'Are you OK?' Will's hand reaches out to mine. 'You've gone pale.'

'Uh… um, sleepless night catching up with me. I'd better get us back – hopefully Cherry will nap in the pram. Thanks,' my voice wobbles, 'thanks so much for the tea. Next time at mine, yup?' I don't know why I say this. Next to this dream house of Will's, our cottage is going to look like a doll's house made in the dark out of a shoebox and sticky-backed plastic. I just need to get out. Get far away from the conversation. Because with everything weird about my life that I've already, unintentionally, shared with these two, I am in no way ready to reveal, 'Oh, yeah, and I put all my darkest mum thoughts into a secret blog.'

No one knows about First-Time Mum. And that's how it's got to stay.

Cherry gives quite the yell of disapproval that she's being taken away from her very own toddler tag team of entertainers, and if I hadn't stumbled on this scary problem, Will would probably have had to forcibly eject me from under his roof in about five hours' time. Olive and Esme are an absolute gift in keeping my fractious wonder calm and happy. To placate her, I find some baby biscotti in the bottom of my bag, only slightly stale, and she gums a chocolate one, the cocoa dribble oozing all over her lovely chops. But the mess is worth it for the peace.

I manoeuvre the pram out of Will's hall without damaging anything stylish, thank god, and start to drag the pram behind me across the gravel. I'm leaving big, deep, unsightly tracks behind me but speed is of the essence here.

Just as I reach the big box hedges that mark the entrance to Will's place, I hear a telltale reflux hiccup and then silence. It's always the silence that's the worry.

Cherry is covered in brown sick, and so is the pram cover. She smiles broadly at me. 'Oh, darling,' I moan wearily, pushing her into the shadow of the hedge so we're out of sight as I whip off the sodden layers and try and assemble something clean from the change bag slung under the pram. 'Your timing, Cherry Alice Cameron, is impeccable, as ever. Couldn't have just waited till we were at home and on the easy-wipe play mat, huh? No, no, no, no.' I'm not really annoyed. Cherry can't help it, poor mite, I know that. I'm just tired. Tired of cleaning up vom, tired of being embarrassed by it, tired of coming away smelling like the last dodgy pint of milk left at the back of the newsagent's fridge. In fact, I think I've just smeared some sick across my forehead. Oh, wonderful.

Cherry is safely in her emergency onesie and I've done the best I can with wet wipes on the pram cover. Now to dispose of the evidence in Will's wheelie bin. Which has its own timber shed thing. Of course it does.

As I slam the lid, a flurry of limbs in pink Lycra passes by my eye line. I don't believe it. It's the mum-mum with ankle-bashing Scooter Boy and an equally lithe and limber mum-mum mate. They're sprinting like gazelles. Gazelles with manicures.

Spare Mum-mum smirks at me and I catch my own whiff again: regurgitated biscuit and curdled dairy. Just as they pass the other box hedge I hear her say to Original Mum-mum: 'Funny, I thought Will and Adrian used the same cleaners as us. New to her profession, by the look of it.' And then there's a burst of shrill tittering as they gallop away.

Just go and fuck yourself, I think. Because I'm scared of confrontation these days, but also of polluting Cherry's little pink ears.

More excellent responses come to me as I march home: 'Nothing wrong with being a cleaner, you know. Better than being a dirty slapper, at any rate.' Or, 'Friend of Will's, are you? Funny, because I was just round at his and he said you were a stupid old cow!' Or, 'Has anyone told you that you look like a Barbie factory seconds sale?' OK, so not exactly excellent, but energetic, anyway.

It's not till we're home and I'm puffed out by the slight uphill push and all my aimless rage and Cherry is back to wiggling on her vom-proof mat that I remember the post. Oh Christ, the blog post.

Chapter 6

I suppose one benefit to Ted being so far away for so very long is that I have the whole place alone to fret, make my hair greasy with pulling on it and no one is here to see me have a large glass of wine with my beans on toast for lunch. Even Ted, with his head-in-his-work iPhone, would have to clock something a bit off with all that.

I keep having to log in and check my blog stats. 8,000 unique views. I don't know if I should count that on top of the Facebook views through the other blogger's page – now at 19,000 – or if these are people who came to my site because they read it first through her and are coming to check me out.

Blimey.

Fuck.

I look at Gin and Sippy Cups' Facebook again. Not just all those views, but around 3,000 comments, too. I start to read some. Loads of fist bump and crying-face emojis, but also longer comments from parents admitting they are in charge/on their own at the moment and absolutely bricking it. One simply says, 'Welcome to my world #singleparent #everygoddamnday' and I realise my post must have seemed ungrateful to people on their own for much longer than a week. Before I know it, I'm replying to their post, about to say thanks for the reality check, when I remember that it would appear under my real name and then the whole sodding game would be over.

I can't have people know it's me. I can't have Ted see all these steaming-mad things I've written about him. Sure, he's not an innocent party right now but I do love him, at the end of the day. He is Cherry's dad and I can't ever stop loving him for giving me this butterball to love. And how would it look to his super-corporate clients that he has a wife so unhappy she vents the details of their family life on the web? Not to mention the divorce papers he'd be emailing over. Can't really see the selling point in being married to someone dull, scared and also secretly bitchy, myself. My mum would have a field day and insist I move to the States to let her take control of my rotten life. Perhaps worse of all, one day Cherry might read these things and think I didn't want her, that I don't love her madly. Which I absolutely do. I just miss being in love with Stevie Cameron. She was fun. She always smelt nice. And I desperately need to try and find her again.

So I pull back from trawling through the comments. Nothing good can come of it. Instead, I scroll back up Gin and Sippy Cups' profile, to see what other kinds of things she posts about, and what kind of reaction she usually gets. Is this big? Is it normal?

Just as I'm absorbing that she's in Cambridge and is a part-time family lawyer, a new post pops up in her timeline, one of those that automatically feeds through from Instagram. It's a picture of a pair of denim-clad legs, drenched in something like foamy coffee by the look of it. And just on the edge of the shot, on the very right-hand side, is a small hand holding a plastic dinosaur, also sploshed with liquid. She's put up a caption underneath:

'So today I'm standing with First-Time Mum. I'm #Notfineactually. Managed to get us out to a chi-chi coffee place, set Littlest Mr up with toys and colouring, savouring the smell of my cappuccino. When Dino Dan fancies a bit of rough-housing. So, just before I pack us up and drag two squealing misters into Primark to get me something, anything to wear, I thought I'd share the evidence that actually not every day is a "fine" one… If you're having a very un-fine day, you're not alone, loves xxx #mumlife #parenting #mumsofinstagram #toddlers #motherof-boys #coffee #reallife.'

A feeling of warmth, a deep tingle, spreads across my collarbone and I can't help it but I hoot one giant, great laugh out loud, alone in my kitchen. Cherry gives a happy squawk from the floor, as if in solidarity.

I scoop her up into my arms and jiggle her on my lap.

'It's not just me, Cherry Baby!' I say through a ridiculous grin, and she gives me one of her long, unbroken stares where I could swear she understands everything that comes out of my mouth. It's strange to feel such a connection with someone who can't talk back, but this gorgeous pudding is somehow completely on my wavelength. And so, it seems, are loads of other mums out there, online.

It's not just me who feels these things sometimes. Not just me who gets vomit on their head and mistaken for a cleaner.

I'm rereading, guiltily, vainly, when another post pops up: 'PS First-Time Mum, where are you?! Can't find you on any social media, no contact option on your blog. Come say hello. I think we'll get on, yeah? xxx'

Cherry can not only stare deep into my soul, she is also a great karmic leveller. As if sensing my slightly inflated pride today, she's decided to puncture it in a grand fashion by refusing to sleep. All. Bloody. Night.

It's 2.13 and I swear the red blocky numbers of the alarm clock have shown those digits for at least three hours by now. I've done bouncing with her on the gym ball, I've walked up and down stairs until my thighs just could not take any more, my throat is hoarse from whisper-singing. At about 1am I gave up and stuck *Frozen* on, which stopped her crying as she got lost in the colours and sounds, but did not lull her off to sleep. I suppose an epic story of sisterly betrayal and love will stimulate you, even at six months. And now, because I am out of ideas and energy and any sort of self-belief, I am swaying vigorously and ssshhhhing as tears fill my eyes. Cherry's arms swing up at me as she cries, as if physically trying to get away from this rubbish mother she has. 'I'm sorry,' I say in a cracked voice. 'Sorry, baby.' I desperately want to be the mum that can fix her problems. I want to be the mum that gets it right. But here I am, failing and crying all over again.

Something our NCT leader said once comes back to me: 'When it gets too much, it's probably because it *is* too much. Practise a bit of self-care. Leave the room for ten minutes and find your centre. If they're crying, they can cry for a little longer and they'll be fine. If you're a mess and wear yourself down too far, nothing will be ever be fixed for you as a unit.'

So with my hands shaking, I lay Cherry gently in her cot by my bed, her legs now furiously kicking at me as I straighten up. 'Come on, my girl, bedtime. Mummy needs a little breather, but I'm not going far.'

I leave the room on tip-toes and immediately lie down on the landing carpet.

I wish Ted was here. God, I wish my mum was here. Even if she just made some of her foul herbal tea and patted me on the head it would be something. I don't want to be alone with this baby that I can't make happy. Just not now. In the daylight it's somehow funnier, but in this soulless, empty, unending stretch of the night I can't see the beginning or end of anything. I lose my whole sense of humour.

My phone digs into me through my back pocket. I've been at this since 8pm so I haven't even had dinner or got into my PJs. My mascara is forming crusty channels on my cheeks. 2.17am the clock display reads. So at 2.27am I will send myself back in there. I'll give it another crack. Something will work. At some point.

But I'm buggered if I know what that is, or when.

Holding a breath in, I release it slowly, trying to fight the urge to cry all over again. Instead, I open WhatsApp.

> Stevie: Don't suppose anyone else is having a mare of a night, are they? Cherry hasn't slept one wink yet. One wink!!!!!! She's getting me back for that unheard-of nap at the parent and baby fair. Little sod.

> Stevie: Who I love unconditionally. And this is not her fault. She's just being a baby.

'Please someone start typing,' I pray. 'Please, please, pl—'
   Nelle is typing...

> Nelle: YES!

> Nelle: To misquote the Kings of Leon, these nips are on fire. I'm on Joe's ninth night feed and this guy is clearly a buffet kind of baby because he has a little bit, gets bored, twenty minutes later obviously wonders, 'Do they have a pudding table? Maybe a cheese board?' And he wants back in.

> Nelle: You can complain about your baby, Stevie. I won't be on to Childline, you know. Goes without saying that you can adore someone and never want to be apart from them, while also wishing they would just chill out and be cool and let you have a shower once in a while.

> Stevie: Phew. I mean, not to your ravaged nips but to it being normal to wish you could just pause your baby for a few hours and come back to them when you're ready and can skip though the boring bits, like an episode of Grand Designs. Did you get any good bookings out of that fair, by the way?

Nelle: Sadly, no. A few nibbles, but nothing really profitable. And those mad diamond anniversary brothers have pulled out because they still can't agree. We've got the deposit but I could have done with the whole event going through the books, if I'm honest. Party planners are not at the top of most people's lists these days. I blame Pinterest! Everyone's making their own piñatas and wedding favours and all that jazz. Chuh. But I can't get into this in the wee small hours – it's too depressing. Joe has finished his latest snack. Let's hope it's his last. Wishing you sleeping pixie dust, too, Stevie. Night xx

As I put down my phone I realise the house is completely quiet. Which wouldn't freak most people out at 2.17am in your average domestic household. But – Cherry?!

I rush back into the bedroom but instead of finding her blue and lifeless, attacked by a fox or a possessed blind cord or some freak spontaneous blanket fire, I see her ruddy and blush-coloured at her cheeks, snuffling her little snore and totally, completely, beautifully asleep.

No way! She fell asleep all by herself? I mean, with some screeching but otherwise unaided by song or jiggle or white noise machine. Magic.

Forgetting how unforgettably angry I am with him, I message Ted straight away.

Stevie: OK, so baby was screaming all night, literally not been asleep all evening and it's now 2.20. I got so desperate I just put her in her cot and walked away. She only went and fell asleep on her own! Maybe she doesn't like being cuddled any more?! Maybe she's got some weird kind of hatred of physical contact but if it means she sleeps I'm cool with that. Oh god, I can take my jeans off now and get some sleep myself.

I do just that: I slip my jeans off without a sound, soundlessly get under the duvet and fall into a deep, cavernous sleep.

—

When I am woken up at 7.15 by a grumpy mewing coming from the cot, for a moment in my half-asleep brain, when I see those numbers on the clock, I think it's the alarm and I need to get up, jump in the shower, pull on a nice Banana Republic suit and get to work. But of course it's not. It's Cherry, realising she is now starving hungry after a five-hour stretch of sleep. Some kind of night-time record for her, but I can't take all that much pleasure in it seeing as it was preceded by a record six-hour stretch of hysteria for both of us. It would be like having a really nice Sunday lie-in after running the marathon twice.

I swing her up into my arms then settle back against the uncomfortable headboard so she can feed away. She latches on like she's never had a drop of milk in her life.

'Ouch! Steady on, baby girl, it's not going out of fashion.'

Luckily, the one rule of Mum Life I have totally cracked is that you never, ever settle down for a feed without your phone in grabbing distance. Sweet, sweet internet distractions.

Breastfeeding may be natural and free and instant and full of wonderful antibodies or whatever but, man, is it dull. It's like you've got to guard a big watermelon on your lap for half an hour (never mind the time it takes to wind and wind again and then mop up little mouthfuls of puke from your PJs). And sometimes they have these great big mammoth feeding sessions, when you seriously think you are going to be medically dehydrated, and twenty minutes later they're hungry for more! When you've barely had a breather to put on some deodorant and play a bit of online Scrabble for sanity.

I wake up my phone and feel a small hit of happiness that Ted has messaged me back.

> Ted: Great.

I have to scroll back up to see what this lame effort is in reply to. Oh, right, my giddy announcement that Cherry had nodded off by herself, a huge milestone in our sleep-deprived lives. And he says 'Great.' Not even 'Great!' Let alone 'WOW! Well done, thanks for raising such an awesome kid, sorry to desert you like an absolute cad but I'm so in awe of how well you're doing on your own, regardless!'

The small hit of happiness fades into a dot of annoyance. Yes, he's got to work and he's got lots to juggle. But this is *my* work and I always find the energy to dig up some enthusiasm when he tells me tales of getting a new client on the books or a pay rise for his best salesperson, Katy.

Cherry is still chomping away, making porcine grunts of pleasure every now and then. Knowing that she's happy and feeding and growing ruddier and healthier by the ounce relaxes me. It's something so basic and natural but it's still a big achievement to keep a baby fed, however you do it.

She's sorted, so what else can I entertain myself with? I flick through my other recent messages and my eyes stop on Nelle's confession that she could really do with some more business right now. I hope she isn't in any real financial trouble. I've really struggled to stretch out my three months of full pay from work and I just have the one kid to manage – she's got three and I'm not sure family businesses pay you for your maternity leave? Not that it sounds like she's getting much of a break from it, answering mad *Moulin Rouge* emails and slapping on the rainbow wig for the Parent and Baby Fair.

She's right, though – people don't use party planners the way they used to. When Ted and I got married I also got loads of ideas from blogs and Pinterest and Instagram – in addition to my PR experience – and spent my lunchbreaks Googling 'Make Your Own Photo Booth' tutorials and where to bulk buy croquet sets for the lawn games I had envisioned. (Such a huge error in the end, though, as seven-year-old nephews can NOT be trusted with wooden mallets.) But there must still be a niche for professional planners, though – just a *new* niche. Not so much mini quiches and string quartets as… well, what? My brain is foggy with a sort of jet lag from my weird bedtime. I open up my notes app and under my to-do list of 'Clean bathroom, buy new lightbulb for porch, find other running shoe' I add, 'Think about how I can help Nelle. Niche parties?!'

I try to find a way to lean my head back without the top of the headboard pressing horribly into the back of my neck. Nope. Every day I think I'm going to tie a cushion here to stop this very thing happening and every day I lose my 'spare' ten minutes somewhere along the way.

'I think just a quiet day for you and me today, Chezza. None of the dramas of yesterday, or *last night*.' I gently pull on her toes through her sleepsuit. 'Just you and me and some tummy time exercises. Then maybe three times round the park at nap time, yup? Quiet. Mummy's knackered and it's not even seven am.'

Huh, I think, *that would make a good blog title.*

And then I jolt forward, knocking Cherry off her feeding supply and sending her purple with rage. 'Sorry, sorry. Hang on, here you go.' I get her latched back on, her jaw working furiously once more, and feel a rush of remembered adrenaline shoot through my system. The blog, the repost, all those reads…

I open up Facebook and head back to Gin and Sippy Cups. Her post reaching out to First-Time Mum is still there, and has 400 or so likes, to boot. What should I do? It has meant so much that she got what I was saying, that she put it out there for her followers and that they also gave it a big cyber nod of recognition. How do I say thanks for that without revealing the 'real' me?

My heart is drumming like the washing machine on spin cycle as I open up my Facebook settings and log off. After a pause, I hit 'New to Facebook?' and make First-Time Mum her very own profile. No details, definitely no pics, just the basics and a link to the blog. I mean, I could be anyone doing this in First-Time Mum's name, but it would be a lame kind of identity theft for a Russian hacker… 'Dimitri, I have great idea! Let's pretend to be slightly depressed, boring housewife with loud child.'

Then I reply to Gin and Sippy Cups post:

> Hello! First-Time Mum here, shyly peeking her head out from under the stinky laundry pile. Thanks so much for the share, can't tell you how chuffed I am to hear from you all. More blogs soon, sleep permitting… x

I bite my lip. Hope it doesn't sound too cocky. Oh, sod it: these parents understand. They get it. They're probably about to face their day on five hours of sleep, too. This is my tribe. These are my people. My phone vibrates in my hand. Ooh, maybe a Like!

But, even better, it's a message from Will.

Will: Sorry to miss the fun (?!) last night, ladies. The girls do go right through the night now, if you consider 5.12am to be the morning. Which I don't. But little mercies etc. It will get better, Stevie. This too shall pass, as my mother always tells me. One day soon you will get a human amount of sleep as standard, it's just that no one can tell you when that will be. The bastards. Anyway, the girls are requesting another sushi lesson from Stewart, which I think must mean you. We're out this morning but do you both fancy another play date this afternoon?

A part of me knows I should counter-offer to host here – the Girl Guide part – but a larger, more exhausted and selfish part of me knows that will involve a mad hour of cleaning, stacking junk and shoving more junk under the sofa and still my house will be nowhere near as stylish and cosy as Will's. Maybe I could just get some nice biscuits from the Co-op on the way there?

Nelle quickly reads my mind.

Nelle: Technically, it could be my turn to host but there are underpants on every radiator here and a job-lot of napkins got delivered to our house instead of the office so the boxes are our new footstools. It's a dump. But if you're happy to have us, Will, I'll be Teasmade while Stewart does her California rolls.

Olive and Esme really need very little instruction before they are deep into Doh concentration, mini furrowed brows so adorable as they roll and cut and line up their produce for their sushi cafe. I enjoy seeing Esme try to claim back a little of the twin power dynamic in this new skill – telling her sister that her sludge-green 'rice' isn't in the right place and that she'd had the cutting wheel for too long, thank you. Olive narrows her eyes and ploughs on, maybe dreaming up some sort of two-year-old revenge. I hope we're out of the house before that goes down.

Cherry is drooling in true happiness; trying as hard as she can to reach out a fat fist and grab some of the shiny curls of the twins before her, she is wriggling with glee on my lap. Real live moving dolls for her entertainment. Bliss all round. It makes my heart happy to see her bond so completely with other children, giving me a glimpse of the world of friendship she'll have as a toddler herself. I would happily allow ten toddlers to tread Play-Doh into my best rug if it meant she had friends who made her as happy as this when she's two.

Will set us up at the patio table outside, seeing as it's a lovely, fine day and fresh air always has the magic power to make any long day of childcare more bearable. He's lounging back in a rattan, boxy armchair, long legs stretched before him and crossed at the ankles. With the end of his slipper he gently bounces Joe in a bouncy chair though from where I'm sitting he looks blissfully asleep still. This is the magic sleeping baby I've heard so much about. I never thought I'd see one in real life, like a unicorn or a leprechaun or an ASOS top you can wear a bra with. I'm not sure whether it makes me feel better or worse to know they really do exist – encouraging and heart-breaking at the same time.

'Jiggling a bouncy chair is one of those things I just can't not do,' Will says. 'I still rock the shopping trolley back and forth while I'm looking for something in the supermarket, even though the girls are long out of those little plastic seats and are most likely two aisles down with their hands in a cereal box. Adrian says he could still make up two perfectly sterile bottles in his sleep. Some parenting things are burnt into your brain, I think. Like it or not.'

'I can't stop myself narrating everything as I go, for Cherry's amusement. And then I realise she's in bed and I'm saying to the toast, "Now will we have some Marmite, do you think, or shall we have Nutella as a little treaty-weaty?" It's a bit of a worry, to be honest. The other day I was explaining the bin days to her when this gorgeous mum-mum busted me and I felt like a fruit bat.'

'Fruit cake,' Nelle says, as she carefully walks out with the tea tray and sets it down on the corner of the table, far away from the girls.

'What did I say?'

'Fruit *bat*, but we knew what you were on about. I've told you, you've got to watch those mum-mums. They will suck the joy and energy out of you quicker than you can say luxury four by four.'

Will shifts a little in his seat. 'They're not *all* bad. You can't dislike someone for having good hair. *You*'re both gorgeous and I like you.'

'Your flattery is well timed and well received.' Nelle winks at him. 'But I don't think you see the real sharpness of their manicures, being a tall, handsome, cultured, stay-at-home dad with a stunning home. You are their ultimate prize and they'd never turn on you.'

He shrugs. 'Sorry, I didn't catch anything after "handsome". You made me swoon. Now, let's crack out the biscuits and you can update us on work dramas.'

Nelle looks uncharacteristically flat at the mention of work. She worries at a thumbnail. 'Do I have to?'

Will looks up at the sky and gives this mock-consideration. 'Well, seeing as how the nearest I get to drama these days is running low on anti-bac handwash of a Tuesday morning, I would say yes. You have to. I know I made the right decision to leave work, leave London and focus on the girls but it doesn't mean I miss real, adult life any less. Now, out with it – have any insults been hurled, any punches thrown?'

'No. It's all gone quiet. In a perfect world, I wouldn't have to worry about any of this with Joe so tiny, but with a family business there literally is no gap between "family" and "business".' Nelle sighs and rubs her hands against her black jeans. 'When Darren and I fell for each other, we were pretty young, barely old enough to drive a car. Back then, having a big family to marry into and work with seemed like a dream – everything taken care of. No scary journey into the big bad world of work for me. But now...'

'Is business really that bad?' Will drops the teasing smile from his face and squeezes Nelle on the knee in sympathy.

Nelle nods. 'It's not just that it's bad, it's that I never really wanted this to be my career, full stop. Party planning doesn't really rev my engine, to be honest. Even less so when no one wants to hire you and your father-in-law is looking over the P&L for last year and making grumbles. My father-in-law is an expert grumbler these days.'

'Can't he help out more?' I venture.

'Not really. It's just one arm of the big family empire; a few local cafes, a small boutique hotel, even a funeral parlour. The idea was the party business would cater to clients of all of those, but demand has just really dropped in the last few years.' She holds up her hands, as if in surrender. 'Smoked salmon sandwiches just aren't drawing the crowds nowadays. It's all bulgur wheat reductions served on a slate tile and I'm bugg—' Her eyes flick to Esme and Olive. 'I'm stumped to even begin to get my head round all that stuff.'

'I always think stick to what you know,' Will says, confidently. 'I once stocked a whole line of sausage dog patterned crockery at Selfridges – plates, bowls, vases. All hand-painted, hand-thrown. Completely beautiful and expensive. I thought, "Everyone loves these dogs, even if I don't, they're everywhere. It's bound to fly."' He shakes his head with a grimace. 'In three months it was all in clearance. I am a cat person, plain and simple. Should have gone for the Persian Blue motif.'

'But that's it – I don't know much.' Nelle's voice was low and gravelly. 'Just parties. And having babies. Even when I don't mean to.' She smoothes one finger over Joe's fluffy little sprouting of hair and a smile flickers back to her face.

Even in the midst of money worries, and nights so broken they are hanging in pieces, and public outbursts, and Play-Doh marathons, there is just something in the sweet curve of a plump cheek or a tiny dark curl falling over an inquisitive eye, or even the fat folds behind the knee of my own little chunk that just makes everything feel better. Like an opium you not only want to take, but must take, everyday. You get that crazy wave of love that sees you meticulously clean and nurture their every patch of flesh while your hair hasn't seen shampoo in a week; you'll buy them overpriced wooden stacking bricks and then ear-grating musical toys and hand-stitched, organic cotton T-shirts when you haven't had anything new since Sainsbury's did 20 per cent off jogging bottoms. They steal your heart, and your credit rating, these babies. And you are happy to let them have it all.

'Babies – you know… *babies*,' I blurt out, sending a biscuit crumb flying from the corner of my mouth. 'People love spending money on their kids. You just need to find new ways for them to spend it.'

Nelle frowns. 'I don't know. That fair didn't really achieve much.'

Will leans forward, his elbows on his knees. 'But that was when you were still selling the usual stuff – anyone can hire a bouncy castle on their tod these days. What if there was something special, more unique you could offer. Like Stevie said, cash in on the fact people can't stop spending on their kids. Emotion gets tied up with money and then there's no holding back. Like when I took the girls to a pottery painting studio and ended up spending £50 on two *beautifully painted* teapots in twenty minutes.'

His lilting tone tells us all we really need to know about how appealing the teapots really were. 'I'd do it again in a heartbeat. I'll keep them for ever, because my girls painted them.'

'I'd love to have something like that for Cherry. A keepsake. I never did get any newborn pics done, or her handprints taken. Just too busy... surviving.'

'Amen,' Nelle says.

'But if there was a more relaxed way to do those things – not in a shop or a hot studio, but in a home with a good changing facility and room to pace with a grumpy baby – I'd sign up like a shot. So... a keepsake party?'

Will points at me. 'You'd get NCT groups signing up together. Hypnobirthing groups. Or post-baby shower parties!'

Nelle sits up a little straighter. 'That could work. And I could just do it at home to start with? Or at one of the family cafes... close up on a quiet afternoon.'

'Yes!' I almost shout with excitement. 'I'll help!'

'We'll all help!' Will adds.

'We'll all help, we'll all help,' the twins chants, banging happy fists into their Play-Doh creations. We'd better keep them away from any precious breakables.

'Blimey.' Nelle rubs her hands together. 'This almost sounds like a plan.'

Chapter 7

From: Sarah Rimmer

To: Steviebutnotabloke@hotmail.co.uk

Subject: Hey yoooou

Hello lovely,

How are things? I realised I didn't hear back from you on that other email and then that sent me into a shame spiral that I shouldn't be sending you work stuff in your cuddly mummy bonding time. I'm sorry! Do you hate me? Have you dobbed me in? Dear IT guys: if you are monitoring my emails right now for a disciplinary, please know that I have photographic evidence of one of you pole dancing at the Christmas party. And I WILL fight dirty if it comes to it.

Anyway, I just wanted to say: I miss you. So much. Can I come out and see you soon, for a weekend lunch? Are you allowed to drink again these days? Shall I bring three bottles of cava or should I REALLY go to town?!

Can't wait to see how life goes down in the sleepy burbs... Do you have a pinny? Do you make your own pastry? The mind boggles!

Love you,

Sarah x

Sleepy burbs. If only Sarah knew. While I've been reading her email and simultaneously tickling Cherry under the chin to keep her happy in the Hobbycraft shopping trolley seat, I have had four more Facebook notifications ping through on my phone. Three friend requests for First-Time Mum, one more comment on my reply to Gin and Sippy Cups. And that's just in the last twenty minutes. Since I created the profile three days ago, I've made 3,267 'friends' and had a gazillion notifications of Likes, replies and mentions. I have that head-swimmy feeling that I've just resurfaced from a scuba dive the whole, entire time.

I should turn off the notifications, really, and just check them at healthy intervals – say, twice a day, rather than between every two mouthfuls of porridge, like I did this morning. But I can't stop myself. It's like the dream I keep trying to wake myself up from. I need proof. Proof that this is all real. That this is happening to Stevie Cameron and not someone with a flat stomach and yet also guts, and a winning social media presence as well as a killer business plan. How can it have happened to the bumbling reality that is me?! I can't find the nous to answer back to a snarky cashier in Co-op but somehow the righteous things my alter ego has typed in the dim light of my bedroom at 4am have really hit home. And people want to hear more. I've copied all my old blogs over to the Facebook page now, but I'm aware I need to write something new. And whatever it is had better be bloody good.

When I was just writing for me, I didn't have this melon-twisting notion. I just let all the mad, dark, stupid, silly, ungrateful, soppy things fall straight from my brain onto the screen. And that was that. I'd give it a cursory reread for typos or anything that could cause offence and away I would go, publishing without a backwards glance. But now I'm a bit... Well, to put it into terminology from my pregnant days, I'm constipated. I'm bunged up with ideas and half-ideas and thoughts I really want to get out, but I don't seem to have the strength to just do it and commit. And no one has invented prune juice for blogs just yet. So my notes folder has a list with a baffling collection of middle-of-the-night thoughts running away with itself:

- I have a theory that Sudocrem is impossible to wash off so the government can easily track the shuffling movements of new parents, in case they crack and hold up their local John Lewis with a sharpened butter knife. It's like that ink that explodes over money when you rob a bank: there is NO getting it off again.

- The world of Bing is MESSED UP. Where are the parents?! Why has an animated sock puppet the size and heft of a guinea pig been left in charge?! There's a talking rabbit, panda and elephant, but mysteriously a tiny cat that is... just a cat. It's too much.

- Stephen King should set his next horror novel in the fetid neck folds of Big Baby.

- I would kill for a really crisp Caesar salad that I don't have to make myself and can eat in a silent room, totally alone. Over four hours.

- Top tips for arguing in code over Big Baby's head. It's not enough to be passive-aggressive and speak in the third person about 'What Daddy's Done Now'. You have to whisper everything, too.

The last one makes me think, of course, of Ted. He's messaged a few times to say he's OK and the meetings are all going well and he even sent a video of himself for Cherry, which at first felt like a lovely thing to do, until I caught sight of the giant bed in the background with his discarded room service tray balanced on the corner. Fucker. A lie-in and a gourmet club sandwich whenever you have the urge?! Fucker. My rage is irrational but complete.

I know I am going to have to smooth things over when he's back in a few days. Or, at least, leave a door open for his apology. And suggest he get a promise in writing from his bosses that he won't do this again without a year's notice and the laying on of a full-time nanny at their expense. Maybe we could spend a special bonding day with Cherry and that would break the ice. It certainly will if she shouts down the local garden centre again. The vengeful looks of the assistant manager last time really helped Ted and me spend quality time together on the way home, spelling out elaborate insults for him in the car. Sometimes a ticking time bomb tot comes with its uses. Well, we'll see when he's back. We'll see how low he stoops in shame and reverence. We'll see.

'Ceramic plates this way!' Will jolts me out of my daydream of Ted prostrate on the floor, throwing roses and bars of Dairy Milk and spa vouchers at me while he begs to be allowed back into the bedroom, while I just casually inspect the my nail varnish that the real me never, ever has the chance to apply these days.

'Right, off we go.' The trolley has an awkwardly large turning circle, not being a nimble supermarket one but a creaky affair Hobbycraft had in the corner of their entrance. Does anyone ever need a full, trolleyload of craft supplies? I suppose I'm about to find out.

Will volunteered us for this sampling and pricing mission on Nelle's behalf: if she could handle the twins plus Joe in the big park near the leisure centre in town for an hour, he and I would speedily scrutinise the wide aisles of Hobbycraft for materials we could use at a prototype keepsake party. Plain ceramics to be painted, boxes to be decoupaged, clay to push little hands and feet into, and anything else that might take our fancy. Nelle warned us not to go too mad – petty cash isn't, apparently, exactly flowing like orange squash round her way. 'It's more like Ribena once a month,' she grumbled, as we waved her off in the direction of the swings.

'Ignore that,' Will had said, once we were out of earshot. 'I've got this.' Not for the first time I felt a romantic tingle, looking at the sharp line of his jaw and absorbing his generosity and kindness. But I quickly reminded myself that not only was Will gay and I'm married, but with a sex life as frequent as a leap year my hormones were bound to look for a new object of affection. He's a good friend, though: Will. Funny, when you need a lift. He listens, when you need to pour it all out. And unfailingly honest: he quickly winced and pointed back at the shelf when I picked up leopard-print decoupage paper. 'No one wants to treasure the memory of their little one turning into a streetwalker, Steve.'

Fair enough.

I pull the trolley to a halt behind him as he inspects plain ceramic side plates, next to the range of specialised paints that can decorate them. 'If we're aiming for little kids, we don't need to go for actual dinner plates, don't you think?' Will holds the plate up to Cherry's fist. 'Definitely covers our Cherry.'

'And she's twice the size of most six month olds,' I say, both self-deprecating and totally proudly. Another odd mix of feelings parenthood brings out in you. I *know* my kid is the greatest in the world, but I don't want anyone else to know I know it, in case they think I'm being some kind of mushy, arrogant dick. But she really is the best.

He rolls his eyes in my direction. 'She's perfect, just perfect. Aren't you, sweet chicken?' He tickles her under her well-padded knees and I swear Cherry does that mock-shy head dip, hiding away to one side and giggling, as if to say, 'Oh, no, not at all. Little old me? But do please keep up the flattery for as long as you have breath in your body.'

I must make a note for a future, grown-up Cherry: gay men can be delicious, but they're not on your menu. And, suddenly, it hits me – the next blog post. Things I need to tell my daughter when she's older. But will most likely forget. I scrabble to dig my phone out again and make a better note.

'You and that phone, love. It's been buzzing and beeping all day, you can hardly drag your eyes away. Doesn't make a guy feel special as he handles his clay balls, you know.'

I bite down my smile. Mustn't give anything away. Way too soon to get into it all. I don't even know what's happening, so how could I explain it?

'Sorry, just… er, well…' The thing is, I'm not ready to confess all. But I'm spectacularly bad at thinking of excuses. When I was hiding my early pregnancy at work drinks events, I went totally overboard and told everyone in excruciating detail that I was taking powerful antibiotics for a UTI.

Will lowers one dark eyebrow. 'Not interrupting a sexting session with your other half, am I? Happy for you, and all that, but,' he drops his voice, '*here*? I applaud you for being able to think sexy thoughts surrounded by so many cupcake boxes.'

'No, no. Nothing like that. Ted is still so far in the dog house he could open his own kennel. No, it's just… anyway, I'll put it away now. Let's get these little espresso cups for painting, shall we? Not too expensive, a quick project for small people who bore easily and I'm sure plenty of our target demographic of middle-class parents enjoy a Nespresso pod on a Sunday morning. And little Obsidian's artwork will make it that more enjoyable.'

'Good thinking!' Will places four carefully into the bottom of the trolley. My phone vibrates again in my bag and he eyes me. But I don't react.

There are three beeps as we debate ceramic paint colour choices (a soft palette of blues, greens and yellows to keep it gender neutral and hopefully avoid the primary colour garish splashes of most craft projects with toddlers), and more vibrating as we turn the corner into the paper-crafts section.

Just as I'm trying to smother more phone alerts by talking up the merits of black sugar paper over white – good for Halloween projects and snowy Christmas ones, and more forgiving of dribbles and snot smudges, maybe – Will puffs out his cheeks. 'Seriously, Stewart.'

'I'm really not keen on that nickn—'

'What is happening? Are you waiting on a kidney transplant? Are you an online bingo addict and this is a cry for help?'

I hold up my hands. 'Sorry! I'll just switch it off – it *is* getting annoying.'

But as I hold my phone in my palm, Will swoops in. 'I have to know just what is going—' He catches me off guard and in a split-second tilts the screen towards himself and squints. 'But this is all... about... First-Time...' He looks at me. He looks so deeply into my eyes that I think he can read all my darkest secrets. Like, the pants I'm wearing today are my very last clean pair and I'm eyeing up Ted's boxers for tomorrow rather than do a wash.

'Do you have a Google alert on her or... but this is her account, her notifications... Stevie, are you...?'

After a beat that seems to last until sunset, I grimace and nod.

'Oh my GOD!' He startles the granny behind us, who is looking at heart-shaped hole punches.

Will grabs me firmly by the shoulders. 'This is immense! This is incredible!'

The blue-rinse crafter has her eyes trained on us now, suspicious we've found the bargain bin deal of the day.

Whereas all I can think is: *You're busted, Stevie, you're busted*.

Will pays for our exploratory haul in near-silence, turning to look at me every now and then with his mouth opening but no noise following. Then he snaps his jaw closed again and shakes his head, shovelling paint brushes and jumbo pencils into his jute shopper. He doesn't even say anything as we troop back to the park, to relieve a now-probably-knackered Nelle.

She holds up her hands to shield her eyes from the sun as we approach. 'Hello, shoppers! Got anything good for me?'

'Oh, you wouldn't BELIEVE!' Will exclaims, folding his long legs down onto a scuffed bench. 'This one has been hiding a very big light under her very big bush.'

Nelle guffaws. 'Wait, what?'

'Will you tell her, or shall I?'

I chew the inside of my cheek. 'It's, ah, it's all a bit—'

'She's First-Time Mum! Our Stevie!' He jabs a thumb in my direction. 'The actual First-Time Mum. The overnight blogging sensation, right under our noses!'

'Night-night, bogey sensor!' Olive squeals, flinging herself into Will's lap. With a skilled hand, he quickly protects his privates from the action. Esme follows suit, locking her arms around her dad's neck and kissing his stubbly cheek. 'Oh, Dad, I missed you so much. What did you bring me?'

His gaze on me is broken and he gives them both a firm squeeze and a matching pair of sloppy kisses.

'My darlings. Have you been good for Nelle?'

'Very much almost.' Olive nods.

'They've been angels, honestly. But, hang on, rewind a bit. Stevie, you—?'

I press my nails into my palms and studiously admire the rusted green paint of the railings. 'It's just been this little hobby, something I never thought anyone would be interested in. But I had to get things off my chest.' I slap my hands to my cheeks. 'Oh god, I'm a really, truly, ungrateful mother, aren't I? I have this gorgeous kid and all I do is moan and complain and harp on about broken sleep and no time to get my split ends sorted. This is' – I look at their blank faces, and then at Cherry trying to get one socked foot in her mouth – 'this is why I didn't want to say anything. I didn't want you guys to think badly of me.'

'Badly!' Will almost explodes. 'This is BRILLIANT!'

'Brill-ee-ant, brill-ee-ant!' the twins sing and Cherry gurgles in glee from her pram. They set off at high speed to do a lap of the climbing frame with their new mantra filling the air and their arms pumping out a mad little dance.

He points in their direction. 'That is the physical embodiment of how I feel about it, actually. You've been saying what we've *all* been feeling. Surely all those Likes told you that? If people thought you were ungrateful that post would have died a death and not become the hit it is. I just wish it was my blog that had gone so big. Or I wish I had been clever enough to start a blog in the first place.'

My cheeks flare. I don't think I've thought of myself in any way clever since one of the last product launches I did, before getting pregnant with Cherry and my brain turned to mush six weeks in.

'I agree with Will. You've just found the way to say what we all know to be true. There are moments you cherish in this mumm—parenting lark' – Nelle catches Will's eye and grins sheepishly – 'and there are moments when you hope – no, you pray – that someone will magic-ally whiz the hands of time forward to a place when your best jewellery isn't pinched to be used as "pirate's loot" while you have one boob hanging out and you're signing for the delivery guy.'

'Or a time when you can poo perfectly in peace, without small hands clutching at your knees and moaning, "But you said we could do gliiiiitter, Dad! Now, Dad, now!"' Will shakes his head mournfully. 'I miss solo pooing.'

My heart rate lowers from that of a hummingbird to a knackered pigeon. 'Or when you could leave cushions and throws on your sofas, nice Habitat ones, without having to move them to a safe, vom-free radius. Mine are now just permanently in the conservatory. I've given up.'

Will lays his hand on mine. 'We should never give up our soft furnishings, Stevie. That's how they win, in the end. They take away our last shred of humanity.'

The laughter that escapes Nelle and me echoes across the park. I flop down on the bench, too. 'So it's OK to carry on, do you think? With the blog, I mean? With all this attention… I'm terrified Ted will see it, somehow. I *don't* think he's going to be as understanding as you guys, given that I have ripped into him and been cheered on by a few thousand people.' I fiddle with my wedding band.

'How will he know? You're doing it all anonymously.' Nelle rubs Joe's head gently as she paces up and down with him, a slight dip in her knees as she does the unconscious jiggling no parent can stop at any time when there's a chance of baby sleep. 'We didn't guess, and you've been right under our blimmin' noses these past weeks. Besides, in what you've said – with all his work commitments and travel – he doesn't sound like the kind of guy who signs up to follow mummy bloggers.'

'No, definitely not. But… it doesn't feel right to keep airing our dirty laundry like this. He doesn't get his say, even if I can't possibly imagine how he would defend swanning off like he did. I mean, Cherry can't control her reflux and throwing up on my best suede handbag or having so many lovely fat folds that she could hold toast in them. So as long as no one can work out it's her, it's a different thing. She's protected. But with Ted – I've got to stop blogging about Ted. Right?'

Will squints and Nelle puckers her lips.

'Or at least give him a chance to put things right before I moan about him in cyberspace again?'

Nelle's lips relax into a half-smile. 'Now *that* sounds fair.'

'Caitlin Moran says if you're going to moan about something for more than five minutes, you've got to be prepared to actually do something about it. I remember that from the days when I read whole books. Or just magazine columns. So, I've had my five minutes of famous-ish moaning. When Ted is back tomorrow, and he gets over his jet lag—'

'And you open what I assume will be a huge and wildly extravagant gift,' Will cuts in.

I roll my eyes. 'We'll see about that part. But when he's up for it, I'll suggest a family day out. And leave the planning to him. And the bag packing. And all the car seat in-and-out wrestling – this kid must be allergic to buckles, the way she fights it. But Ted can tackle it. See if that helps him realise how "fine" it is to do it all alone.'

Nelle now full-on grins. 'Oh, so when you said a chance for him to redress the balance, you really meant a chance to punish him! Ha! I love it.'

I can see I have wandered away from my karma-balancing intentions and am now more a little bit more in the an eye-for-an-eye territory. A blood-shot, sleepless eye, to be exact.

'If I really want to punish him, I'd make him pack *my* bag so I could disappear to a boutique hotel for the weekend. Eeep, speaking of disappearing, I should make tracks so we don't fall into the dreaded 5pm nap death trap.'

Will sits bolt upright. 'Christ, is it getting that late already?! I am not risking that either, not for a month of Sunday lie-ins. Come on, ladies, let's hustle.'

As we walk away, an unlikely line up – like the *Reservoir Dogs* but with sleek buggies rather than suits – I let myself dream of a blissful family day. Maybe a walk by the river, feeding the ducks, sipping hot coffee that I haven't had to make myself while Ted points out interesting things to Cherry – boats, weeping willows, non-traditional family structures. My gorgeous girl and the man I married. A perfectly solid unit of three. A time for us to breathe, relax, do nothing but work on everything. Talk, listen. I really think, right about now, that we need it.

Draft blog post

First-Time Mum

Things to remember to tell my daughter. Which I will forget.

I'm not sure I have *any* big chunks of wisdom I could confidently pass on to Big Baby. If I was truly wise, I'm sure that I wouldn't forget my PIN number every fortnight. But sometimes, as I'm doing one of the mindless bits of parenting: putting on my third load of washing of the day, warbling away with 'Incy Wincy', cleaning fluff out from between tiny, pudgy toes, these odd little details about life come to me and I think, 'I MUST remember to tell my girl this. It will save her precious moments of annoyance when she grows up.' So I'm going to keep a running list. And this is where I start:

Chapter 8

Ted had been really receptive to the idea of some quality family time when he got back, smelling of peaty whisky and taxi air fresheners. He'd bought a really lovely plush panda for Cherry, which she took to her heart straight away, trying to gouge out and eat its eyes. His business exec blanket from the flight was for me, because I'm 'always cold'. I decided to let that slide and focus on the fact he'd thought of our girl first and foremost. Some brownie points there.

'OK, well, I'll leave it all in your hands, then,' I'd enunciated slowly. 'Where we go. When. What stuff we need in the change bag. Yeah?' I'd been so casual about it, so cool. Not at all the trap-laying wife.

'Hmm? Absolutely,' he'd replied, bunging his suitcase contents into the washing machine – darks, whites, woollens. Ted has a severe case of laundry blindness and I've given up trying to lead him through it.

And so, are we sauntering by the River Thames, hand in hand, sharing a honeycomb ice cream? Are we at the Roald Dahl museum, teaching Cherry her first revolting rhymes as a harmonised family unit? Are we just at the local park with a picnic already prepared, simply enjoying the lovely area we live in?

Are we fuck.

We're at Twist and Bounce. A place so wholly demonic that they took the hell that is an airless, windowless soft play centre and added trampolines and random bursts of Euro synth dance music, which upon hearing you're supposed to drop everything and run into the central play area and join in a crazed 'flash mob' Macarena. I don't come here on a Tuesday, let alone a weekend. But this was Ted's best idea. Some might say, rightly, his only idea.

The noise pummels my ears as screams and screeches ping off the hard painted walls and right down my ear canals. The coffee is – frankly – shit: watery and thin. I'd rather have my usual stone-cold instant at home. At least I'd know the cup had been properly cleaned. And it wouldn't have cost £3.50.

This place is not at all relaxing for me and it's way too much stimulation for Cherry as a six month old. Large toddlers whoosh and wheel around her, dangerously close to treading on a precious fat finger. Her head whips this way and that as she tries to take them all in and I can read her little squint: *Hey, how can I stare at you if you run so fast! Come here and let me chew an item of your clothing until we're friends!* And as she licks one red ball from the pit, and then a green one, and then another red – as if tasting whether the colour has any effect on flavour – I shudder to think what human substances have been left behind on those balls and in which decade they were last cleaned. Judging by the smell of urine hanging around, barely covered by air freshener, I'm not altogether confident.

But I won't go in and rescue her from this berserk place. No. She's not in any real danger and Ted has made his choice, so he's in charge. Even when he picks up Cherry and looks over to where I'm sitting and pulls a wonky grin, as if to say, 'Am I doing this right? Do I look weird?'

I choose to pretend I can't catch the drift and I just send a jaunty thumbs up back. No, this isn't right. Yes, you look weird, your lanky frame awkwardly squeezed into a ball pit meant for the under-5s. But on your head be it.

I'm going to sit here, upgrade myself to a can of Diet Coke and do nothing and try not to even think anything. Not – is she hungry for lunch yet? Shall I start warming the pouch in some hot water? Not – is she having a bad reflux day? Are the wipes close by? That is all on Ted today, whether he's appreciated it or not.

When I come back to my little table with my nicely chilled can, I take a long, slow breath. Mindfulness. Calm. First World Problems.

Yes, OK, this isn't a pottering-about session in Marlow with a cream tea, but I'm here, we're all well and we're lucky to have the disposable income to do family trips like this. Even if they are to a mostly abandoned industrial estate just outside town. I have a cold fizzy drink to sip alone and that is a very fine thing in itself.

I take a quick snap of the can on the table, just to remind myself to stop moaning and start enjoying the details. Just then, something flashes up in my First-Time Mum Messenger inbox.

> Hi First-Time Mum! I'm a junior features ed at the Metro. Wondering if you'd write a short piece for us about parenting in the blogging age, or another angle if you've been thinking of one, thanks. We can provide a standard fee. Let me know. X

My mouth goes dry and I knock back some of my drink, the bubbles threatening to burst out of my nose. *Metro?* Short piece? FEE?!

I take a screenshot and ping it to my WhatsApp group.

> Stevie: OMG, GUYS, WHAAAAAAT DO I DO?

After ten twitchy minutes I get a reply.

> Will: WHAH! Amazing!!! You do it, of course. Money and fame – what's not to love? You're High Wycombe's answer to Belle du Jour!

> Nelle: Hang on, I'm doling out fish fingers for lunch. Belle Whosit? And yes, DO IT, STEWART.

> Will: Belle du Jour was a secret blogging call girl who made a mint from her 'sexploits' (ugh). I think our Stevie could be quids in here. First stop Metro, next stop: Glamour! Psychologies! Red!

> Nelle: Will she have to do sexploits?! I didn't think we'd forgiven Ted that quickly... ;)

Despite the hand clamped over my mouth, I am giggling hysterically through my fingers.

'What's so funny?' Ted almost makes me leap out of my plastic seat.

'Oh, um, nothing. Just… Will saying I'm a call girl. Everything OK?' I blunder on speedily.

'Yes, fine. A call girl?' Ted's eyebrows begin to fuse together.

I wave his frown away. 'Just a silly joke. How is the little squeezer?' I poke my finger into Cherry's sweaty grip and try not to wince at how sticky it is from the ball pit transfer.

'Maybe hungry?' Ted says, half-convinced. 'She's gnawed on me a few times. Is this the right time for lunch?' He flips his wrist, his fancy computer watch coming to life.

I smile and shrug, noncommittally.

Ted blinks. 'I could get her some toast. And I think they've got a fruit bowl on the counter. A banana?'

'You didn't bring a pouch, then?' I keep my voice level and light.

'Shit, no. I got the nappies, though.' He says this as if it was the parenting version of *The Da Vinci Code* to bring spare nappies and he cracked the complex puzzle before finishing his Weetabix.

'Toast and banana it is, then.' I sit there, glued to my chair with stubbornness. I'm not going up to order it, no sir. When I take Cherry out solo I have to juggle her, shopping bags, fiddling my credit card out of my purse, a tutting queue in any average cafe – so he can experience a taste of that today.

'Come on, gorgeous girl,' he says, standing up and repositioning Cherry face-out at his front, one arm safely beneath her bottom and one under her arms. This is her favourite way to view the world – at adult height and not nose-to-cleavage like she is in the Baby Björn, missing all the real action. She loves to nose at people and trees and cars and lampposts. She wants a front-row view.

I subtly turn a little so I can just about see him at the snack bar without it being obvious I'm keeping tabs. He plonks Cherry gently down on the counter, ignoring the disapproving look of the fifteen year old on the till and the fact that she is now in grabbing distance of a pot full of sugar packets. In a flash they are everywhere – mostly on the floor. Something behind my knees flinches and tries to send me standing and dashing over there to help with the clean up. But nope. Not today. Ted keeps one wide hand on Cherry's tum and crouches down to fish the packets up, handing them over with an apologetic smile to the teen. Whose face does not crack even by a millimetre.

As the surly sixth-former shuffles off to prepare Cherry's, ahem, gourmet and totally balanced lunch, I watch Ted do his silly little 'dislocated thumb' trick for Cherry, to her droolly delight. Do they pull dads aside at the hospital to teach them that? Is it statutory, like having to prove your baby is securely clicked into their car seat before they let you take them home? 'I'm sorry, sir, but unless you can pretend you can detach and reattach your thumb at will, you cannot be trusted to parent this newborn.'

Cherry is loving it on its twelfth go, her arms waving ecstatically in his direction, whether in an attempt to clap or get a nibble of his hand, I'm not sure, but either is a genuine sign of love from our girl. It fills my rib cage with a pure kind of warmth, a sense that everything will be OK if we can just hold on to silly moments like this. OK, he might not get some things right, but Ted is trying. He is really trying and they are having their time, some real quality bonding for the first time in a good while. The backdrop isn't the Boden catalogue shoot I'd hoped for, but who cares when you can see the flash of pure happiness in your daughter's bright eyes?

I'm not the only one appreciating the scene. A lady, probably in her fifties, audibly coos as she trundles past me on her way to the till herself, her eyes on my family. I feel my heart grow in my chest. When she's moved off, I think, I will take a sneaky little pic when Ted's not looking. Maybe put it in a nice frame for his birthday in a few months' time. Something to have on his minimalist desk at work.

The lady smiles and winks at Ted as she lines up behind him. 'What a lovely baby!' She wrinkles her nose at Cherry. 'Aren't you a poppet?'

All the tensions of the last week seem that bit further behind me, like I'm on a raft drifting away from the desert island where I was alone and having to fend for the two of us with nothing more than a flip-flop and two coconuts. It's in the past now. Ted is back and we're a unit. We're in this together. Two parents, one baby. Somehow when you're in it with someone else, you can laugh about sick trickling down inside your bra or about this small person who gets so angry at the injustice of you trying to gently remove faeces from its bum. Because it's not just you in this bizarre, baffling alternative universe. You're finding your way through together. Whether it's a romantic partner or your own parents or a best friend: parenting is like tackling a flat-pack wardrobe. Unsafe and exhausting if attempted alone.

Cherry and Ted's admirer is still at it as she waits for her coffee. The teen hands over a tray to Ted with toast, banana and a bottle of water on it. I can see Ted looking puzzled at his now-full hands and at Cherry sitting where she is. How is he going to handle both? I'm already enjoying watching the cogs turn.

'Oh, here, let me!' The lady does not wait for an acknowledgement, let alone an invite, and reaches out her arms towards *my* baby. She's going to put her hands on my baby! This stranger! WHAT?! My fingers flinch as if I could activate bear claws.

Ted dumps the tray on a spare table behind him and steps in her way. 'Oh, ah, that's kind but I've got it covered. I'll get her settled in her high chair and come back for the food. But you're very kind!' he over-enthuses at her disappointed face. Atta boy, Ted. Compliments are all jolly and happily received but if I don't know your name, let alone your criminal record status, you're not entrusted to pick up the most precious, delicate substance the world has ever seen. Thank *you*.

She recovers and hoists her handbag further up her shoulder. 'Fair enough. Good on you for babysitting. Good dad, you are. Mum putting her feet up, is she?'

Ted simply smiles magnanimously.

And I think I nearly black out. Rage level: Hotter Than The Sun.

Cherry hoovers up her smashed banana on toast and I quietly thrum with anger. I can't say anything to Ted about it because he'll know I've been snooping on him. But REALLY? Babysitting?! I feel every cell of my blood as it rushes around my body, jacked up on adrenalin and outrage.

I breathe out in a weirdly controlled way through my nose. There's only one way to dissipate this anger: *Metro* lady, you are getting your piece, and fast.

'I think Cherry could handle another ball pit session, yeah?' It's not really a question; it's a politely phrased order. Ted leaves the chaos of the lunch tray without so much as tidying it into one heap at least. He wipes some buttery crumbs from Cherry's chin with his index finger. 'Once more unto the breach, eh, baby chops? I think Daddy is brave enough for one more session and then it could be Mummy's go, maybe?'

My lips are sealed together with fury at the world but I don't let it show. OK, it's not strictly Ted's fault I'm so cross – and I'm not going to direct it at him – but it's got to go somewhere before I burst a blood vessel. And he didn't exactly set that biddy straight.

Maybe Cherry's penchant for getting angry is not such a mystery after all – maybe she just takes after her mother.

As soon as they're deep into the slithery, rainbow-coloured balls, I start to type as fast as any human has ever typed with two thumbs on a tiny screen.

LET'S GET SOMETHING STRAIGHT – IT'S NOT 'BABYSITTING' IF THEY SHARE YOUR DNA

I can't count the number of times I've been taking Big Baby to the supermarket, or pushing her around the park, or wiping up a puddle of sick from a GP's surgery floor and someone has said, 'Oh, babysitting today, are we?' I can't count them, because it never happens. Because I'm the mum, and this is the natural order of things, right?

But the minute my OH so much as raises a wet wipe, someone is patting him on the back for 'babysitting', 'helping Mum out', being 'so hands on' and he's basking in the glory of a job well done. Positively glowing like a Ready Brek commercial. But it *is* his job, too. He helped make this beautiful mess so he's totally, legitimately responsible for half the clean up. Not because he's generous; not because he's doing me a favour; but because it's his job. I sure as hell didn't conceive this lovely tot on my own. No angel in my bedroom that night – it was most definitely OH.

Yes, he's working hard to earn a regular wage while I'm on the rice-and-beans statutory maternity pay, and I would never diminish that. He's juggling stress, physical tiredness and the expectation of his superiors. But while he's at his desk or in a plush meeting room facing all these small battles, he's also able to grab a lunch of any denomination he fancies. He can go to the toilet alone. He can drink hot beverages. And when he powers down his computer and waves Nigel the security guy a cheery goodnight, his job is done and he's off the clock.

In my day job, there are some similarities: I'm still stressed, I'm tired from a broken night but I'm being loudly micromanaged by an overbearing, if totally perfect, infant. My lunch is whatever I see first in the fridge. I will realise at 3pm that I'm dying for a pee because I meant to go at 12 but then washing and feeding and changing all happened in a blur. And there's no logging off for me. It's 24/7.

So when we're both at home on the weekends, I'm squarely of the view that everything domestic or baby-related gets split 50/50. Not because my OH is a 'good bloke' or a 'modern man' but because that's fair. The DNA makeup is split 50/50 and that's just how the chore roster should be too.*

And it can't just be frustrating for the female parents (if it so happens that the stay-at-home parent is female, which I know is not always the case); dads must be gnashing their teeth at every little backhanded compliment, too. The implication that it's a major achievement for them to provide the basic domestic care for their children, like they're cavemen smacking their heads against their spears because they can't figure out which way round the nappy goes. Like making fairy cakes would give them an aneurism or knowing all the extra verses to 'Hickory Dickory Dock' requires a PHD in Music Theory. The jobs in everyday parenting aren't hard; they are just CONSTANT. And no one should be expected to do them alone if there's help available.

So the next time you see a dad pushing a swing or putting beans in the trolley with a few children by his side, don't be tempted to commend him. Just remember: he's no hero, he's just doing his job.

* Except for the bins, because I will never, ever take them out.

I read over my brain-dump a few times, my eyes flicking up between each paragraph to check Ted isn't heading back here.

I'm not going to chicken out. I'm going to send it to the *Metro*. Now. Job done. It might not be what they're after at all or they could hate the tone or just generally think it's pants, but it's real, all right. It's raw. It's First-Time Mum agenda.

I place my phone face-down on the table as if putting my alter ego to bed for the day. She's blown her gasket, she's worked through her anger, she needs to recharge. And, so does my actual phone. I'm now at 12 per cent. Using a mindfulness trick of counting my breaths in and out, I try to find a little calm. I try to focus on the positives. Here I am, having time to think. Having time to *write a feature for a London newspaper*. In my PR days, if someone we were representing had this kind of exposure for free I would be dropping hints to my boss about a raise. Causing a news-worthy stir is what it's all about. Starting a conversation. And even if First-Time Mum is my mouthpiece, rather than stepping into the spotlight as myself, I have got a chance to say some important things.

And, as Will pointed out, maybe make even some money. There are some big mummy bloggers and Instagrammers out there who've done well for themselves by showcasing their lives: some glam and some more down-to-earth. Obviously I'm not going to be snapping Cherry and me in matching rose-gold Adidas anytime soon, and I'd be nervous about exposing her too much to the internet (her real name, her actual picture), but if I could support us more financially by talking anonymously about our experiences… well, that feels like a worthy pay-off. If she ever randomly found out as a teen, a little nest egg for university or a car might redress the balance. Not that she will know. Not that Ted will ever know, for that matter.

But if I could keep blogging, if I could work out how you sell ad space and if I write more pieces, all under the radar like this, that would be a way for me not to have to go back to my old job. No blanching in boardrooms, no crying in loos after a simple conversation. I'd be safely behind a laptop, but I'd be paying my way. I wouldn't have to leave Cherry behind while I join the commuter hordes again. I could just tell Ted the money's coming from freelance PR. And it would be, technically: I'd be the PR for First-Time Mum. And apparently she's a hot ticket right now.

Look how well it's worked out today, for starters – family time, with an article squeezed in during soft play time. Perfect! I'm having it all!

I get an all mighty shock as Las Ketchup starts booming from the speaker right over my head. 'It's twistin' time, everybody!' the pre-recorded voice croons. 'Get up on the dancefloor, boys and girls, mums and dads! Let's boooooogie.'

I watch Ted do some exaggerated hand jives from Cherry, who has turned an angry shade of purple at the noise. Oh dear. It's all a bit much for her, little chubby love. But soon Ted clocks that everyone else is heading for the central area – toddlers pushing past him clumsily and parents following in their tracks – and, doing the dutiful dad bit, he clambers to his feet and picks her up. He beckons to me and mouths over the noise, 'Shall we?'

The thought of my new mumpreneur future softens a little of the baked-on anger from earlier. And for a minute I'm reminded of the first New Year's we spent together, just a few months after we met, where Ted had called me to the dancefloor. Still in that stage where both of us were pretending to be ultra cool and sophisticated, I'd booked us tickets to see the New Year in at a bar near Old Street. I hadn't been before but some of the office girls have been raving about it. Turns out they loved it because it was 'so vintage'. Or at least the DJ was. He played the very stinkiest Eighties and Nineties cheese, I think in order to be ironic. But he'd gone that step too far – with a Steps medley, in fact. The hipsters were shunning the dancefloor in disgust.

Ted took one look at the yawningly empty space as the last beats of 'Deeper Shade of Blue' faded and midnight approached. 'The Final Countdown' crashed around our heads. He took my hand and said, 'Shall we?' as if it was a tea dance at The Ritz – and we owned that floor. Just the two of us, jumping around to the synthy sounds and even air guitaring at one point. And I remember feeling this click inside me, not like a lock closing but like a tricky maths formula falling into place. *Oh, you're not cool*, I remember thinking, *you're real and you don't mind occasionally looking like a berk. Yes. You're the one for me.*

That night was one of the best nights, ever. I haven't thought about it in so long. I even arranged for our string quartet to play 'The Final Countdown' as I walked up the aisle to Ted. It made everyone in the room laugh, as if it was his last chance to leg it, but he and I locked eyes and we knew. We knew it was playing the moment we fell properly in love.

I nod quickly and kick our bags under the table.

But my breath catches in my throat as I see Ted turn and start to gingerly climb out of the ball pit's low, cubbyhole entrance. Spreading up the back of Cherry's T-shirt is an unmistakable korma-brown colour.

Poo-splosion.

And from the look of how far it's got around to her sides and up to her neck, I would say it's not happened in the last thirty seconds. And if it's had time to spread through her clothes it may well have got—

'SHIT!' I yell hopelessly at Ted, as the tinny music drowns me out.

He frowns and cups one hand behind his ear.

'POO!' I yell. 'Poooooooo!'

He shakes his head. I'm not getting through at all.

I swipe my arms drastically like an air traffic controller and then hold one hand palm up, praying he will read this as Stop in Your Goddamn Tracks for the Good of Mankind.

Sprinting to the snack bar, I resist the urge to grab the teen by his collar but instead shout right into his face, 'Poo in the ball pit. Shut it DOWN!'

Like a well-trained autobot, he turns straight to the stereo controls under the coffee machine and in a second the music has abruptly stopped. Then he speaks into a little mic and his reedy voice comes over the PA.

'Ladies and gentlemen, we have a… faecal situation in the ball pit. Please evacuate the surrounding area. If you have been affected, please remain where you are and a member of staff will be with you shortly.' He rushes out the next bit. 'Twist and Bounce cannot accept any liability for ruined clothes, shoes or accessories, or any subsequent illnesses. No refunds will be given at this time. Thank you.'

I turn to see Ted, frozen to the spot, his face as lacking in colour as Cherry's outfit is now stained with it. And then she starts to cry.

–

I'm not sure which moment that followed was the absolute pinnacle of humiliation for me: watching the assistant manager daub my husband all over with anti-bacterial wipes before she'd let him fully out of the pit; watching him strip a wailing Cherry naked while still knee-deep in plastic balls, passing the wet and soiled clothes out to me to go straight into a bin bag; or maybe it was the fact that during the entire charade, we were watched by about twenty other families, silent, peeved and judging us for all they were worth. They were on pause until the place was sterilised, so I suppose they had to get their kicks somehow, but I felt like the mother of the chimp who throws faeces at the zoo. Not one for the family album. And maybe not a story for the blog either.

My face burnt as we left, heads down and speed-walking to the car, Cherry wrapped in a travel blanket as I couldn't face spending another ten minutes in there trying to manipulate her into her spare set of clothes.

I'm re-dressing her on the back seat, giving her another once-over with wipes to make doubly sure there's no faint tidal marks of poo-nami still on her.

'Ssssh, ssssssh, Cherry Bomb. Humpy Dumpty sat on a wall...' I start to sing, but my voice cracks and my eyes blur. Even six months in, I have an eggshell-thin defence to public shame when my baby screams the house down, and this time with an extra pooey whiff.

Ted is in the driver's seat, tapping the wheel erratically, seemingly oblivious that I'm about to lose it. Why have I leapt in like this when he could be sorting her out? Now my anger wells up again, fighting for space against the shame and anxiety behind my ribs.

'Ted,' I say, through tightly clamped teeth, 'I need five minutes right now. Please come and dress your daughter.' I clamber out of the car awkwardly, bum first, and just start walking. I hear Cherry's cries go up an octave and there's a twist in my stomach as I realise she wants me, that she thinks I'm abandoning her, but I keep walking for self-preservation. Better at a distance from my girl than breaking down right in front of her.

Keep going till you get to that bus stop, I tell myself in an eerily calm serial-killer kind of voice. *Don't get on the bus. Don't get on the bus. Just sit on the bench. Breathe.*

Once I've counted some breaths in and out, in and out, and I can hear Cherry has calmed down to a basic whinge-cry level, I start to walk slowly back. Ted has Cherry on his lap and she's gumming the steering wheel between complaints, smacking the knobs on the display panel as if they somehow caused her gastro-pyrotechnics.

Ted looks at me, creases running along his forehead. 'OK? I'll clip her in, then we can head home.'

Numbly, I follow him around to the other side of the car. Cherry gives her usual kicks of protest at being safeguarded from terrible injury but Ted ploughs on and soon she's in. He turns around and pulls me to his chest.

It's the first prolonged hug between us that I can remember for quite a while. It feels so good. His arms have me locked in, snuggly, like the baby's car seat straps. We need to do this more often. Not the public shitting, but the consolidating afterwards.

'It's all going to be fine,' he says into my hair, and for once that word doesn't trigger a flare in me. For once, it's nice to hear someone say that and feel – even if it isn't totally accurate – that they're going to steer the ship for a while and I can just leave it all in their hands. I don't have to be the captain of mealtimes and bath times and poo management and scream diffusing. That's all I really want out of Ted: not some unrealistic dreamboat that polishes the floor as he walks through a room reading poetry, but just to share the burdens on weekends, as well as the good bits.

'We're all clean now. She might zonk out in the car on the way back, if we're lucky. If I'd shat out half my body weight I'd be pretty tired. And then how about we do some *real* good old fashioned family fun while she's asleep and hit the McDonald's drive-thru, yeah? A couple of cheese burgers, just like Mum used to make. And an apple pie to incinerate the roof of your mouth. Good times!'

My chest loosens and I press my head further into his polo shirt. I let out one big lungful of air.

'And, you know, it makes me think of that mindfulness stuff you tell me about – this whole… adventure.'

'It does?' I crane my neck back to be able to look him in the eye. I had no idea he was even taking it in when I've talked about it.

He nods, deadpan. 'Think about the bright side to today: we never, *never* have to show our faces here, at this awful place, ever again. In fact, I think they would *actively* prevent it.'

And now my jaw loosens, and I can smile. 'Excellent point. Come on, I'm craving synthetic cheese now.'

–

There are some weird moments of happiness in family life. Ones I did not see coming. There are the predictable ones and they absolutely have their merits – when Ted throws Cherry into the air just by a few centimetres and catches her smoothly; when she sees her own reflection in the hall mirror and goes wide-eyed and freaked out, then melts into a cheesy grin for this beauty she's spotted seconds later. But the weird ones have the extra layer of joy because they sneak up to you at the oddest times.

Like just now, when I jolted awake in the passenger seat, probably from my own snores, and came to in the car foggy with burger smell and full of the people I love to the ends of the earth. Cherry is open-mouthed and dead asleep. I check my watch. Forty-five minutes, I'd say. Not too shabby. Maybe as she's getting older she's napping just that bit longer? Ted has bunched up his coat and is using it as a pillow against the driver's side window. I must have nodded off after emotionally eating my greasy, cheesy delight and instead of taking us home and nudging me awake when we got there, he's pulled into the McDonald's car park and joined in this communal nap.

So, here we are: perhaps not a Hallmark card snap but a picture of total happiness to me nonetheless. Is a baby ever as delightful as when it's silent and immobile? Can you love a man more than when he facilitates snacking and sleep?

Recharged with a micro-nap, I use the last sliver of phone battery to write a quick micro-post for the Facebook page. OK, so maybe combining a blogging career with family days isn't going to be a blissful walk in the park. It's probably going to be more like a roll in a shitty ball pit, but sometimes weird is right. For me, at least.

The Beautiful Oddness of Parenthood

When you have a rubbish, tearful day and it's rescued by chips and a car nap.

Picking up the 'grown-up' jokes in Shrek. If you've got to watch something thirty-seven times in a row, it might as well have hidden penis gags in it.

Your baby lunges at you for a random chew and you get a gumming on your arm which is oddly warm and relaxing, like a very localised hydrotherapy treatment.

The white noise sheep/owl/whirring of the fan is actually pretty peaceful to sleep with, TBH.

You'd forgotten Play-Doh is really great.

The Moana soundtrack. I mean, I literally feel bad for people who haven't heard it. You're welcome.

Being in the park on a sunny Thursday mid-morning. OK, you're not being mentally stimulated and you might have put your coat on over your PJs just to get out of the house, but isn't it a bit great that you're enjoying this lovely day, in the fresh air with a rosy-cheeked babe, and so many other suckers are stuck in a windowless office staring at a spreadsheet?

Sucking up leftover fruit purée pouches. If you sploshed a bit of Cava in that, boom, you'd have a wicked Bellini. Not that I'd recommend too much of that while in charge of a minor etc, etc.

So, come on then, parents the country over, what's your weird moment of joy?

I haven't put a shout out like that before, actually asking for feedback, and it still makes me wobble as I hit 'publish' but there's a bit more confidence there now, a little bit of past evidence that people are keen to engage. So let's see. Let's see how far First-Time Mum takes me. Because Stevie Cameron's career definitely needs a new direction and this might just be it. Like Nelle said, in her terrifying clown get-up, my confidence has been stripped away by the early baby days. To be myself again and to be the best mum to Cherry, the best partner to Ted, I need to bring that confidence back. In a big way.

Chapter 9

Nelle's house is just how I pictured: messy and vibrant and full of life. It would make a perfect backdrop for a Shirley Williams children's book: you want to shove aside the newspapers on the sofa and snuggle down in the warmth of this family household and be absorbed.

'I haven't done anywhere as much tidying as I meant to last night!' Nelle apologises straight after opening her front door. 'So why don't we keep everyone in the living room, hide the unfolded laundry and, er, everything else in the kitchen with the doors closed. Now, get Cherry settled on the play mat in there and we can get the kettle going and our asses into gear.'

I open my mouth to give my usual disclaimer about my darling and her reflux ruining material things, but Nelle beats me to it. 'I don't care if she's sick on it. It all goes in the machine anyway.'

I take Cherry out of the buggy and carry her through into the living room, carefully laying her down on the red and black striped play mat, underneath the dangling jungle creatures. You never know with Chezza whether she'll find something interesting enough to keep her amused or just too much stimulation which sets off some noise, but we seem to be on the safe side here. She swipes and kicks at a fuzzy blue chameleon without a peep.

Nelle's carpets are a lovely light biscuit colour and a shudder hits me as I think of our weekend family *fun*. Surely that won't happen again? Well, the Co-op is only a ten-minute drive if I need to make a dash for carpet cleaner and stain remover, and then there's the local church for the holy water. I'm sure with three kids, Nelle has seen it all, not to mention the job of cleaning up after other people's parties. I'll take the risk today. I put my hands on my hips and survey the room. It's a really good size: a long living room with two giant sofas and a few armchairs at the far end. An old PR skill creaks into life somewhere in my brain: sussing out a room for mingling and comfort potential. We could pull the armchairs up a bit, closer to the sofas. We'll need some low coffee tables for the crafts and some higher ones for drinks and nibbles. Plus still leave floor space for small people to move about without tripping over handbags. The room will be inviting and functional – lots of kneeling space for the tots at the tables, lots of throws and cushions on the sofa to make the mums (and dad) at home while they create some special keepsakes.

'Have you got an oil cloth or camping ground sheet, Nelle?' I call through to the kitchen.

Her face pops round the door. 'She can't have been *that* sick, surely?'

'Don't speak so soon. Actually, I was thinking of something to put down for the pottery painting. I think that paint would be a special kind of hell to get out of fabrics. And any kids' tables kicking around?'

She counts off on her fingers. 'I got Darren to hose down the two tables from the garage – plastic numbers that I'm happy to get trashed. And then there's one still in Amy's room that she used to do her water beads on. But mention that to her these days and she'll deny it forever. *So uncool.*' She flicks a pretend lock of hair over her shoulder and rolls her eyes. 'Do you think that'll swing it?' I hear a faint cry crackle through the baby monitor on Nelle's hip, just as the doorbell goes.

'I'll get the boy if you get the door? Hopefully it's Will and not some mega-keen early bird.' I've yet to see Nelle in anything but high, bouncy spirits but today I can tell the stress is starting to worry at her can-do attitude. I've had days when I burst into tears in the middle of the street at how exhausted and lost I feel, and I have just the one baby and no real money troubles to fret over. Nelle is juggling three children, the emotional complications of working in a family business and the practical worries of that business not working. It definitely makes me realise how lucky I am in so many ways.

Luckily, it is Will and the girls, who are already wearing painting aprons with funny little elasticated sleeves that cover their arms, like Victorian surgeons. 'You can never be underprepared for craft time,' he informs me seriously. 'Right, what's to be done?'

We've got three mums coming, with one toddler each. Will recruited two through toddler groups he goes to, and Nelle found the other through a notice she put in the family's cafe window. Nelle, Will and I have decided on a charm offensive over our warm-up teas – we'll each all stick to one of the mums, chatting and crafting together, making sure they have a really good time and tell all their mates. Plus, we can sneak some under-the-radar market research out of them at the same time, to help inform how Nelle might price this for a proper party.

There is a cold twist in my stomach as I think of having to talk to a stranger. OK, a big cold twist. But, I remind myself, it's just *one* mum, and – much more importantly – it's for Nelle. She's a mate. Did she leave me sobbing in the loos at the Parent and Baby Fair? No. It would have been easier for her to do so, less weird most likely. But she stuck it out for me. And I'm determined to do the same for her today. Besides, if I feel myself clamming up, this time I'm going to think: *What would I be typing about if it were the wee small hours and I was in my bedroom, post-feed? What would First-Time Mum say?* All those Likes and comments have made me realise that we're all up for the chance to spill the beans on our real child-rearing experiences, and not just the ones worthy of a spot in the family album. So if I can steer us onto a universal subject like 'When Porridge Becomes Concrete', we should bump along together just fine.

Joe is happy in his sling, his tiny head bobbing gently in the direction of Nelle's movements. 'So this table, painting plates or little cups. This one, handprints in clay and, here, decoupage. Not that I'm still very clear on what that is,' she says.

'Middle-class cutting and sticking, basically.' Will shrugs. 'To make a trinket box thingy. They'll love it!'

'And you will give me that receipt for Hobbycraft so I can refund you, yes? I've only said it a million times.'

He studies the ceiling.

'Shall I make more tea?' I offer, to change the subject.

'Why not? This is a British household, so we should, by rights, have tea coming out of our ears by the end of the afternoon. Blimey, I hope everyone has a good time.'

I sling my arm around Nelle's shoulders. 'With company like this and a jumbo supply of PVA glue, how can they not?'

Half an hour later, and two of the mums had arrived. I went back to the kitchen to sort them out with drinks while Will got them settled, and Nelle got their toddlers stuck into something sticky and entertaining.

Even without the clown make-up, Nelle can project this big, energetic personality that little ones can't tear their eyes away from. 'Who will pass me the biggest piece of paper, hmm? Will it be you, Charlotte, or you, Finn? Let's see!' I hear her saying jauntily, through the walls.

When I carry the teas back through and put them safely out of the reach of small hands, I can see Will is already deep in conversation with his allotted mum. She has flawless black skin and can't be more than thirty. She's leaning on the arm of her armchair to listen to Will, sitting in the other.

'... but aid agency work. Wow. I mean... that's so noble of you. So brave!'

She waves his praise away. 'No, not at all, really. You should have seen how much we used to drink, how we partied once the day was over. I mean, there's not really much else to do in some places – just seek out some home-brewed moonshine and hope it doesn't take the enamel off your teeth!'

Will catches my eye. 'Hey, Stevie. This is Bernie. I was just asking her how she met her other half and she said while in the Sudan, sorting out clean water. Isn't that... well, I think it's incredible.'

'Oh, absolutely, absolutely!' I enthuse. So maybe this isn't going to be the mum that I get blabbing to about our favourite nappy-rash creams, or how quickly a talking Peppa Pig toy can drive you completely bonkers. She seems to have a fantastic, grounded sense of humour, but

I just feel like a lowly whiner in comparison. Happy to let Will handle this.

Nelle is now perched by the other mum and they're both helping the two tots lay strips of tissue paper onto little cardboard boxes coated with big blobs of PVA.

'Your tea is just up there.' I point. 'I'm Stevie, by the way.'

'Louise,' she says. 'I would shake hands but I think we might get permanently attached!' She holds up a hand almost glistening with glue.

'I think that's my cue to grab some more baby wipes!' I reply, happy to have a task to keep me on the move. Clearly whoever the third mum is will be my craft buddy. *You've got this, Stevie*, I tell myself. *It's not like before. You're in a nice house, Cherry isn't yelling, you're with friends. You can do this.*

I spend the next twenty minutes helping the twins and their extra buddies – Eloise and William – push their sweet little hands into flat discs of clay, before the doorbell goes again.

The sight on the doorstep mutes my cheerleading internal voice instantly.

It's that bloody mum–mum. The one whose son nearly broke both my ankles, and the one whose mate 'mistook' me for Will's cleaner. Oh deep, deep joy.

But this is for Nelle, remember? So game face, Stevie. Game face.

I pull a thin smile together and welcome her in. She has an immaculate little girl with her, probably two or so, her chocolate brown hair neatly plaited by her ears, a checked pinafore dress that looks like it's been actually ironed. 'Mills, shoes off,' her mother says, in a perfect Sloane accent.

The little girl obediently removes her shining Mary-Janes and places them next to her mum's spotless wellies.

Say something, Stevie. Break this Arctic ice!

'Gosh, I love those wellies. I've never seen a pattern like that before – are they Cath Kidston?'

The mum-mum looks down at them, as if it was a totally bonkers thing to talk about. 'No, they're actually customised Hunters. One-offs. My husband knows I love bluebells so he got them hand-painted for me when we were in Cornwall at Easter. Thank you,' she adds, almost as an afterthought.

'I'm Stevie, by the way, nearly forgot that important part!' I laugh a hollow little tinkle. 'And are you Milly?' I ask the little girl, who dips behind her mother's legs.

'Millicent, or Mills,' the mum-mum quickly corrects me. 'And I'm Chloe. Thanks for having us.'

I slap my hands against my thighs in an odd, matronly kind of way that I instantly regret, before I turn towards the living room. 'You're so welcome! Come on through, everyone's having a good old messy time, Mills, and there's lots of space for you, too. Guys, this is Chloe and Mills.'

'Chlo! Lovely to see you,' Will says, as he hops up to give her a peck on both cheeks.

Chloe looks around the room and blinks, her face not giving away a shred of emotion. 'Is Teresa not here?'

'Oh, no, she cancelled yesterday. Did she not tell you?'

The mum-mum chews the corner of her mouth, taking off some of the subtle gloss from her bottom lip. 'No. Hmm.'

'Well, we're so glad to have you. Take a seat and I'll fetch you a tea.'

'I can do tha—'

'You've made buckets of the stuff, Stevie. It's definitely my turn. And, besides, I can see Mills eyeing up that clay you were showing the others. Shall I fetch you an apron, poppet?'

'Oh, yes, please.' Chloe coos at him, now positively melting in relief that there is, in fact, someone here that she can clearly tolerate. 'That dress is vintage.'

Then why wear it to a crafternoon? the First-Time Mum in me seethes. *Bloody show-off.*

Esme pulls at my hand. 'Steve, Steve, come and help me.'

I could not love her more.

I've given Chloe two of the best openers I can muster – some of the best conversation starting I've done in six months, in fact – and she's replied monosyllabically to both: I complimented her on how verbal Mills is for her age and asked, 'Is she in any kind of childcare? I hear that's so good for language skills.'

'She's with me. At home. Sometimes the nanny helps out,' was all I got in reply.

Fine.

After she shuts down my asking about Cornwall and where she'd recommend there for a family holiday – 'We go to my parents' second home in Polzeath, so I've never been anywhere else. Sorry' – I decide I've made my effort and I'm going to find my level with the children instead. Chloe has clearly decided this is not her kind of social gathering, so she feels like a lost cause in trying to spread the word amongst her similarity snobby mates. And someone with hand-painted wellies is not going to give a fig whether a paint-your-own pottery painting is twelve pounds a head or fifteen.

I've moved to the decoupage table with the twins, Eloise and Mills. William, poor soul, though a keen joiner has been forgotten about in the all-girls chatathon that is four two year olds, and has decided to make faces at Cherry instead, which she's enjoying studying with her bright, intelligent eyes, and which suits me just fine. She's done one thankfully solid poo so far today and only lost a bit of a mouthful of milky sick after her lunch, so we're achieving. We really are.

Eloise is laying thin strips of blue and green tissue paper on her trinket box, letting the long strands at the ends stick out at all angles. The twins have me ripping up strips of their desired colours at will, which is pleasing but mindless work, so I decide to join in the chat.

'I love your pattern, Eloise. It looks a bit like mermaid hair.'

Four sets of eyes turn to me.

'What's that?' Olive asks, coming to stand right in my personal space. As I'm sitting on the floor, back resting against the sofa, she comes up beyond my shoulder height and is oddly imposing.

'Well, you know mermaids have long hair in all colours, a bit like seaweed. That's what Eloise's box reminds me of. And it's lovely.'

She colours and giggles.

'Can we all do mahmaid hair?' Esme pipes up.

'Of course!' I reach for the ocean palette of colours and start tearing.

'We could make YOU mahmaid hair!' Olive yells happily, right in my ear.

I see Will's eyes widen from across the room. 'Well, no, I actually meant to stick on—'

'But we're boooooored with stickin'.' Esme now comes to stand at my other side, also unnervingly close. I feel like the Krays are interviewing a new getaway driver.

Olive looks to Mills and Eloise, who silently nod in agreement.

Got to make this work for Nelle, my cheerleader pipes up. *Besides, it's just a bit of paper twisted in your hair.*

—

Three hours later, I am bending over Nelle's bath while she busily scrubs shampoo into my roots.

'PVA is great for surfaces where you can peel it off, but hair follicles not so much, huh?'

I feel another tiny yank at my scalp. 'I really could… sort this at… home.' I struggle to talk through the water and bubbles running down my face.

'Nonsense! I got you into this mess – I'd hate myself if I didn't send you home looking peachy again. Just' – she pauses for a second – 'don't blog about this, OK?'

I burst out into laughter and swallow a mouthful of suds as a result. 'Some things… not even First-Time Mum would share. Like getting a… mermaid wig glued to your head!'

Through my screwed-up eyes I can see the water running with splashes of blue and green into the plug hole as the dye runs out of the little bits of paper still tangled into my hair; the paper I thought would be innocent fun to let the girls place on top of my head. The paper that had devilishly absorbed the glue from their hands, and which had probably been peeled from some of their art projects in the frenzy, too.

I should be humiliated. Maybe someone else would be angry, in my shoes. But actually, I think the whole afternoon was a great laugh, PVA conditioning treatment included. Probably one of the best bursts of fun I've had in a long time, now I think about it.

When Nelle finishes rinsing me and hands me a towel, I wrap it around my head and sit back on my heels. Cherry is strapped into a bouncing chair on the landing and I give her a little wave, just to confirm she hasn't been abandoned. 'I can pick the rest out later, thanks. I don't think I've got the core strength to bend over that bath any more! Shall we get on with the cleaning up?'

'Oh, sod that, Darren can do it when he gets home. He's just as responsible for trying to pick up this business as I am. And we've definitely done our part today. You were a star, keeping those little ones engaged. I actually loved having a grown-up mum chat with Louise. That was a treat. And you gave it a shot with Chloe, at least.'

I pull a grimace. 'She was harder work than eating toffee through braces. I have to admit I gave up after a bit – sorry. I found my level with the two year olds.'

Nelle leans back against the towel rack. 'It wasn't you. Not at all! She seems… very closed off. A bit of a cold fish, if I'm being mean.'

Will thumps his way up the stairs. Maybe another thing they teach dads on day one of official parenting – how to make as much noise as possible coming upstairs. Honestly. 'Wait, wait for me if you're being mean! I want in. What are we talking about?' He fills the doorframe with his height.

'Er…' I scratch at my prickly scalp.

'Chloe,' Nelle states.

Will narrows his eyes ever so slightly. 'I know she wasn't very chatty, but when she's more relaxed she's actually lovely.'

Nelle folds her arms. 'Well, what's not relaxed about sitting in my living room, drinking tea while someone else entertains your child? She could have joined in a bit more. At one point she even started scrolling through her phone.'

'Yeah, I can't really defend that. Bit rude. All I know is that I've been with her at a few playgroups where she's been a lot chattier, when she knows more of her friends.'

'Her mum-mum friends,' I add. 'And, you know, horses for courses. We tried and it wasn't her bag. Fair enough. But the others seemed keen, so that's positive.'

Nelle nods. 'They did have a good time, I'm pretty sure of that. And they all took home some wonky little treasures to keep for ever and ever. Bernie kept trying to pay, bless her, so I said they could both fill out an email questionnaire for me instead, and that will be a real help. Try and make a template out of today for other keepsake parties.'

'I keep thinking about something Louise said when she was leaving,' Will chimes in. '"That was amazing fun. It could only have been better if I hadn't had to get my hands dirty – give me a sun lounger, a book and a glass of something fizzy while my kid is up to his eyes in glitter and clay and I would gladly remortgage for a slice of that action." Something like that. Maybe there's another angle to the parent pound, one we've missed so far. You've got to entertain the children BUT also give the parents what they want, you know, as *people*.'

'Ahhh.' Nelle runs her hands through her short hair. 'Interesting. Treating parents like people…'

Cherry yelps and jiggles herself in the bouncing chair. It's almost 3pm, so it's well past her mid-afternoon feed slot. I'd better find somewhere to park myself before she works up a full head of steam. 'Do you mind if I feed her downstairs quickly? Then we'll scoot and get out of your hair.'

Will nods. 'The girls are silenced with a baby biscotti each but then we'll do the same. I'm a bit worried I'm next for the Ariel treatment.'

'Hang on!' Nelle waves her hands. She takes my hand and pulls me towards Will, circling both our necks with a fierce hug. 'Thank you both. Thanks for everything. Even if we don't get anywhere with this, even if the business stays down in the dumps, it's been so good to be in it with you guys. Wait, did I say that right? I didn't mean that I like seeing you dragged down into my misery, just...'

'That a problem shared and all that,' I say, in the midst of our huddle. 'The longer I spend as a mum, the more I'm convinced no one's supposed to raise a baby alone, let alone hold down a job and a relationship, too. It's a team sport.'

'Amen,' Will agrees.

Just then a squeaky shout of, 'That's mine!' reaches our ears, followed quickly by some heartbroken sobbing. The noise clearly gets on Cherry's last hungry nerve as she pipes up with her own wail, and that in turn starts Joe thrashing and mewling from his sling.

With a raised eyebrow Will turns to head back down to his girls and referee whatever dispute is going on. 'And sometimes that sport is WWF wrestling.'

Buoyed by our team talk, I walk the long way home with Cherry in her pram so that we hit the greengrocer and butcher. Maybe I will dig deep for some extra energy to make Ted and me a proper dinner tonight, from scratch. He used to love my Greek-inspired grilled lamb chops, with a Greek salad on the side, before pregnancy put me right off the idea of any red meat so much as touching my lips. I haven't cooked it in so long, but I must be able to remember it.

Cherry was amused by gumming a whole lemon while I pointed out the chops I wanted, and the greengrocer even had some fresh dill, which was a winner. Cherry went down easily for the night after her mega-stimulating day of toddler entertainment – just fifteen minutes of mild protest from her cot. Now that I know that she can fall asleep on her tod without always having to be cuddled and bounced, I'm trying it out more and more. It doesn't always work, but it's a light at the end of the tunnel. And tonight, life almost feels like the dream I had for my maternity leave – a contented baby, homecooked meals and awaiting my beloved husband to come back and catch up on the day with me.

But by the time I place two warm plates of my best Mediterranean cooking on the table, the colours of tomatoes, peppers and red onion all bright and fresh and inviting, Ted is already craning over multiple screens at once – one his work iPad, the other his 'real' iPhone. Apparently nothing beats an Apple product. He looked at me to say hello coming through the door and dumping his bag, but beyond that he's been scratching his stubbly beard over emails and spreadsheets while I witter on about today's crafternoon. With such a closed-off recipient in front of me, the warmth and confidence I'd walked away with today seems silly and thin out of context. I might as well go back to discussing the fake hanging flowers outside the GP's office.

'Is something going on at work?' I ask, as he finally turns his focus to gobbling down the food.

'Hmm? Oh… no. No, it's all going really well, actually. Very well. Keeping me busy!' He smiles and shrugs like he's giving a banal answer to an uncle at a family do, rather than an honest one to his best friend.

The last crumbs of my good mood disappear along with the last mouthful of Ted's lamb. It's taken him less than five minutes to gobble up something it took me forty minutes to prepare. And he hasn't even said so much as a 'Yummy!' About it. Charming. Tomorrow it's back to jacket potatoes in front of *Masterchef*.

'So, anything else going on, then?' Let him carry a conversation for once. I've done all the small-talk I can for today.

'Well,' he inspects the ceiling for a moment, 'I did hear about this great cheese festival coming up, in Aylesbury. Rob was talking about it at work – he went last year with some mates. One of those foodie things where it's totally acceptable to eat way too much because it's *artisanal*. Wine and beer, a bit of live music. Could be really fun. What do you think?' He hands over his phone with the site 'Live For Cheese 2018: from here to fromagerie!'

I tap the About Us and Facilities tabs, scrolling past the pictures of smiling, glassy-eyed twenty-somethings dropping whole wedges of Brie into their mouths and swilling back beer.

'What are the changing facilities like?'

'Um… hang on a sec.' Ted takes back his phone and swipes around a bit. 'Dunno, doesn't say. But I bet they'll have somewhere.'

'Hmm.' I spear a last half-moon of cucumber. 'Not necessarily.'

'Well, I could find that out, ping them an email. We haven't been to a food festival in ages. We used to go to that French one on the Southbank all the time. I could definitely make room for some serious dairy and bread, then wash it all down with a beer. And some wine. Bit of whisky…' He winks.

'And so while you get sloshed on all that I'm going to be the one responsible for Cherry, I suppose? And sober enough to drive us home, too? Nice.' I can't even remember what a good mood feels like now, and I'm sharpening each word as if to slice through Parmesan. Which, no doubt, Ted would enjoying snaffling down between shots, as I change a pooey nappy on a wet Portaloo floor.

His eyes retreat back to his phone. 'Maybe we don't need to take Cherry just this once? There are these babysitting apps now, I read about, we could—'

'I don't think so!' I spit out. 'A stranger looking after *my baby*? How can you even think of something like that?!'

Ted pushes his chair back, grabs the plates and lets them clatter into the sink. 'I'm not talking about handing her over to the first person I see at the bus depot! You can check references, first aid certificates, all that, and then talk to them before—'

'No.'

He folds his arms. 'Right then. Let's forget it, then. We can take her with us.'

'If – *if* – it turns out to be baby friendly. With some-where to warm food. And somewhere for me to sit and feed her, of course. And…'

'It sounds like you're finding excuses not to go now. If you don't fancy it, that's fine. I was just suggesting something fun for us all to do together.'

I puff out my cheeks. 'But what's fun for you at things like this is a different experience for me altogether. I have to think about how Cherry will sleep – with all that noise and crowds of people, she'd never drop off on a pram walk. How I'll get a good lunch in her. What if she has another poo explosion and I've got to somehow wrestle her out of shitty clothes, clean her up and re-dress her in a smelly toilet cubicle? You'd be sampling Stinking Bishop or whatever and I would just be stinking. And stressed.'

Ted rubs one foot against the other. 'OK. OK. We'll cover all that. We'll pack five bags of back-up stuff, we'll bring a pack horse if we have to, and you can tell me what I have to do to help.'

I feel my energy evaporate through my shoulders. Suddenly I just want to go to sleep. For twelve straight hours, rather than three. Funnily enough, the idea of packing up half our lives for a single day trip and barking out orders all day doesn't really make me feel relaxed.

Ted's work phone vibrates, sending a shudder through the kitchen table. Just before he picks it up, I see the green box that says *From: Maddie Forrester Re: Hong Kong*. Ted takes it to the sofa to do more rapid-fire replying, and it seems our discussion is over.

I don't want to have to tell you how to 'help', Ted, I imagine saying to him, with the bravery I can only muster through the written word. *I just want you to do half of what's yours by rights. And that's all.*

Chapter 10

'Can I not do this bit online?' I half-shout over Cherry's cries so that the bank clerk behind the glass has a chance of hearing me.

'Sadly not.' She smiles sympathetically. 'Some bits we need to have you here in person to do, in order to open a new account. But it will just take ten minutes, once we book in the appointment with a customer services manager.'

'OK, OK.' I nod while she clicks through some calendar options on her computer.

'Friday at three?' I run through the timing variations of Cherry's nap schedule. Oh, to have a baby who takes regular three-hour naps to work around, and not scrawny, hard-earned thirty- minute ones that could come at 2 or 2.45 or 3.27 on any given day.

'Let's say four, if you have it.' And I'll just have to hope she's well rested because clearly this bank decor is not going down well. Or maybe it's the stuffy, hot air or the bright lights. Or maybe Cherry just woke up in a stinky mood today. Or maybe her stomach is rolling ahead of a major reflux session. The thing is with babies who can't talk yet is that you'll never really know what the problem is: you just have to try every godforsaken thing until you accidentally hit on the solution.

'That's fine,' she says, and I grab the forms to fill in and leg it, taking my human police siren with me.

The fresh air startles Cherry into pausing for breath and I decide to keep up momentum and head to the park. Something must be able to cheer her up over there. A big dog, or some school children on their way home, even another drooling baby to stare at would do the trick. Sometimes, when Cherry's reflux bothers her, distraction is the only way.

'Not the Golden Ticket moment I imagined for today, kid,' I say gently down to the pram, 'but we'll cash Mummy's cheque another day.'

The payment from the *Metro* had arrived in the post this morning and I'd had to squeal with excitement into a cushion so Ted wouldn't rumble me. They'd said they could pay via a bank transfer, and it would be much quicker, but I knew that way they'd have an account name and I'd be well and truly rumbled. No, thank you. Snail mail and paper money would do just fine for the incognito First-Time Mum.

I couldn't wait to get down to my local branch and open an account just for my blogger earnings. I've been watching YouTube tutorials at night, with my headphones in while Cherry drops off after her feed, all about monetising your blog and driving Facebook follows. It's a whole other world and it might be my world, if I keep at it. The thing I've realised is that I have to supply a steady stream of 'content' or I'll lose this wave of interest I'm riding. So I've started a Twitter account for First-Time Mum, too, and linked up my Facebook posts so they automatically feed out there. When I'm fully in the swing of it, I'll have to get good at churning out proper, unique Tweets but, right now, that just feels like one task too many. I do get a little blip of thrill when anyone follows me, though, and I tend to follow them right back, health shake company or spam bot, whatever. I'll take a follower!

Quite a few other requests have come in via my Facebook Messenger over the last week, and I've been snapping them up like a Hungry Hippo: other bloggers asking me if I'd like to do a Q&A for them ('Sure! But I am NO expert on parenting/careers/relationships/pretty much anything bar *Homes Under the Hammer*'); an organic clothing company offering me some free vests for me to try on Big Baby and review ('OK! But I'm going to be REALLY honest about how well they repel sick stains'); and even a digital feminist radio station suggesting I do a phone interview down the line for a podcast. This one I couldn't just drum out an instant big fat YES to, because it made me a lot more nervy than the others. What if someone recognised my voice? What if I slipped up and said Cherry or Ted's real names? It would be an amazing way to speak to loads of other parents in the same boat, but I'm more comfortable with First-Time Mum on screen for now, rather than creeping onto the airwaves, too. I said I'd think about it and let them know.

And when I'm not thinking blogging, I'm thinking Nelle and the keepsake party. Father's Day is in two weeks and she has got one of the family cafes booked out for an entire Saturday just before, so mums (and dads) can drop in to make something special for the following Sunday. We decided more decoupage would be the way to go, even though it took me three days to get the last nub of green tissue paper away from my head. The materials are relatively cheap, the craft process is simple enough for parents to help the tiniest tots choose where to glue their patterns or for older toddlers to be let loose on their own, and the clay and pottery turned out to be far from shatterproof in the end. Nelle didn't fancy enforcing a 'If you break it, you buy it' policy on guests, so we've stocked every colour of paper under the sun and three sizes of trinket boxes. And I'm going to keep my baseball cap close by in case Esme and Olive pincer me with another one of their wigs.

Will volunteered to be stock co-ordinator and I'm writing poster and flyer text for us to put up around the town and surrounding villages. I *must* finish it tonight, in fact; I promised Nelle she would have it yesterday. Will's done his part and I don't want to let my new mates down. If this works, it could be a revenue shot in the arm for Nelle's business, and something she can repeat for the summer holidays, Halloween, Christmas, Mother's Day, Easter... We just need bodies through doors to kick this first one off.

'Hey, Stevie!' I hear a familiar voice call my name. Nelle is rounding the corner with her own pram to push. She puffs over to the play park. 'Seeing you has brightened up my school run no end. How are you doing?'

'Good thanks, love. How about you? How are your nights with lovely Joe?'

Her eyebrows shoot up. 'You know how it goes. You get two good nights and you think – here we go, we're on to a winner. Plain sailing from here on in. Then the next evening it's cluster feeding and random screaming and that sinking feeling that you're totally out of your depth at 2am when all they want to do is look at you and blink. Not sleeping.' She leans down into Joe's basinet and says this last part gently. 'So I set off early today to see if I could sneak more napping from him on the way. It's not working and I'll be fucked if I've got the patience any more. And because I'm rattled I had a stupid row with Darren over some deck chairs, if you can believe it. I mean, that's perhaps the most ridiculous subject I think we've ever rowed about. And I can't even remember what the context was now...' Nelle spaces out and I can see all-too familiar grey shadows under her eyes.

'Snap. Except our argument was about cheese.'

'Hah! That is a good one. Maybe we should start a list for the blog!' She nudges me in the ribs. 'So, how did you fall out over cheese? Did he snaffle the last Babybel? Swine!'

'He wanted us to go to a cheese festival, for a family day out.' Now I say those words out loud, I worry that I'm sounding pretty ungrateful. And slightly mental. 'But... he doesn't get all the work that'll be for me. Trying to sort out a clean nappy in a temporary loo someone might just have heaved in. Having nowhere private or comfortable to feed. What if it rains? I have to factor this stuff in. Ugh, maybe I should have been gentler about it. He's been in a right sulk ever since.'

Nelle pats me on the arm. 'I'm sure you were entirely reasonable. Festivals aren't for parents and that's the sad truth of it. Not real festivals, anyway. You get your special festivals for kids and everything they like, but it's hardly Glastonbury for us grown-ups. Having to spend over the odds for macaroni cheese and listen to *Justin's House* songs. Not quite the same thing as the Stone Roses after a hash cake. Ah, good times.'

'You've been to Glasto, then?'

She lets out a long sigh. 'Hard to believe to look at me, but yes. It was 1998, I think. A few years before we actually got married. If I knew then what I now know, I would have savoured every lazy minute of it: drinking, lying on the grass, getting sunburnt and henna tattoos. Not having to watch out for anyone wandering off or accidentally drinking absinthe. I have heard Glasto can be great with kids and they love it but, like you said, more work for us. More lists, and anxieties, and if you're not mostly pissed when you sleep in a tent I just don't see the appeal of it.'

'If they could just take the kids off into a little fenced-in bit, with no booze allowed inside, everything covered in crash mats and one huge screen playing CBeebies, then we could have our own area. Where it gets messy. Until 9pm. Because no one can magically whisk those early starts away, even if you do have a VIP pass.'

Nelle snorts. 'ParentFest.'

'What?'

'A ParentFest. That would be awesome. I mean, don't lock the kids in a cage, but can we put *our* fun first, for once. Because, you know, parents—'

'Parents are people, too,' I say before she can, echoing Will's words from the keepsake party between us.

As if he knows he's being quoted, my phone vibrates and I see it's a message from Will. The image has a 'play' triangle so I press it, baffled.

It's a GIF of Will holding up a copy of the *Metro* and swaying side to side, a huge, excited, open-mouthed smile fixed to his face. Nelle peers over my shoulder and soon neither of us can talk for laughter or see straight for the tears in our eyes.

Will: *Tracked down a copy!!!! Come see!!! You're famous, love xxx*

When she's recovered, Nelle pushes me towards the gates. 'You need to get over there and see your words in the actual newspaper. I need to collect my rabble from school. I know who I'd rather be right now!'

I'm shaking my head and tsking like mad, but also unlocking the brake on the buggy to speed-walk over to Will's. I need to see it for myself or it just won't be real. None of this really seems like it's actually happening to me, still.

–

I smooth out the crackling newspaper gingerly, the faint light of Cherry's rabbit-shaped night light making it impossible to read the words. But I pretty much know them by heart.

I wish I could tell my mum about this. Or Ted. Or the newsagent. But First-Time Mum can't leave this house, not unless it's by high-speed broadband. This half-page of paper will have to go somewhere special, somewhere secret. But even if no one else knows it's there, I do. And it feels as weighty as a university diploma. This proves I can do something. This proves there's some sort of person underneath my stained baggy shirt and past-their-best leggings. A person people want to hear from. A voice worth listening to.

I tuck the paper under my side of the mattress very carefully and then tap the Twitter app on my phone. It feels like a good time to Tweet any other mums out there, stuck in the small hours wilderness.

@First_Time_Mum: Who else is awake? New parents, truck drivers, nurses on the graveyard shift? We're all desperately trying to keep awake for one reason or another, right? Say hello if you're about. I always like a friendly tweet! xxx

@First_Time_Mum: But if it's 'friendly' advice like 'Get all the sleep you can while the baby's sleeping!' you can DO ONE.

My inbox announces a new Twitter DM.

@BBootsMum: Hello, FTM. I'm here. My babies aren't exactly tiny any more, but I just have this horrible insomnia most nights. So I'm downstairs ironing, if you can believe it. Do you ever get so lonely that you start talking to the iron?!

My heart lurches as I read this. Yes, I have been that lonely and, yes, I've half-cloaked it in humour before. But it doesn't stop it being real. I quickly reply.

@First_Time_Mum: Morning! Or is it still night? It should still be, but if your brain is whirring with stuff it won't really listen to you pleading to go back to sleep, I know. Put that iron down, though, and get yourself to a Netflix account. Immediately. If you're going to miss out on sleep, it might as well be for some awesome, trashy US telly. And message me if you ever want to chat.

@BBootsMum: Thanks. That means a lot xxxxxx

I chuck my phone onto the duvet and rub my hands down my dry, flaky face. I remind myself that the next time I'm lovingly rubbing E45 into Cherry's neck and arm folds, I'd better slather the leftovers over myself, too. Some top-notch self-care if ever I saw it. Boots' message is not the first one of its kind and I feel both heartened and saddened by that. Heartened – that I'm not the only person to feel overwhelmed by motherhood. Saddened – that so many of us feel so down, and that we only feel we can talk about it via social media.

I've started to get all these messages from women, telling me their mum stresses and asking for my opinion. Besides the fact I can't teach anyone *anything* about parenting – except maybe the best biscuits to eat job lots of without feeling sick (Digestives, Rich Tea – but don't go beyond three custard creams or you'll barf) – these messages are sacred. It feels like such a treasure they are trusting me with – their inner gripes and worries and longings – that I want to respond, but I'm not sure how. And if I carefully respond to one – and it might take me a good thirty minutes to think of just the right thing to type – do I have enough hours in the day to go back to them all? I mean hours in the night, really, seeing as I grab my chances to write on my phone while Cherry is zonked out and Ted is asleep in the bedroom.

Reading back through some of the readers' messages, a theme starts to poke out at me:

'*I love your blog. THANK YOU for admitting it's not just me that feels lost.*'

'*So many times I've nearly said hello to another mum by the slide, or in the Tesco car park, but then I bottle it. What if they ignore me and I look like a bell end?*'

'WHY is it just MY baby that screams during the baby massage class? The time when you're supposed to be all calm and bonded and my little boy is squirming like he hates me. Why can't I have one of those lovely, calm babies?! I think your Big Baby and mine might be long-lost cousins, or something.'

We all feel so alone. We all feel like it's just us finding nature's greatest magic trick – creating a whole person from the tiniest cell – absolutely impossible to pull off, and the audience is hating us silently.

Even though I know I should finish Nelle's posters and press release – and I will, in a second – I let my fingers fly over a new blog post.

IT'S NOT JUST YOU, IT'S THEM, TOO (EVEN THE PERFECT ONES, HONEST)

Hey mums, dads and any combination of the two,

I just had a lovely 3am chat with my new Twitter mate @BBootsMum and, you know what, it made me feel a lot better about things. (So, @BBootsMum, is your account name from the fact that you work in a Boots or that you wear crazy killer thigh-high boots?! I like to think it's both. Seeing as you don't have a profile pic it's just how I have drawn you in my head, stacking Lemsip boxes in creaking PVC. Sorry, not sorry.) Sometimes that little connection with someone in the same boat can mean so much.

And it's hard, right, finding those connections—? I've wittered on to you all a million times about how hard I find baby classes and sitting in a cafe when my baby turns into a screech bomb and trying to think of anything, anything interesting to say to a fellow adult when your brain is barely running on caffeine and cat naps. But now I've met you lot through the life-saving channels of social media, I know it's *not* just me. So many of us feel lost and lonely and at sea.

Tricky not to feel these things when you see a Pampers advert with a mum head-to-toe in spotless white, looking orgasmically happy to be changing her thirtieth nappy of the day. It must just be me that near-retches at saffron-orange poos welded onto a tiny bum cheek, then. Or at the baby class – all those smiling, engaged tots loving the nursery rhymes and coloured lights, while yours just wants to try and eat the fire extinguisher and yells with pure rage when you pull them away. It must just be me that has the weird kid who will grow up to have no friends and live like a hermit in our shed, surrounded by well-chewed fire safety equipment. Or, heaven forbid you should come across a Perfect Parent type, who is dolling out unflavoured rice cakes and carrot sticks as 'treats' to a brood of immaculate offspring, while the chocolate-button-drool racing down your baby's chin is joining approximately thirteen other stains on their vest. It must just be me that always means to pack, but totally forgets, a Tupperware of halved grapes for the car. And I should have been soaking my kid's entire wardrobe in Vanish last night but I just wanted twenty more minutes of RuPaul's Drag Race. I am selfish. And lazy.

But you know what? It's not just you. It's everyone. The Pampers woman isn't real — she's a childless 24-year-old model who was probably smoking a fag and looking longingly at a quiche during breaks in the filming. You can eat a quiche whenever you fancy it, because you are a real person. If you delighted in scraping gluey faeces from under your finger nails then I would be very, very worried about you, my dear.

And EVERY baby in that class has had a meltdown at some time or other. Fact. Even the most Buddha-looking babe has gone purple at some point for no reason at all. The reason those mums look so happy and at peace in that class is because — for that forty-five-minute slot at least — they're dodging the bullet and they're just grateful to get out of it alive. As you would be, right?

Likewise the Perfect Parent: maybe they look like they're raising the Von Trapps in matching Joules pinafores but behind closed doors you don't know what epic tantrums over screen-time go down. And all the time they're putting into chopping raw veggies and steam-pressing pleats, they're missing out on the best drag queen make-up tips and fiercest put-downs. Pity them. Pity the fool with no time for RuPaul.

So try and remember, if you can, that you are not alone. Say it with me: I am not alone. Write it on a Post-it and stick it on your alarm clock. Put it on the fridge door. Embroider it on a pillow, if that's your thing. I am not alone.

Parenthood is hard. We're all just about surviving, albeit with different methods, rates of success and levels of hair-washing. When you're too nervous to approach that smiling mum at the soft play for a bit of a chat, just remember that they too have an inner voice telling them, It must just be me... You might make their day by saying hello. Wouldn't that be amazing?

And I'm always here, for pre-dawn moan sharing. But @BBootsMum you'd better have stepped away from that ironing by now!

Love,

First-Time Mum x

Chapter 11

I can feel all eyes on me at the weigh-in and, for once, I love it.

OK, so it's not because I have the most perfectly behaved baby in the room (Cherry managed to be sick on her red health book; I have no idea how). And it's not because I look crazy stylish and well kept (hello, Dorothy Perkins jade jeggings for the millionth time). It's because I'm sitting next to Will and everyone is trying to work out our deal. Are we a couple? I am clearly not gorgeous enough to have produced Olive and Esme, and I would have had to have waited a full five minutes after their delivery to get pregnant with Cherry, so maybe all the other mums are marvelling at the HOW?! of that scenario. I know I would be.

It's been four weeks since we met at one of these weigh-ins, and it's mad how different I feel now; still like I'm a C-mum at best, but able to laugh about it, which I think is the real key. Will had suggested we come back after his last attempt went awry – he needed to get the girls weighed as part of their two-year health review and because he's about seven months overdue getting this done, the health visitors have sent him a stream of snarky letters. When his GP called because they had been alerted to 'irregularities' in the girls' records and Will picked up a hint of condescension from the female GP, as if a dad could not understand the importance of these things, he decided to show them what was what. And that his girls were perfectly healthy, thank you.

'That new post was spot-on, Steve,' he says quietly, out of the corner of his mouth.

'Thanks,' I whisper back, enjoying even more this covert conversation and how it must be sending the watching mums absolutely wild with intrigue. Ha!

'And the views are going through the roof. Have you checked them? When I read it yesterday morning, it was at 6,000.'

I don't want to say that it's now more like 11,000 because it's just nuts to say out loud. Plus, it exposes me for the obsessive egomaniac blogging has apparently made me. I check my stats constantly, like I've just won the lottery and the millions have been transferred over to my account. Somehow, if I don't keep checking, all those precious pounds will drop out and roll away. Twitter Follows, Facebook Likes, blog reads: it's all racking up and I feel made of mental energy. Like I could tackle anything! I mean, my washing basket is still fit to bursting but I could write you 300 words on the five easiest ways to pass off pyjamas as outdoor clothes right now before breaking a sweat. I've got many other half-written blogs that have come to my hyped-up brain and my fingers itch to get back to them. I haven't even really noticed that Ted has been away for the last few nights with work again, this time in Denmark. It doesn't seem to drain me at the moment. Our level of conversation hasn't really picked up again after Cheesegate: I ask him about work and he grunts a response. Occasionally he asks if Cherry has turned over yet and I get huffy and defensive as if he's implying that she's taking her sweet time about it. I'd much rather be in my blogging world, thanks very much.

In fact, I was so pumped up last night that I replied to Mum's latest passive-aggressive email to say pretty clearly that a flight to the States with a six month old was not on the cards, but here was a whole month's worth of snaps for her to enjoy. End of. And I invited Sarah over for Sunday lunch in a few weeks' time – it has been far too long since I saw her and maybe she can be trusted with my secret identity and even give me a few pointers from her professional point of view. I have missed her wicked sense of humour so much and I've been rubbish at letting her emails remain unanswered for so long. I didn't make any reference to taking on Fierce Beauty and coming back to work. I don't want to ruin our reunion by admitting I might never be back in that office, that the old Stevie is now just a person in photos and this is the new me, part-Stevie, part-First-Time Mum, and it's going to be a career, if I can make a go of it. Right now, I feel like I could make a go of anything. Even getting Cherry to eat spinach purée.

Speaking of impressive feats…

'Hey, Nelle and I have been meaning to run something past you. A new idea for the party planners.'

I hand him my phone, open to the draft for the Parent-Fest press release I've worked up. I finessed the Father's Day keepsake party one first, before I let myself loose on this. But the idea just makes so much sense to me that I keep thinking of it – at the sink, unpacking groceries, hunting out clean knickers in the morning. I want to *be* at the festival but, more than that, I want *us* to run it. It's what the legion of fellow frustrated parents out there want. No – they *need* it.

PARENTFEST – COMING TO YOU FOR THE VERY FIRST TIME IN 2018!

When was the last time your idea of fun came before your kids? If you are thinking of something that happened before the invention of the iPhone then you need ParentFest. And we need you!

ParentFest is not a family-friendly event. Don't get us wrong – it's great for kids and all their needs will be catered for: food without 'bits' in, changing facilities that don't give you the shivers, a large screen for Peppa and Blaze and Paw Patrol marathons. Plus live music and games – sports, clown skills, dance, bouncy castles. All that energy-draining activity will be included in the ticket price per child.

But this is where it gets seriously parent-friendly. The children's area will be entirely separate from the adult's festival space. The children will be looked after by qualified childcare specialists and the adults will be looked after by craft beers and New Zealand wines. We'll supply you with a beeper so that if your child is distressed you'll be immediately alerted. Music in the parents' section will not be something you've heard before on a Disney movie. The food on offer will be served hot, sometimes spicy and is not designed to be shared. There will be deck-chairs, picnic blankets and bean-bag sofas. Sitting still is very much encouraged.

Our festival will kick off at 10am because, let's face it, you've been awake since 5am so why not make a head start? It will close at 8pm because the kids need to get to bed and you'll be awake again at 5am the next day, so you can get a head start on that hangover.

We'll set up a taxi rank to take you home or back to the train station. There'll be a secure pram and car-seat shed. Contactless payments for everything. Proper recycling facilities so you can eat too much and drink too much guilt-free.

But, BEST of all: parents go free. You just need to pay per child, per beer and per henna tattoo.

See you at ParentFest!

And if there's anything that would make your day easier, or more enjoyable, you let us know: contact@parentfest.co.uk

(There must be one adult per child. Over 18s only in the adult section.)

'Wow,' Will breathes. 'Can we really *do* this? I mean, all these clever ideas – are they even possible?'

I slip the phone back into my bag. 'I think so. In theory. With my old PR experience and the fact that Nelle has a whole team of people trained in supplying food, booze and music at her disposal, we have a good shot. Plus a certain former Selfridges buyer who knows how to make things fly and have people positively throwing their credit cards into the air in glee. If we want to try and squeeze it in at the end of September this year, we're going to need all hands on deck plus a whole lot of luck.'

Will squints as he does the calculations. 'That's about eighteen weeks. Blimey. Well, nothing ventured and all that.'

The Scottish health visitor with the white bob clears her throat and calls, 'Twenty-three!'

'That's us, girls.' Will nudges the girls up from the chairs next to him, where they've been deeply absorbed in Peppa Pig Top Trumps. Not that they can read any of the stats, but they're making a good show of pretending to.

There's a minor disturbance as Olive and Esme insist on only getting on the scales together. I see Will pinch the bridge of his nose.

'Well, now.' The Scottish lady looks over the top of her blue-framed glasses. 'Do you share most things at home, girls?' They nod dutifully. 'Then why don't we weigh you together and split the result down the middle, share it out between you? No harm, no foul, eh, Dad?'

'That is a great idea, thank you.'

Will waves us a goodbye as they head off for their toddler French lesson. In many ways he is so much classier than I will ever be. And that's mostly OK.

Before I have long to contemplate whether a second language is really that much of an advantage in a Google Translate world, my number is called and I lift the heft of Cherry out of her pram. I used to panic week to week when she was a newborn that she would lose weight, that I wasn't feeding her properly and that if she was wasting away Social Services would swoop in one night and take her away. I never told Ted this, because I could already hear in my head how mad it sounded. But now, with the benefit of time, I can see it was all hormones, tiredness and the first flush of proper 'Mama Bear' maternal love.

Now those hormones have died down a bit and I've adjusted (as adjusted as anyone *can* be) to the broken nights, it is clear to see even without the help of digital scales that this chunk is healthy and hearty. No doubt. She's a beautiful butter ball of rude health. I have fed her well.

This thought makes me pull my shoulders back and stand that bit taller while she's lying naked on the disposable paper sheeting. I may not be finding it easy, I may well be a rookie still, but I am doing a good job as Cherry's mum.

Just then an almost comically perfect poo emerges from Cherry's plump bot, like someone squeezing brown toothpaste from a tube.

'Whoah there!' I laugh and lunge forward, grabbing the anti-bac wipes from the desk.

The health visitor laughs. 'Oh, my! Haven't had one of those in a while. Straight into the offensive waste bag under the table, thanks, dear.'

I somehow manage to whip the paper out from under Cherry without ripping it, like a restaurant magician, ball it up and get it in the waste bag pronto. I check my hands, wrists and T-shirt for any transfer that could cause problems (this ain't my first poo rodeo, after all) and then check the baby all over for the same.

'We'd better try that again, hadn't we? You might have lost an ounce or two.' She smiles down at Cherry. 'And everything OK with Mum?' she asks. 'We haven't seen you in a while. Everything all right?'

The bubbling ParentFest ideas flash through my brain, as do those recent Likes and Follows. I think of Nelle group-hugging Will and me in her bathroom, while I still had glue in my hair. I think of Olive and Esme's sushi factory and how my sweet, inquisitive Cherry could watch them silently for hours at a time. I have a brief thought of Ted and how I'll have to try and patch things up with him – again – when he gets back from Denmark tonight – well, not every single thing can be coming up Stevie, I suppose.

'Everything is good. Really good. Thanks.'

The Scottish lady jots down the figures in Cherry's weight chart. 'She's still doing wonderfully – ninety-fifth percentile for weight! So, unless you have any problems, I wouldn't say you need to visit us again for another few months. Or just at her one-year review? I'd say, all in all, you're doing nicely.'

For all the warmth that flooded my heart, she might as well have said I'd been granted an honorary Oxbridge degree in Motherhood and simultaneously crowned Ass-kicker of the Year by the Feminists' Association.

We are doing nicely. Not perfectly, but I think nicely is a much better measuring stick.

–

All the messages about ParentFest pinging back and forth between Will, Nelle and me have really made me wonder about parent fun and why it seems so taboo to our generation of baby-makers. I don't think our parents felt any guilt at enjoying the rare chances they had to go out, get sloshed and live it up once a decade. And on their precious weekends, they didn't want to sit in a cheesy gymnasium watching us do rhythmically challenged gymnastics – they wanted to be in a beer garden, half-watching us play giant Jenga and half-listening to their own friends' chatter. Did they have a smarter sense of parent—life balance? Have we become so obsessed with giving our offspring the best of everything that it's been to our own detriment in some way?

Dinner tonight is two posh pies from the supermarket, warming in the oven, with the readymade mashed potato and buttered greens waiting for their time in microwave heaven. It's not freshly prepared but it's not beans on toast, so that's something. And while I'm waiting for Ted, I can do some more flexible working and crack on with this latest post. It's a treat to get my actual laptop out and not be reducing my thumbs to tired nubs by typing on the phone.

WHAT'S IN IT FOR US AGAIN?

We all know parenting takes a lot out of us. Read through my list below and nod if any of these apply to you

Physically: knees creak from so much lifting and carrying. Back aches from swaying and jiggling to sleep. Teeth rotting because you keep forgetting the normal human times to brush your teeth e.g. not at 3am and then again 10.30am. And DON'T even get me started on the horror show that is birth injury. That is for another post when I've had two whiskies for courage.

Financially: the Bugaboo. The Snuzepod. The Baby Björn. I might not be able to spell them all but I am surely paying for them. Sorry, Visa people. It's going to be a long time before my balance sees anything like the colour black again.

Emotionally: how balanced can you feel when within the space of one hour you've gone from, 'This sleeping baby is the single most beautiful thing on Earth and I think I believe in God now' to 'Forty-five minutes of crying! Why does this demon child hate us so much?! Why won't it just CHILL OUT? FML!'

Romantically: look at the three reasons above, combine them, times them by ten and then imagine how sexy you feel.

Socially: either you can't finish a conversation with a mate because you have to keep stopping to fish bogies out of noses, put a nipple into a mouth or snake charm a burp, or you change the subject on them so you can discuss how you have the most advanced baby in the world because they can get their foot in their mouth on the first try. You might move to Cambodia? Oh, cool, yeah, but Big Baby can almost roll over! Let me show you seven different video clips.

Sore neck, right? Me, too. Parenting takes a lot out of us. And what do we get in return? That's what I'm wondering tonight.

Now, before you sharpen your pitchforks and call for my head, let me just put the big old caveat out there: we get to keep the children. That's what we get. And we are f*cking lucky to have them, we're f*cking lucky that we got the golden ticket of biology to create ourselves in miniature and then watch them turn into mind-blowingly unique characters.

I'll never not be bowled over with love and gratitude for Big Baby.

But even if your job was to guard and restore and occasionally dust the 'Mona Lisa', every now and then you'd think, 'Oh, to put my feet up all day in front of a blank wall. That would be a holiday.' Parents are locked in, round the clock, to their domestic, emotional and financial responsibilities. And even though you have been blessed with a beaut of a child, a day off would not be such a bad thing.

But the minute we so much as catch a whiff of a break, a decent hair-down session, here comes the guilt. Because you shouldn't be thinking of yourself: you should be focusing on little Billy's fine motor skills or scouring every high street store for the one perfect party dress that Jemima will love but one that also doesn't give her damaging gender role messages for the rest of her life.

Did our parents worry about this as they played darts down the pub? When they shipped us off to grandparents for the summer so they could just go to work, cook dinner and – brace yourself – have sex that was both noisy and enjoyable? I think that kjshftyww

'Hello there.' Ted's voice suddenly sails into my ear from over my shoulder. 'What are you up to?'

I slam the lid of my laptop closed and he winces.

'Uh. Not much.'

'Looked like you were going ten to the dozen on a press release. Is that a work thing?'

'Y-yes. Yes, Sarah sent me something she was struggling with. For an old client of mine. Said I'd take a fresh swipe at it.'

Ted dislodges his bag, coat and shoes into one heaped mess on the floor. 'Huh. Well, I hope they pay you for it. Could do with a shot of life for the credit card, if I'm honest. What's cooking?'

A few weeks ago I would have silently rankled at this response: no interest in the work itself, just the revenue. Not valuing my own professional skills, just wondering what he can shove in his gob. But since I am so shitty at covering my tracks, tonight I'm glad of the instant subject switch.

'Pie. Mash. Standard.'

'Don't apologise. Sounds great.'

I wasn't apologising, actually...

'Do you mind calling me when it's ready? Just a few work things to sort. And then I might head up again after eating, for an hour or so. It's full-on mental at the moment. How's the chunk today?'

I slip the laptop under a cushion, convinced it might open and scream out my secrets, like the tell-tale HP. 'Good. We went to the weigh-in. Cherry's still way up there on the ninety-fifth. Health visitors say she's all tickety-boo.'

'Good, good.' Ted puts his hands on his hips and rocks back and forth a little on his heels, like he's got something to say. 'So...' His eyes drop away from mine. 'I'd better get on.'

Ted leaps quietly up the stairs – thank god – and then I'm alone with my rants once again. Bliss.

—

'Coffee, you sexy bastard,' Nelle says throatily, taking a big gulps of her latte. We're at one of the family cafes and have magically got Cherry and Joe to nap in sync, next to each other in their prams.

'Long night?'

She nods. 'Boy, oh boy. I felt like my life was one of those long-winded Russian novels they turn into BBC dramas. It took me, I don't know, two months to fold some laundry yesterday afternoon. And then the night stretched out into several decades with Joe deciding the Moses basket was suddenly not as comfy as my chest. With the first two we were so strict about this kind of stuff, but now I just need the whole household to get some rest, so I found myself – having lowered him ever so gently into his bed, already asleep – with my hand caught behind his neck and I'm too damn scared to remove it but I'm so damn tired I might just pass out right there on the bedroom rug. Which needs hoovering.' A waitress with stripes of green dye in her hair brings over two big wedges of carrot cake. 'Oh, Bea, you are a love.' Nelle smiles at her like she's been sent from above. 'With this and the caffeine and the three-hour nap Darren arranged for me this morning, taking Joe to see his folks, I think I may be a real, live person again. And he pitched ParentFest to them – they love it!' Nelle tings her cake fork against mine in a toast. 'We'll make a great mark-up from the booze and there's the perfect field we've used for a big marquee wedding in the past – a bored farmer who doesn't really mind if you tear up his ground because he's only going to put potatoes in, anyway. Saves him a job. You know what, I haven't felt this worked up about an event in ages! Such a genius move of yours!' The smile reaches all the way up to her eyes, knocking any tired shadows out of place.

'Are you sure that's not just the sugar high talking?'

Nelle uses her cake fork to poke me in the arm.

'Ow!'

'Take a sodding compliment, Stewart. Or I will call you Stewart until my dying day. I will have it chiselled into my gravestone, in fact. "Excellent person. Beloved wife and mother. Dearest friend of Stewart." You need to give yourself credit. We're all grafting on this but you gave it life, OK? Suck it up – you did good, kid.'

I shovel more of the perfectly dense, slightly spiced cake into my mouth so I don't have to actually reply.

Nelle rattles out more of the prospective plans, sticking a finger out for each one. 'Our mate at The Jolly Good is going to give us the names of really good local guitar bands – ones that don't mind playing faithful covers of late nineties Britpop. The circus performers will be under strict instructions to stay in the kids' area and not spook any of the grown-ups' – she shoots me a meaningful look – 'um, and we're going to source one of those HUGE paella dishes, bigger than a duck pond, for a massive paella stand. Chef is totally excited about trying one of those. We've got your excellent press release, of course, and we're taking out some local paper ads and even some digital ones. To be honest, seeing the way your blog has blossomed has made me twig that our punters are more likely to react to something like this if it jumps out at them on their scrolling time and they can click through and buy tickets in a flash.'

I clear my throat. 'I could… I mean, First-Time Mum could mention it, nearer the time? I'd have to say that I got sent some comp tickets, so that it seems like a standard blogger product review thing, rather than revealing me as your mate. But if you think it might help—?'

'That would be brilliant!' Nelle beams. 'But only if you're sure? And you're really happy to?'

'Sure as sure can be. I want this thing to work, just as much as you guys. I need all the proof I can get that my brain still has functional parts.' Nelle rolls her eyes. 'But I need to be super careful. Ted nearly busted me, right in the middle of writing a blog last night. Not that he cared much after I said it was a work thing I was helping out with.'

Nelle carefully scoops the foam from around the rim of her cup with a teaspoon. 'So, he's *never* going to know? About the blog? I mean, you did say you were going to come clean with him about how you've felt in the mum life.'

I look over at Cherry, still snoozing, a bubble of snot inflating then deflating with weirdly hypnotic beauty from her left nostril. 'Well, some of that I feel better about these days. Like, talking to humans; that doesn't make me want to tear my skin off quite so much. And I can't be so completely boring if people like my posts. Even the ones that hate them – at least it proves I'm not totally irrelevant.' I pick at a thumbnail. 'Sometimes I don't even know where to start with Ted. We get these two-hour slots at night to be together. And if he's not emailing or watching phone clips of rugby injuries, we're just swapping domestic info. It's all… transactional. "Did you get any dishwasher tablets on the way home? Did your parents confirm that date in September for us to go up? Is it time to move Cherry into her own room?"'

Nelle nods as I talk. 'I know what you mean. A lot of being married with kids is making sure the diary works and there are fish fingers in the freezer. But you're still in the new baby phase. Things even out. You find your rhythm again. It gets fun, honest! Like, when you both step back and look at the ridiculousness of it all and you can't help but laugh. I remember our eldest, Evan, being so cross with us as a toddler because we bought him the wrong Ninja Turtle for Christmas. If I ever want to get a smile out of Darren, I just whinge 'Raphaeeeeeeel!' and we're in stitches.'

'We did laugh after the poo in the pit,' I say.

She shudders a little at the mention. 'There you go.'

'But that's the first time I can remember us properly laughing in... oh, months, most likely. Ted's not usually there to share the really ridiculous bits. Fair enough, he's working hard to support us. I try and remind myself of that every day. He's knackering himself out flying off to Vienna or Cologne or he's at his desk upstairs, slamming the keyboard keys stupidly loudly and waking the baby. I don't find those moments all that charming, I must admit. And, besides, I never want to say when something is super-gross or annoying or boring, in case he looks at me like a monster for resenting any part of Cherry's existence.'

Nelle glances at me over the rim of her cup as she drinks. 'I think you're actually crediting him with far more emotional intelligence than the average man possesses. He would never think that! He knows you too well.'

The cake is all gone now. I could have polished off three slices. 'Maybe. And maybe it's more like I haven't known "me" for a while. But maybe he won't enjoy First-Time-Mum me now, if he came across the blog somehow. She pulls no punches.'

Shaking crumbs from her lap, Nelle nods. 'And that's exactly why we love her.'

–

Nelle's in the back, chatting to some of the cafe staff about earning overtime by working at ParentFest, and I am poring through messages, tweets and emails. Who knew that all of a sudden *not* being cripplingly lonely could be just as overwhelming? I think I'm going to have to limit myself to five replies a day and hope that keeps me mentally balanced. Otherwise I think I will drain myself of verbal energy.

One message from the early hours of this morning instantly catches my eye:

> @BBootsMum: Hey MM, how are things? I have banished the iron and am now obsessed with Gilmore Girls for my 4am insomnia. Have you seen it?

> @First_Time_Mum: Love that show! Got me through my so-pregnant-I-can't-leave-the-sofa weeks. One day soon let's have a big Jess/Dean/Logan debate. Glad to hear you're finding the bright side of shitty sleep. You're an inspiration!

I think I'm going to need folders to organise all these messages, so I start tapping like mad to set them up, suddenly aware that Cherry's 45-minute maximum nap time is about to be reached. She's due to wake up any minute and I want to be ready for her, to give her my undivided attention. But I'm interrupted by new WhatsApp messages dropping down from the top of my screen, getting in my way.

Ted: Are you in tonight? Maybe I'll pick up dinner and we can catch up properly.

A faint smile crosses my lips at the thought of one major job off my list today (our store cupboards are down to Cup-a-Soups and tinned salmon), plus a real chance to talk, and then I'm back into my folder frenzy. Shove these messages in there, flag these with a star, not sure about that, come back to...

Out of the corner of my eye, it feels like someone is heading my way. A very blonde someone.

I look up and my eyes lock on Chloe's, but then a second later she steps back, looks determinedly away, a hand to her lips in concentration, her beautifully painted lilac nails drumming against her lip as she studies the cafe blackboard. Nope, not after me. Probably a soya latte. So I go back to my organising.

Jeez, Stevie. Not everyone is interested in you these days. Big head, much? Clearly a mum-mum has no interest in you — you look like the classic lazy mother ignoring her kid for another game of Candy Crush. Not that that's totally wrong. Right, now file this—

My breath catches as I scan the first line of an email

Re: Have you ever thought about writing a book?

It must be spam. It must be a Nepalese government official offering me a unique investment in a... printing press—?

Or it's an autocorrect fail for 'writhing about' and I'm about to get loads of weirdo porn filling my screen.

But I should just check.

> Dear First-Time Mum,
>
> I love your posts! Totally could have been me, eight years ago now (my son wouldn't let anyone but me push his pushchair and used to hide his head under my top when he was shy. This went on until he was five!).
>
> I'll cut to the chase. I'm a literary agent and I've worked with a few social media talents to help them turn their brands into books. You might well have already had approaches and might be meeting with other agents, but I'd love to beg a meeting with you, if I may?
>
> I had lunch with a really good friend of mine who's a big non-fiction editor at Random House and we both brought you up at the same time! She'd be really keen to see any sample material you might be able to write. Based on your blogs, I think it could be an absolutely hysterical guide to parenting. REAL parenting, mind you! The 'Coco Pops as a bribe' kind.
>
> If you'd like to meet, let me know when and where suits you.
>
> Best wishes,
>
> Francesca Blair

I let out a yelp that doesn't sound like my actual voice. And when it continues, and gets louder, I realise it isn't mine

– it's the Cherry Post-Nap Grumps. For a minute I am genuinely torn between reading this amazing email again and scooping her up for a jiggle and a cuddle. If she'll put up with one. But my girl needs me, and she always comes first.

I hold Cherry at my front, facing out – her favourite position for a distracting nose about at other people. But it's not working – her cries are now shrill and almost constant. Joe wriggles in his pram and starts to mew along.

'Nelle!' I sing-song call. 'The kraken has awoken and so has your Joe, sorry!'

Chloe is clutching a cardboard cup and inching closer to my table. Her face has flushed red and she's eyeing up the chair I've just vacated. One of the random skills that having a tricky baby has installed in me is being able to instantly read the body language for 'Your kid is ruining it for the rest of us: can you just not get to fuck?'

Fine. Message received.

Chloe's delicate lips part, but before she says pointedly, 'Are you leaving?' or whatever, I roll my eyes and blurt out, 'Yes, the table's yours. We're going.' I start clumsily three-point-turning the pram with Cherry still bawling in my arms. Nelle appears in the kitchen doorway and I mouth, 'Off home. I'll text you later' in an needlessly over-exaggerated way – she could probably have heard me if I'd just said it normally.

The bright June sunlight seems to stun Cherry into silence so I take advantage of her shock and clip her back into the pram pronto, speed-walking in the direction of home. Caffeine, sugar, book deals, screamfests – the adrenaline is knocking about in me like martini ingredients in a cocktail shaker: potent, intense, ice cold.

A book? Could I write a whole book?!

I mean, I wouldn't know where to start. But then, six months ago I didn't know how to write a blog, either. Maybe I could take my posts as a jumping-off point and expand on them. There is always more to say on the topic of the best ways to clean up a car-based vomit session when you only have a scarf, three dried-up wet wipes and a copy of *Elle* with you. And I'm sure this agent would steer me in the right direction if I'm going totally off the boil.

A *real* literary agent. Blimey. She must think there's some money in it, then, or she'd hardly be wasting her time or her publisher mate's time. Money. Like, career-building money. I could pay someone to pimp up my blog. I could take some evening classes in digital marketing, maybe. Get a flash laptop.

But how would I explain the money to Ted? A small drug-dealing operation, maybe. Or that I'd sold my left kidney. Either would probably seem more plausible to him than, 'Someone thinks I'm smart and entertaining enough to write an entire book' coming from the wife who drones on about Cherry being two sizes ahead in nappies than another six month old at the weigh-in, and thinks she's made an effort by brushing the egg off her sweatshirt and taking her ponytail out.

Maybe this is the moment to tell Ted; maybe this is when I come clean? But what if he really disapproved? What if he didn't want our lives examined in print, even anonymously? Obviously I would never choose a book deal over my family, but this good feeling I've been building through the blog, this confidence – so much more like the old me – it's too fragile to risk someone else's disapproval right now.

I can't deny that the thought of bringing in some real money again – not the piddling statutory maternity pay which just about covers my biscuit expenses – fills my skeleton with something like molten iron. I'll be a provider again. I can buy a new top without two weeks of guilt.

I get us home, for once not noticing the steep incline of the way back as my mind rattles through chapters – maybe little illustrations, and a list of all the shit NOT to buy. Baby bath? Pah. By the time I got myself together enough to give Cherry so much as a once a week bath, she was too big for the damn thing. And now it acts as an awkward laundry basket. Whose contents never get sorted or put away.

Before I give my anxieties enough time to find 3,000 reasons why trying this would lead to certain DOOM for all of us, I reply to Francesca.

> Hello!
> God, I'm so flattered and YES I would love to try my hand at a book. Meeting right now is tricky (baby juggling, plus the whole anonymous thing) but how about I get you a sample and we could take it from there. How many chapters would you need to see?
> Nervous and excited,
> First-Time Mum x

The voice of anxiety is just starting to warm up minutes later – *Way to sound professional, Stevie, you might as well have asked her to be your new BFF and come round and braid your hair in front of* Dawson's Creek. *You really are just winging it, aren't you?* – when Francesca sends back a quick response.

Excellent! I'm leaving the office now but I would say 10,000 words would be a really good sample – something I could interest publishers with. And if this is all new to you, just try and keep one core message at the heart of it. To bring the whole book together. What I took from your posts was a rallying cry against the 'perfect parenthood' that gets shoved down our throats, but you need to find the message that rings true to you.

Plus, I would really rather we meet before I officially offer you representation. We need to see if we'd click, for both our sakes! Maybe if we're both happy with the sample when you send it in, we could chat on the phone and take it from there? And let me know if you do decide to go with another agent, as a courtesy, thanks. But I do hope you'll pick me!

F x

With my heart pounding my ribs, I send back:

Thanks for this. Not talking to any other agents and won't until you've had a chance to see what I've written. Thanks for reaching out. It means so much!

FTMx

Oh, come on, Stevie! Are you going for your hostess badge at the Brownies?! I mean, you sound like a silly, litt—

Shut up. I'm doing this. First-Time Mum is going to try and get into print!

Chapter 12

There were all sorts of things I swore I'd never do as a parent. Lose my temper at my kids. Give them anything less than sugar-free, salt-free homemade snacks. Use the TV as a babysitter. That's when I had parenting down to a T: the parenting of my fictional, future children, that is. I wonder who got those imagined kids of mine? The ones taking care of their organic cotton T-shirts and thoughtfully munching on raw red pepper while I read the new Kate Atkinson in a separate room. I wouldn't swap Cherry for the world. Maybe a solitary weekend, but not full time, anyway.

She's not perfect and that makes two of us. Peas in a pod. I have broken one of my own cardinal sins of pre-parenthood and have propped her up on the sofa, with the change bag on one side and my balled-up raincoat on the other, to be entertained by the Twirlywoos. So that I can type like a madwoman. While the adrenaline is working to my advantage, I might as well harness this pumped-up level of unnatural energy and get some ideas down. Like Francesca said, I need to find my own message to join everything up. And she was not far wrong when she mentioned the myth of perfect. But I need to put it in my voice.

WHAT THE F*CK IS PERFECT, ANYWAY?

I'm First-Time Mum. You might have heard of me if you are awake between the hours of 1am and 5.30am without any alcohol, amphetamines or serious jet lag in your system. That is to say: if you are a parent. This is me writing a book.★

It's a book about parenting. But it is not a parenting book. It is not me telling you what to do. Because I'll be fucked if I know what to do when it's my kid, let alone yours. And I spend all day with mine and she's still more mysterious than a Sphinx (only with neck folds), so I would never tell you what to do with your kid(s), seeing as I have never met them, let alone counted the layers of their under-chin fat.

But this is a book about the parenting I have experienced and the small ways in which I have been trying (not always succeeding) to get through it sane and sober(-ish). It's meant to distract you, reassure you and possibly give you a small laugh. And it's going to remind you, hopefully on every page: you are good enough.

If you're anything like me and someone tries to compliment you on doing a good job with your kid, you probably quickly thank them and change the subject. But really, you don't believe a single word of it. Because how can you be doing a great job when your life is nothing like those Instagram shots, those Baby Björn photos, those amazing mum-mums who bounce down the road with a troop of immaculately dressed children following in her suede-heeled footsteps? You don't measure up to them. And they are perfect. So therefore you are crap.

Well, I am here to throw a pooey nappy in the face of 'perfect'. It's a myth. It's a lie. It's as real and obtainable as 'me time'. Parents, all we have to be is good enough. You don't need to have a Walton's-esque day in the park with your family, blowing dandelion clocks and linking arms as you skip through a meadow. If you've made it to the swings and someone comes home with a grazed elbow? Good enough. You got out of the house and there was no A&E trip – achievement. Your children don't need to be raised on hummus and quinoa alone and blink in confusion at the sight of an Oreo. If one vaguely colourful piece of vegetation is sneaked into their system on a daily basis, you're winning. If it's followed by a few Jammy Dodgers in front of Pointless, you still won today.

I've struggled with so much guilt over Big Baby's sleep patterns – they are far from what the perfect parenting books say. She does not 'drop off' when awake-but-drowsy. She does not self-soothe. She has to be rocked, pram-pushed, jiggled and begged to sleep for the shortest times. I am her 'crutch', these books tell me. I am setting up bad patterns for life.

For the first months of her life I thought her sleep patterns were all because of ME.

Because I was failing, because I wasn't trying hard enough, maybe even because there was something wrong with my maternal gene, deep down. It's taken an agonisingly long time; it's taken non-stop tears and middle-of-the-night panics; and finally it took the wise words of some crucial parenting friends in my life to make me see – this is just it. This is the parenting life, sometimes – messy, unpredictable and nothing like the books. It can be hard, but that doesn't mean you are weak. It can make you loathe yourself, but that doesn't mean you don't TOTALLY love your kid(s). It can feel endless, but one day it will get better.

But first, and say it with me: 'Fuck perfect. We are good enough!'

Solidarity,

First-Time Mum x

★ I know, right?! TRIPPY.

I'm actually slightly panting as I type the last few sentences. This introduction just seemed to pour out of me, like I was the medium for some clever, dead person's thoughts. But damn it, I've typed them – they're mine now. And instead of feeling exhausted after this mental blast, I actually feel totally revved up. Adrenaline feeding adrenaline. Cherry has hardly made a peep as the tubby little felt family roll about on the screen. We're all on the up. Seems like tempting fate to stop now. *If she cries, I'll totally take a break*, I promise myself.

I start a new page under this first draft of the intro and type 'Contents'. Maybe if I just freestyle some pertinent parenting topics, I will see a pattern emerging and will be able to pick the most appealing bits for this sample.

Under 'Contents' I write 'Funny. Raw. Honest. ALWAYS honest' to make sure I don't lose my thread of this first bit.

And then it flows, as my fingers bash the keys:

Sex after kids: er, come again? Or – more aptly – come at all?!

Early risers: black-out blinds, Groclocks, white noise. Whatevs, mate, you're pretty much stuffed. Invest in a Nespresso instead.

Gender bullshit: watch out, they're coming for it all – blue muslins for boys, pink pram covers for girls. Why we should all say stuff it and raise unicorn babies.

The boob brigade: what you do with your tits is up to you and you alone. Flop 'em out. Or don't. It isn't political, it's personal. And formula is very good. Almost like they designed it to properly feed infants. (GASP!)

'Are you sure it's not twins?!': the weird and wounding things people feel A-OK about blabbing at you when you're pregnant, or just after having your baby. Top ten quick-fire responses, including: 'Are you sure you're allowed out on your own? Shall I call the ward?'

What the HELL is that down there?: you thought the freaky rollercoaster of bodily changes ended after pregnancy? You were

wrong. Piles. Tears. Blocked ducts. A chapter
to leave open if your OH looks askance at
being asked to do the dishwasher again.

I'm just sinking a cool glass of wine post-bedtime when
Ted walks in.

'Rough day?' he asks.

I look at the inch of sauvignon blanc left in the glass and
give it a swirl. Just this once, it's actually a reward rather
than a rescue. Just this once, it's a celebration. But I don't
know how to explain that to him without delving into a
whole heap of trouble. '*No, darling. Actually, it's been a mega
day because the secret blog I've been writing has really taken off
and someone might want me to write a book. And pay me for
it. Of course, the blog is all about our lives and my frustrations
and Cherry's ability to vomit over a four-metre radius, but don't
worry your sweet face about that. In fact, one of the longest posts
was slagging you right off. Beer?*' Maybe not.

I shrug noncommittally. The coward's response. But
the safe one. With the book ideas and ParentFest and all
this social media attention, I can't possibly find a decent
space in my head to work out how I break this to Ted. But
I will. When the sample is sent and I have one big thing
ticked off my list, I'll cook the best meal I can muster,
maybe a nice Thai green curry, and we'll get it all out in
the open. Somehow.

Ted holds up an M&S bag. 'Got us one of those nice
meals for two. With the apple pie my mum always says is
such good value. I'll bung it all in, you relax.'

'Oh, thanks, love.' I give him a quick peck and dash
back to my laptop on the sofa. Relax? Pah! I could get a
good start on the first chapter while he's rotating dishes in
the microwave.

'Earth. To. Stevie.'

Ted is standing in the doorway, a tea towel over his shoulder and one hand scratching the back of his head.

'Sorry?'

'I've been calling you for five minutes. Where have you been?'

Lost in my recounting of the baby blues – two months' weeping on the sofa with a similarly weeping baby, a million boxes of tissues and the sinking feeling we should just have got a dog.

'Still… uh, helping Sarah with this work thing.'

'Well, your moussaka is going curly at the edges. Come on.'

Ted pours me another glass of wine as I sit down, but I shake my head with a smile. I want to be sober enough to hit a decent word count between night feeds. His plate is already half-cleared so I start trowelling it down like a teenage boy at boarding school.

'Hang on!' He laughs. 'I thought we'd have a bit of a catch-up, what with work being so mental recently. You haven't told me what you and our girl have been up to this week.'

If you only knew…

'Mmmm,' I say through a mouthful of lukewarm – but still very lovely – lamb mince and white sauce. 'Promised Sarah I would get her something for the morning, though. Deadlines, pitches. You know.'

He sticks his tongue in his cheek briefly and blinks. 'OK.'

'Actually, I might take this to finish off in the office as I go, if you don't mind? As long as you weren't planning on doing emails up there or anything?' I have my plate in one hand, cutlery in another, and I'm raising my eyebrows hopefully.

Ted lays his knife and fork down on the rim of his plate. 'Nope. Wasn't going to work at all tonight.' He clears his throat.

'Great! Thanks, love. This is delicious!' I call as I launch myself up the stairs.

—

Ted called a soft goodnight at about ten and I knew my first night feed of the night wasn't far off, so what was the point in stopping? Besides, I was deep into the Sex After Babies chapter and it took a lot of my mental powers to work out exactly when we might have last had sex. Was it a birthday? A bank holiday? I feel like there was a concrete reason why I took the plunge, filled with the fear of my delicate parts being ruined all over again after Cherry made her unsubtle way out. But I do know for sure that we've only done it twice in seven months. The first was so angsty and fumbly and painful (for me) that when I wimped out I could see the overwhelming relief in Ted's eyes (well, I would have been able to see it if I'd allowed the lights on). The second technically counted as full sex but it wouldn't make the Mills & Boon cut, put it that way. Hang on – *three* times if you count the one I made Ted do when I was ten days overdue and had heard a very unique male secretion could bring on labour. I don't know if that counts as sex. I think, to Ted at least, it might count as cruel and unusual punishment.

I've written nearly 2,000 words today, between Cherry's tea and now. So if I bash away at it every day like this for a week and then allow myself a week of editing and revision, in a fortnight I should have something worthy of Francesca! I just can't let up. I'm feeling the momentum. And sleep is for suckers.

I sneak out another two paragraphs before the familiar whine begins and quickly builds up into a full-lung moan. Creeping into the bedroom and unhooking one side of my grey and bobbly feeding bra, I pick up Cherry, get myself comfortable as best I can against the evil headboard and she's away, greedy little love.

'Mummy's just been building her literary career, Chicken,' I whisper down at her. 'And then tomorrow we can do the supermarket shop. And two days after *that* we'll go singing at the library, shall we? With Nelle and Joe. Looks like you've got a mumpreneur, eh?'

Cherry doesn't flinch as her jaw moves rhythmically, hypnotically. I suppose my career choices don't really affect her snack supply. But they sure as hell make me feel better.

–

I'm still busting with the potential of book ideas three days later, as I speed-walk Cherry in her pram to the library. Nelle is loitering outside the double doors for us.

'Where's the fire?' she says, taking in my semi-sprint.

'I was just making a few notes on my phone in the car park, lost track of time. Nearly forgot my parking ticket. Doh!' I smack my palm against my head.

'You OK?' Nelle's eyebrows slide down a touch.

'Amazing!' I trill, bouncing on the balls of my feet. 'On a mission. Writing *loads* and I'm even sixty per cent sure it's not crap. I might… I might send you a bit to read, you and Will. If that's OK?'

Her eyebrows shoot right back up to her hairline again. 'Are you kidding? I'd bloody love that! And I have plenty of material, should you need any extras.' She rubs her fingers gently over Joe's impossibly tiny earlobe. 'So, how much have you been able to write?'

'About seven thousand words. The agent said ten, in total. So I'm cracking on.'

'Seven thousand?!' Nelle squeaks in alarm, as if I've just said that was how much I paid for my sagging blue leggings. 'How the bejesus have you managed that in just a few days?'

I shrug. 'I can make notes once Cherry is asleep in the car, for about half an hour. And then I can get a good two hours in between night feeds.' I chew the inside of my lip.

'Stevie!' Nelle almost growls in protest, as if I've just confessed to the last time these sad blue leggings were washed. 'That's not good, hun. *When* are you actually sleeping?'

'When I need to. It's fine. I'm fine. And hey, might as well capitalise on having broken nights, right?'

She doesn't reply for a beat. 'Let's work something out for tomorrow where Will and I take the Cherry pie and you have an hour to yourself to write. And consider yourself excused from ParentFest duties while you're spinning all these plates. But in exchange, NO burning the candle tonight, *capisce*?'

I nod obediently. I mean, she won't *know* if I work in another quick blast… 'Come on, nursery rhyme chanting calls. Maybe this is the week it truly turns into a cult and we have to sign away all our earthy possessions?' I beam out a smile, mostly fuelled by coffee and nervous energy.

Nelle is suitably distracted from her chiding. 'They wouldn't want what I've got, believe me. And you'd better join in with my version of "Five Little Monkeys" if it comes up.' She pokes me playfully on the shoulder. Nelle has slightly rewritten this old and bonkers song in her head so that instead of mummy monkey calling the doctor, we sing loudly over everyone else, 'Mummy WAS A DOCTOR, and so SHE said' because, as Nelle puts it: 'If this chimp lady has the guts to have five kids, I bet she's got it in her to tell them herself to sodding well stop ruining her mattresses or they can bloody well drive themselves to A&E with a head wound.' Not a line of reasoning I find fault with, myself.

We shuffle into the library and join the ramshackle circle of mums and babies forming on the brightly coloured, partially stained carpet. Before meeting Nelle this was one of THE scariest places to bring Cherry, for fear of a very loud meltdown. Screeches and screams bouncing around a bustling coffee shop is bad enough, but being the only noise within an otherwise perfectly serene library? No thanks. It's like walking through an exam hall with a police siren strapped to your front.

Now that I know I have an ally to deflect some of the shame and self-consciousness, I'm at least readier to give these sessions a shot. If I have to make a mad dash for it, so what? I can try again next week. And I have someone to at least laugh it off with. And should Nelle experience a poo-slosion with Joe that leaks through his clothes and the sling and onto her cardigan, I'm here for her too; holding the soiled items with one finger as she removes them in the disabled loos. That is what mum mates are for. Knowing I have two real parenting friends (and quite a few faceless ones online, now I think of it) puts that bit more steel into my resolve. I'm far from thinking that my days of burning cheeks and escaping bodily fluids are behind me, but now I know it's not really the worst that can happen. Plus I really am not alone in how I feel. That makes all the difference.

I'm feeling so at home on the carpet, surrounded by the low carts of well-creased picture books, that I barely react as I spot Chloe and her polished pals swaggering through the door with their NASA-designed prams. The first few times I bumped into her, her sky-high bar of parenting had made me feel so lowly, like I could limbo under a gate. But now I just think: *Good for her. You do you. And I will do me.* That's the sum of it.

Cherry is plonked down in front of me, facing the rest of the group to be in her ultimate nosey position, and Joe is lying just in front of Nelle, safely out of Cherry's grasp. The sweet lady that leads the singing is still fussing over a sheet of stickers at the library desk, so Nelle and I break into whispers.

'What have you been writing about then? So far?'

'Um,' I mutter out of the side of my mouth, 'well, one of the first chapters I've completed is about… sex.' My eyes go wide in mock-horror.

'Oh, I've heard of that,' Nelle replies in low tones. 'That's the thing young people do instead of watching *Corrie*, right?'

I laugh silently into the heel of my hand. 'Sounds like you can skip over that chapter, Nelle.'

She shakes her head. 'Ha! As if. Hand over your phone, let me take a look.'

I oblige. 'Press that pen app, it's in there. Synchs up from my laptop.'

'Fancy.'

The singing lady takes her seat on the little red stool at the front of us all. 'Hello, happy faces!' she begins, and

Cherry's head whips round in her direction. I have this feeling she is going to be a total teacher-worshipping nerd at school, if her devotion to the health visitors and the library lady is anything to go by. As if to prove my thesis, she starts rocking back and forth on her fat thighs, trying to propel herself further towards this authority figure, however tenuous.

'Shall we start with "Wheels on the Bus" today?' the lady asks, and Nelle cackles just beside me. Quite a few of the mums look over at us in confusion and I smile apologetically. I think Nelle may have just read the bit about covering any bedroom mirrors with the nearest thick dressing gown. Because no one needs a reflected recap of their nethers if they're braving sex again, let alone having to look at your engorged boobs if you can bare to have them set free from their bra-hammock. Mine are covered in these horrendous dark, thick veins that look like the scary Underneath monster from *Stranger Things*. Which I have admitted in the chapter.

Nelle is gently vibrating with swallowed giggles right now, hiding my phone by her crossed legs but keeping her eyes glued to the screen. Despite the fact that I feel bad that this is somewhat throwing the singing lady off her jolly tunes, and also embarrassment that Chloe and her gang are throwing narrowed glances our way, I can't help but feel a glow of pride. Nelle likes it! It's ringing true! Maybe Francesca will like it, too; hopefully she'll have the odd laugh. Maybe her editor chum will race through it and make her a stonking offer over the next lunch and I can be a lady author and never have to worry about office life ever again and…

I need to calm down. I tune back into the lyrics for 'Hickory Dickory Dock', focusing on keeping up with the extra verses (which until I had Cherry I had no idea existed. To be honest, they're a bit thin and it's not only the mouse saying 'No more!' by the time you get to the fourth one). *Don't run away with yourself, Stevie. You need to get the words down, do a hell of a lot of editing and then cross everything that is still flexible enough to cross over.* Nelle is bound to be kind about it – she's a mate, and she's super-lovely.

Clearing her throat and wiping a tiny tear away from under one eye, Nelle slips the phone back to me. 'Dynamite, Stevie. Dynamite.' I squeeze her hand briefly before she pulls it away and gets stuck into winding the bobbin up.

Feeling like the naughty girls that have just thrown spitballs all the way through year nine History, we're in no rush to be the first through the doors once the singing has ended. I hand Cherry a touchable board book on ducklings that she immediately starts licking. Oh, well, maybe you can absorb literacy that way. Nelle has wrapped Joe back up in his trusty sling and is looking at the DVDs by the entrance, which I think must be the library's version of that trick when supermarkets pump fresh bread smell at you as you walk in. Hook you with something a bit tempting and naughty before you are swamped with periodicals or fresh cabbages and blindly shove them in your trolley.

A loud duck quacking alert makes her fish her mobile out of her handbag. She rolls her eyes at me. 'Preteens. I suppose I'm lucky they don't set the language to Mandarin, or something.' She looks down at the new message. 'Ooooh! Hey, are you up to much this afternoon?'

'Just the usual bikini waxing, and I can always cancel my Italian lover,' I drawl. The tiny, hunched male librarian by Street Maps and Atlases gives me a filthy look. I return it with a hard stare. *I'm having fun, mate, give me a break.* Just a month ago this kind of an exchange would have me twisted with anxiety for weeks after, berating myself for having done the wrong thing yet again.

'Great! There's this local band we like for ParentFest and they say they can come and play a mini acoustic set for us at the pub today, so we can see if *we like their sound, yeah.*' She says this last bit in a roughly Gallagher-like accent.

'Private acoustic set?! Blimey, it's like our very own Live Lounge. Count me in! What about Will?'

'Messaging him now,' Nelle replies, eyes down and thumbs moving rapidly. 'Meet you at The Jolly Good at 2pm?'

'Perfect. Maybe we should have a pint of snakebite each, just for full authenticity? I must have a tie-dye T-shirt at the back of a drawer somewhere still.'

The moody little library gnome clears his throat loudly and obnoxiously. *Jeez, I'm joking about having a pint, not downing a can of Foster's here and now!*

I follow Nelle out of the double doors, glad to be out of his miserable earshot. 'I haven't listened to live music in… just for ever. Maybe they're like the next Ed Sheeran or something, and we can say we saw them first?!'

'Four Ed Sheerans is a bit of a weird thought, though, isn't it? And if they cover that "Irish Girl" song I'll be having words. Rude words. I'm hoping for some classic Springsteen, Van Morrison. Clapton, if they've been well schooled by their parents. Coldplay and maybe—'

'Excuse me!' I wheel around on the spot at an angry croaking following us down the street. The gnome is huffing his way the ten metres from the doors to where we're standing. Instinctively I pat my pockets. Did I slip a book in there and forget to check it out properly? I'm all for supporting libraries, not robbing them.

His whole face and neck are a livid puce as he reaches us. 'You forgot...' he wheezes.

Oh god, I have unintentionally nicked a book...

'...your baby,' he eventually finishes.

My breath catches as I look at Nelle's sling. But Joe's stripy beanie is visible, poking out above her cleavage, and he can't mean—

'CHERRY!' I scream, running past the little troll, almost knocking him over, my lungs now devoid of oxygen and a searing pain tearing through my calves.

She's sitting on the carpet, still sucking all the juices from her board book. Tears stream down my face as I scoop her up. 'Oh, baby, baby,' I cry into her neck. 'I'm sorry. Mummy's so sorry. I didn't—I wouldn't—'

But I did. Didn't I? I forgot my baby.

–

Even at 2pm, I'm still shaking. My hands, my legs, my brain. Whatever steel I thought my resolve had gained recently has melted in fiery-hot shame and now I'm a puddle of a person. I left Cherry behind. I breezed out of there without a care in the world, easy as you like, making stupid, stupid jokes about getting drunk in the daytime. Full of myself. All the while, my beautiful, defenceless baby just sat there in a public space, waiting to be snatched. I might as well have listed her on Freecycle: *Baby to collect. ASAP.* What if the staff hadn't noticed?! What if someone unscrupulous had got there first? What if I had to make one of those awful public appeals on television, with Ted barely holding back the urge to throttle me there and then for being so careless, so stupid with this incredible, precious gift of life.

I'm at the bar in The Jolly Good, ordering three coffees, and tears drop quickly into my cappuccino. Nelle spots me and comes over.

'Love, please, don't beat yourself up. It's such an easy thing to do and you've been working all these crazy hours…'

I hold up my hand, not even turning to face her. I'd rather she put hot coals down my bra than be kind to me right now. Kindness just makes the shame burn even deeper. I am an awful person.

She takes the hint. 'OK. OK. Look, the band's about to start… try and allow yourself to be distracted, if you can. Just listen to the music and let it drown everything else out.'

Will puts his arm around my shoulders as I take a seat at the little round pub table. The girls are doing one of their first nursery afternoons and he can barely contain his giddy joy, even though I know he's trying his best to sympathise.

I pull Cherry's pram closer to me by a few inches. This girl is not leaving my sight. Ever. Possibly not until she collects a pension. Luckily she seems unfazed by the abandonment ordeal I put her through this morning. Sure, she had her usual shouts and cries of protest at being wheeled about for a nap after lunch, but it was no louder or longer than any other day. I'm definitely putting off moving her into her own room now, though. Maybe I'll do it in October. October 2035.

'Ooooh, here we go.' Will rubs his hands together as some tuning twangs come from the lead singer's guitar. He has super-tight acid wash jeans on, which finish promptly above his ankle, and a lot of quiffy hair on top with a number one shave around the sides. Young. Cool. Maybe this is the perfect distraction from my mothering fails – I can use this guy as portal to reminisce about all my teenage crushes: Damon Albarn, Leo DiCaprio, the boy with the ice-blue eyes who used to give out the shoes at the bowling alley. Every week I'd go and rent those sweaty flats so that I could chance brushing my hand against his.

Nelle sits just behind us and gives the band the thumbs up. The Isolated Pawns, apparently. They can't be more than twenty-three at the oldest but they seem so self-assured, so composed. Standing with their cool T-shirts and instruments in a corner of a Berkshire pub at 2pm on a weekday, looking like a Top Man shoot that's got hideously lost. I envy them that confidence of youth. Or maybe it's the confidence of talent? Or good hair? But they seem to just belong, to fit perfectly, and I miss that easy, impossible-to-fake sense of belonging. Just when I thought I was hitting something like a stride this week with the blog and the chance to write a book, all alongside caring for Chezza, I go and slide right back into Beginner Mum territory…

Hang on. Distract yourself. Don't start crying again in front of Nelle and Will. Or The Isolated Pawns. They're too young to handle a middle-aged meltdown.

Some gentle chords start to float out towards us, and I'm sure I remember this song. From sixth form. Kind of romantic. What was it? Not Nirvana. Not REM. Foo Fighters, that's it. The strumming goes on and I feel my shoulders loosen as familiar notes fill my head. What was it called? I hum along a bit just to myself, seeing if I can get to the chorus before they do.

Oh. 'Walking Back to You.' That was it.

Karma really has it in for me today. *Thanks, universe. I get it. Might as well do my own cover called 'Running Hysterically Back to You' by the Custody Battle Fighters.*

To keep myself from more ugly sobs, I unlock Cherry from the pram and lift her into my lap for a good head-sniff. I hope I never lose the memory of what her hair smells like: part custard powder, part fresh laundry, wrapped up together in the smell that can only be called Warm. I get these smells best post-bath time, when she's squeaky clean and we're settling down for her bedtime feed. They're few and far between during the day because sadly the sour-milk taint of regurgitation trumps Warm smell, every time.

My daughter wriggles and kicks away from me, not wanting to be enclosed in my desperate arms but to be lunging towards these strangers and their mysterious big toys which she could slice her fingers on and cover with her drool. 'Geerrrrghhhh!' she yells, as they wind the song down.

Nelle looks at me out of the corner of her eye and then yells, 'Got anything a bit more up tempo? But same era?'

The lead singer nods without making eye contact and soon an acoustic version of 'American Idiot' has us up and out of our seats. Now *this* is distracting music. I bounce up and down with Cherry on my hip and her pudgy arms wave in no apparent rhythm, but she's loving it just as much as I am. After a few verses she yanks my hair and grins. These are the moments I should hold on to, I realise. Not the utter fails but the relatively normal, happy triumphs. When my girl and I are jigging about like loons and having fun together. The moments when I feel how closely we are connected, how unbreakable is our bond. If I'm going to write this book, I'd better practise what I preach. Today this feels like a momentous fuck-up of nuclear disaster proportions but in a week, in a month, next year, will it feel like something knobbish I could actually laugh about? I mean, David Cameron left his kid in a pub and he was still allowed to be prime minister. One of the worst ones, in my opinion, but he wasn't chased out of Downing Street with pitchforks and flaming torches for that forgetfulness. And, right now, the only one pointing a sharpened garden tool in my direction is *me*.

Nelle is pogoing around the limited space, her eyes half-closed in joy, and Will is pumping his arms about wildly, stepping side to side. I think it might have been a while since he was last clubbing. And that makes three of us. But who cares?

I switch Cherry into a rocket launcher position, crouching down her then zooming her up in the air and over my head. She wetly gurgles out laughter, louder with each whoosh. This girl might leave a white, sticky calling card wherever she goes, she might burst the eardrums of cafe patrons, she might not sleep like the books say she should, but she's happy in this moment. And she is utter perfection to me.

The band leap straight into Garbage's 'Stupid Girl' without even taking a breath. 'Yes!' bellows Nelle. 'Absolute classic!' And I don't even let that snarky little voice in my head pass comment about the relevance of the song title to today's misadventures. I just keep twirling and hopping and shimmying with Cherry held at my front. When I have to pause for a slurp of coffee, I get an image of myself at the end of the year six disco, the first one I ever went to. Those huge stretchy headbands that were de rigueur, making us look – in hindsight – like we had serious head injuries. I shuffled awkwardly about the dance floor with my mates to this song, feeling so grown up to be at a *disco* in my best Tammy Girl stirrup leggings, without my parents, listening to grunge. *This is proper adult stuff*, I'd thought. Which, of course, it in no way was.

But here I am now, decades later, a certified adult with a baby of my own (though always yearning for those stirrup leggings – they were a pure grape purple) and, at times in the parenting game, I still feel like I've been let into my first ever disco. Excited, overwhelmed, out of my depth. Like everyone else is so cool and so ahead of the game. But it's OK not to have mastered it all. It's OK to not follow some kind of master plan. It's OK to trip over in the middle of 'Oh, Carolina' and then get up and try and shrug it off like some very rare body-popping move.

I will remember The Event at the Library for as long as I live. It will ramp up my levels of protectiveness, caution and double-checking under seats by 120 per cent, I imagine. But I will also remember it as the day my friends helped me shrug it off and then dance around to guitar music in the same afternoon. I've got to write a chapter on Mum Mates. Even if it scares the bejesus out of you to find them, they are a lifesaver.

Nelle leans against me, heaving happy breaths of exhaustion.

'Working hard, are we?' a gruff voice calls out behind us.

'Hello, love!' Nelle beams in the direction of a stocky guy with sandy-blond hair standing in the pub doorway. 'Come and meet Stevie and Will. This is my Darren.' As he approaches, Nelle places her hand on his chest, rubbing a brief circle on his flannel shirt. It's both affectionate and protective. These are couple goals.

'Hello, heard lots about you all. All good, of course. Um, love, you know that dentist appointment the kids had for today?'

Nelle frowns. 'What? No. I didn't make one. Did you?'

'Yeah, uh, the thing is' – he scratches the back of his head – '*someone* might have mentioned to the kids that we were trialling a live band. And then that same someone got worn down by begging and pleading. So that soppy someone made up fake dentist appointments to get them out of school early.'

Just as Nelle is taking aim to smack him on the bicep, Darren yells, 'Kids! Your mother is fine with it!' and through the door barrel two very excited children, both with the sandy hair of their dad: Evan's is buzzed all over in a close crop and Amy's is long and parted on the side, with a *Hunger Games*-style plait in front of her ear.

I can see Nelle biting back the admonishment she'd like to give her other half and instead she just shrugs and smiles. 'Oh, well. You're here now. But *only* one lemonade each. And you must work really hard, deciding if this band is any good. Look, they're about to start up again.' She pulls a frown of mock-concern. 'But I don't know about these guys, what do you reckon? Hmm. I really think we should get them to play at least three more tracks.'

'Four!' Will does a cheesy double-finger gun towards us all. There's a smattering of sweat beads on his forehead and he's thrown off the inky blue jumper he was wearing.

'I would say the success of ParentFest categorically depends on it!' I chime in.

'Yay!' Evan and Amy chorus together, gleeful at playing hooky with their parents' consent and probably looking forward to showing off to their mates at being inside a pub, listening to a band.

And I can see us all there at ParentFest: at the front of the crowd, faces thick with festival glitter and shoes slopped with white wine as we bop about without a care in the world to the tunes of our youth. We're going to put on an awesome shindig for the parents of this place. This place which is really starting to feel like home for me.

Chapter 13

We danced and nattered and bargained a rate with the band, high on nostalgia for the past, excitement for the future of the festival, and more caffeine than is strictly good for you. In fact, we were having such a blast that I suddenly realised the pub was filling up with after-work drinkers. It was 5.40pm and I hadn't even given Cherry her tea!

With some swearing and apologies, I high-tailed it home, praying to the patron saint of Parenting, The Lady Annabelle of the Holy Purée, that there would be at least one ready-to-heat food pouch in the cupboard for Cherry. I didn't have time to defrost any of her frozen homemade cubes of smush if I had any hope of catching up with the normal evening routine. And it would be so nice to have a relatively normal night of it tonight, to hold on to the lovely, bonkers shine of this afternoon. Just for a little while.

The front door swings open and Ted's pale face turns to greet me. Not with a friendly smile, but with a relieved grimace.

'Where have you been?' he snaps, and my hackles rise.

'Out with friends,' I shoot back, shoulders pulling back. 'Which, last time I checked, was allowed without my husband as chaperone.' I flick my eyes to the clock on the kitchen wall. 'You're back early. It's not even six.'

He gets up from the table and paces around it. 'I've been back since four. To see you. Only you weren't here. And you didn't answer your phone. I have been thinking the very worst thoughts about something having happened to you, or to Cherry.'

I bite my lip. Now is not the time for a confessional.

'And the Champagne I opened has lost all its fizz, I think.' His voice tapers down into a flat tone.

'Champagne?' Two crystal glasses are out on the table, wedding gifts we haven't thought to use since I successfully weed on a Clear Blue test.

Ted flops into a chair, his paleness being slowly replaced by a healthy, pink, more-Ted-like colour. 'I got promoted!'

I finally wheel the pram the rest of the way in and hurriedly slam the door behind me. Cherry, by now hangry and not having time for my loud noises bullshit, breaks instantly into an ear-splitting wail. 'Argh. Sorry.' I whip her out and jiggle her about, my knees creaking with the effort after so much dancing this afternoon. 'But yey!' I say loudly over the din. 'So you're now...?'

'Global Head of Strategic Client Success.' He dips his head.

'WOW!' I hope my semi-shout of enthusiasm over Cherry's red-faced screams will compensate for the fact that I don't totally understand what that means. 'Blimey, global! That almost sounds a bit jet-set!'

'Well...' He smiles shyly and twists his watch on his wrist. 'It is. It's based in Hong Kong.'

'Sorry?' The baby's cries have not even started to peter out, and for a moment it sounded like he was saying... 'HONG KONG?'

He starts ticking things off on his fingers hurriedly. 'It's a huge pay rise. Huge. You know,' his eyes roll to the ceiling, 'Bahamas holidays huge. They'll give us a resettling payment and sort out everything – they can choose our house, if we like, fill it with furniture. They'll even compensate us for a nanny or au pair. That's pretty standard out there. And, later, private school fees. Literally, they've thought of everything.'

My hands tremble and my face burns as I squat down to the bottom of the pram and fish out a sandwich bag of emergency baby-friendly gingerbread men. I shove one in Cherry's loudspeaker and she's quiet at last, orange drool spouting from the corners of her mouth.

They've thought of everything, have they? They've thought of everything. Well. Wow.

With Cherry weighing me down on one hip, I turn back and look at Ted. My husband. The father of this precious kid. The man who wants to drag us halfway around the world, away from everything we know. The man who apparently can't see anything wrong with this plan.

'Ted. Hong Kong. I…'

He comes over to us and puts a hand gently on my forearm. 'I know it's a lot to take in. And I didn't want to say anything until it was completely in the bag – just in case it fell through and you got disappointed. But now it's official. It's so much more financial security for us… you don't need to worry about working again, you can be with Cherry all the time if you want.' He blows out a deep breath and smiles. 'It's going to be great. I know it.'

'Could there be something you're overlooking?' I say very calmly, very quietly.

He runs his tongue over his teeth. 'Um, the money, the house, the childcare. Don't think so—? I'll have to buy my mum a stiff drink when I tell her, but I'm sure they'll come out and visit. It's not as if we ever get to see your folks as it is. It'll be a whole new life for us, Stevie.'

I slip Cherry into her high chair and move over to the store cupboard, keeping my back to Ted as, eerily calmly, I go about the routine of finding a packet of baby food, slopping it into a bowl, stirring it a bit and pinging the microwave on.

'You haven't *asked me* if I want a new life. This is a new life for *you*, and we're coming along. In your plan. A plan you have signed, sealed and delivered without even consulting me. It's the other side of the world, Ted! This is where we live, here!' My voice gets louder and higher as I jab a green plastic spoon for emphasis, sending shepherd's pie splattering down the back of Cherry's chair.

He blinks as if no part of his mega-clever brain ever considered I wouldn't be doing cartwheels and throwing flowers at his feet right now. 'But it always seems like—'

'Like what?' I cut across him.

'Like you're *not* all that at home here. We don't see our London friends really, you keep saying that you're not sold on going back to work and that you want more time with Cherry. I found a way for that to happen.' His hands are open, palms up, at his side.

'Your way. Not my way. And maybe between all your emails and late-night work sessions you haven't really noticed, but I have friends here. Friends *here*, who mean a lot to me and I mean a lot to them. And I'm actually—'

I stop myself short, leaving my mouth gaping open, as I realise I can't tell him about the blog, or the book opportunity. Or ParentFest, even. So instead I grab the warm mush as the microwave dings, sit down and start shovelling it into Cherry.

'I'm actually really fond of these guys. I don't want to leave them behind.'

He sits down across from me, reaching for my hand. 'But you'd make friends anywhere, Stevie. You always do. You're so great with people. It'll be a breeze. They have soft plays all over the world. And you could do freelance PR from wherever you are.'

The voice I hear from Ted right now sounds like some corporate management, creepy calmness: he's level, softly encouraging and oh-so-confident that I will bend to his will. I wince as I look into his eyes, trying to peg this guy onto the one from the New Year dance floor – or even just our recent poo-splosion experience. But to me, right now, he looks as blank and soulless as a business card. Not someone I recognise. 'It'll be home before you know it.'

'NO!' The voice I hear erupting from my mouth tells me exactly where my daughter gets her riotous rages from. 'Stop trying to manage me! Do you see anything that happens in our house these days? I am NOT good with people, not any more. I have panic attacks in public bathrooms. I still want to cry when Cherry has a public meltdown. Did you know that? No, because you're in Amsterdam or Seattle or Scunthorpe, enjoying a 7am wake-up call.' Cherry is watching me, her eyes wide and her cheeks packed with mashed potato. Mummy has never gone this ballistic before. But I can feel myself still building up steam, still hurtling through everything I've wanted to say for so long but haven't known how. Driven by a panicky vision of saying goodbye to Nelle and Will, and the book deal and the *Metro* pieces. Swinging from the joy and the pain of today into a volcanic anger.

I press my balled-up fists against my thighs. 'I'm not the Stevie from London, from smooth product launches or Islington bars at 2am. Sometimes I don't know who I am. But recently I was beginning to see myself, through my mates; realising it isn't just me worrying that they're a gigantic fuck-up. *They* are the people making me feel good right now. When very little else,' my eyes take in the kitchen with its sticky worktop and rammed-full bin, 'does. You think my whole life is just soft plays and coffees and putting my feet up. My life is more than that and it's *mine*. You are not taking me away from here – or my daughter. You're taking me away from the bl—'

The blog. You have to tell him about being First-Time Mum. You have to tell him this is who you are now and it means too much to walk away from.

But I don't. I burst into tears, snatch up my coat and walk out of the door.

–

Seeing as we moved here when I was waddlingly pregnant, I never had the chance to decide on my favourite local pub. But for now, The Fox and Gherkin will do.

I had no plan on leaving the house other than To Get Out, and I was too pumped up to admit I was a hysterical woman walking along the streets alone without a destination or a handbag. I was not turning back now. Let Ted finish the baby's dinner. Hell, let him bath her and put her to bed if he can remember how. There's an expressed bottle in the fridge, if he can think that far. My hands instinctively come up to cover my boobs. Oh lord, please don't let me spring a leak. Not now.

I think drying thoughts as I storm on – sand, towels, unbuttered toast – and soon realise the lights of the pub facing the park are beckoning to me. If I do start to go, there'll be loo roll there. I root around in my pocket and find my keys, thank god, and a few receipts. Five coins. A lip salve. No phone. It's OK. It's enough. I can make this work.

The double doors to the bar swing easily open and present me with just the kind of place I need right now – pleasantly noisy and full, but with a tiny little table still free in the corner. Yes. Everyone too happy and busy to ask any awkward questions of the red-eyed woman by herself. I just need to get a drink to hide behind for an hour while I take in this mad fuckery and let my lungs breathe normally again.

I bring the five coins out and count them in my wobbly hand. £3.70. OK. Great. Enough.

Plastering what I hope is a winning smile on my sweaty, tear-streaked face, I lean in to the barman. 'What's the most alcoholic thing I can get for £3.70?'

He must be all of nineteen and he squints just briefly as he thinks of his reply. I hope it's not: 'Should you really be out on your own in this state?'

He lays a hand on a tap handle just to his left. 'This week the Halemead Brewery are doing a special local promotion – two for one on their new cider. It's a really good dry one. £3.70 would get you two pints of that.'

'PERFECT,' I say, a bit too loudly, slapping the coins down on the shiny woodwork. *And* it's dry: it was meant to be. I may not have a husband who at all understands me, but the cosmos is totally getting my needs tonight.

Two pints is the perfect cover – no one will talk to me because they'll all assume I'm meeting someone immin-ently. I slurp a good mouthful off the top of one glass and hurry over to the corner table.

I'll hide out, I'll drink, I'll try and process what the hell just happened. *How* could Ted think this would be good for us?! How the *hell* could he do all this behind my back? All this time and he hasn't just said: *I might get an awesome promotion but it would mean we live on a different continent indefinitely.* I can't believe he could keep this all ticking away...

As the second gulp of cider hits my empty stomach, I feel something curdle. Not the booze so much as the tiniest spot of clarity – I've been keeping things from him, too. I've been hiding away a secret life, a secret plan. Haven't I?

But it's different. Right? My plan wasn't going to wrench our family unit away from everything we know and love. In fact, if I can keep making money out of the blog and maybe even a book, it would only help me keep our family foundations stable. I'll be with Cherry, she won't have to go into childcare. I'll be working from home. All the better for Ted to ignore me from when he comes in, dumps his shit in a pile and sprints off to the office. My stomach is churning again but now it's anger layered on guilt layered on booze. Suddenly half the pint has gone and I feel very spacey.

A sweet little lady in a red cable-knit sweater vest is standing in front of my table, shaking an old-fashioned pint glass full of pound coins. Eh? Granted, it's been a long time since I was 'out' in a pub, but this is the politest, neatest request for spare change I've ever seen.

'Are you playing?' she asks.

In my over-wrought brain, all I can think of is that we're all going to launch into 'Rhyme Time', and my heart hurts for Cherry. *I shouldn't have stormed out. She could be heartbroken at bedtime without me. Ted won't sing Humpty in the right way. She's probably screeching the place down and the neighbours are calling Child Services. Yet MORE abandonment today. Write that chapter up, you heartless cow. You don't deserve to be Cherry's mum.*

'The quiz?' The OAP tries again. 'Two pounds per person to enter. Lots of great prizes!'

'Oh,' I pat my pockets in the international symbol for *I'm making an effort but I am totally skint*. 'Sorry, no. I didn't realise… do you need this table for someone else?'

She bats my concern away. 'Of course not! You can just play along in your head, for fun. But maybe try it out properly next week, it's ever such a lark and,' she lowers her voice to a half-whisper, 'I made them drop the Sports round. Such a bore.' She tilts her head and moves off to the next table: a mixed group of friends who can only just be legally old enough to drink here. They have three bowls of chips between them and my mouth waters.

God, I'm hungry. Carbs would be such a good mood stabiliser right now. Something to absorb the anger and hurt and fear and guilt. Two bowls of chips would do it. If I had any money. Maybe I should completely finish this pint and then walk around shaking the glass, hoping for some pitiful donations? But would my table get nicked? Does that sort of thing still happen in pubs? I've forgotten all the social rules of drinking etiquette. I feel like an awkward exchange student in this warm, mellow pub: one that left their phrasebook in their other bumbag.

I will just keep sipping this cider. Slowly. There is no need to rush back. Mostly because I have no idea what to say to Ted right now other than: 'Fucking fuck! What the fuck! You… Why…? Fuuuuuck!' And also because: I am out. That's something. OK, my head is swimming with alcohol units, my boobs are tingling in a threatening manner and my face is blotchy with swallowed anger and spent tears, but I'm out. If I had my phone, I could have sent an invitation to Will and Nelle to grab some cash and join me. I bet we'd make a killer quiz team.

Speaking of which, there's a tapping on the mic at the front of the bar and the little old lady does a gentle shush. 'Hello, everyone! We'll be kicking off with round one: the picture round! So we'll give you about ten minutes with these tricky puzzles, then we'll dive into round two!'

All around me, the quiz-goers dip their heads and start a happy buzz of conversation and scribbling. This is what adults do. Adults not in a bonkers sleep pattern. Adults not thrown into surprise emotional attacks by their partners. Adults who do not leave babies in libraries.

If I sit very still, if I hardly blink, I can pretend I Am An Adult.

'Hang on, say that again.' One of the eighteen year olds next to me is talking to his mate with long ginger hair.

He sighs and says slowly, 'What's the connection? There's a picture of a cartoon pig, a blank space, then a picture of Frank Skinner. I think we have to work out what links them. The pig and Skinner.'

A curvy girl in a clingy striped top giggles. 'He hasn't ever, you know… with a pig, has he?' She goes bright red and collapses into more laughter.

The ginger guy cuffs her playfully behind the head. 'No, that's Cameron. He's the true pig fuc—'

'OK, OK,' the first teen cuts across, looking over his shoulder. He clearly can't get used to the idea they are *allowed* to be here and won't be thrown out for the first minor indiscretion. 'So, first of all, do we know the pig?'

'It's a woman. A female. In an orange dress like an umbrella.'

Oh, FFS. This was all so lovely and adult, as well.

'Mummy Pig.' I can't help myself. I say it loud enough for them to hear.

'Sorry?' Ginger Rocker turns to me.

'The lady pig is Mummy Pig, from *Peppa Pig*.' I'm acutely aware of how many times I've just said 'pig'. And that my lips are going a bit numb. I should really pace this second pint. 'And if you're looking for the connection between her and Frank Skinner, it's David Baddiel.'

'It is?' The curvy girl looks confused.

I nod sagely. 'The actress who does her voice – Morwenna something – is married to David Baddiel. And he used to be in a double act with Frank Skinner. You know, *Fantasy Football*.' As I say this, I can see myself – the same age these guys are now – sprawled on the sofa, laughing uncontainably at the very rude jokes woven through football references I was happy not to get.

But they all blink at me in response.

'Shit. Before you were born. But I'm really sure I'm right. Really sure.'

This seems enough of a promise to the ginger guy and he writes down the answer. 'Thanks! Don't suppose you fancy joining our team, do you? We could do with some more experience beyond A Level General Studies. And Mike actually failed that.' He points the Biro across the table at his mate, who goes red to the tips of his ears.

I smile. What I wouldn't give to be eighteen and have uncomplicated fun. Even uncomplicated misery, come to think of it, but just a day when things were simple. 'I would, but I've stupidly come out without my money, so I was just going to drink this and then...'

'Pssht.' The girls flaps her hands. 'You've already paid your way with that answer. I'll cover you. It's what my

Dorothy Perkins wages are for.' She winks and pushes a bowl my way. 'Fancy a chip?'

—

I had such a genuinely good time that I didn't notice we were winning. But at 10.30pm, Lovely Old Lady announced that it had come down to a tie between our team – Quiz On My Face – and a large group of very serious white-haired quizzers called HMS Victory. I thought it was a lame team name and they seemed to shudder every time ours was read out, so game on.

My new teen mates grinned with total glee, their eyes flashing with joy and Guinness merriment. 'We're fucking winning!' Ginger Guy crowed, and HMS Victory shuddered all over again.

'A *local knowledge* question,' our compère read out slowly. 'I will give a point for the nearest answer and I'm looking for the year here. In what year was the town's last workhouse torn down?' Her eyebrows rise. 'Jolly question, that. Anyway, five minutes to discuss, then I will take your answers.'

Ginger Guy frowns, his eyes now almost crossed with drunken concentration. 'I think it could be a trick. Pretty sure they had work houses in *Oliver Twist* and that was, you know, a musical. Not real.' He crosses his arms like he just found the Holy Grail in the back of his sock drawer. Job done.

I'm also feeling pretty well smashed – the guys stood me two more pints of the cider on offer and even with a bowl of chips in my system the fizzy booze is taking charge. But a little sober voice is telling me I know this. Has someone talked to me about this? Did I read a book…?

'Oh!' I put my hands on my head, as if to stop the knowledge floating out. 'It's 1890-something. There's a plaque, just by the library. I see it every time I take my daughter out for a walk in her pram. Which is four times a day. It's, like, 1893 or 1894. I remember, because it doesn't seem all that long ago, for something as awful as an actual workhouse. They'd put you there and pay you fuck all if you were poor.'

'Fucking Teresa May,' the other bloke mutters into his pint glass.

'Do you have a baby?' Curvy Girl coos. 'Where is it?' She looks under the table.

I gulp. My throat is suddenly very dry. 'At home. With my husband. I don't usually come out... I don't usually drink in pubs at night...' I feel a pressure on my chest, around my ribs.

I'm not a teenager. I have a family. What if Cherry hasn't settled in all this time? I haven't thought about her at all. I just stuffed toilet roll down my bra in the loos and continued with Round 4: Foods from Around the World. She could be breathless from hours and hours of tears; she could have made herself hot and sick with them by now. Ted might think there was something seriously wrong, he might have rushed her to A&E and she's caught MRSA off a trolley and he can't call me and she needs her mum and I'm swimming with cider and trying to bag a twenty-pound voucher to the local Chinese.

Stuffing my arms into my coat, I blab, 'I really should go. But put 1890. Good luck and thanks for the drinks. Nice to meet you.'

I make it home in about three breaths.

The lights are all out. At least there's no sirens flashing. I stumble in the front door, suddenly feeling all the more drunk in the chilly reality of our kitchen.

There's a scribbled note on the table. Oh god, oh god, something happened. This is all my fault!

> Stevie,
>
> You went without your phone. I'm pretty fucking worried. But I also have to be up at 4am for a flight so I've taken a sleeping pill and gone to bed. When they offered me the job they suggested I should fly out ASAP and meet the team, see if I'd gel on a daily basis with those guys. Which makes sense. Also, I can look at houses and things to get a feel for it. Didn't get a chance to tell you before you stormed off.
>
> I know you're not all that keen but maybe if I can send you some more deets it might help you see the full picture? Then we could talk some more.
>
> See you in ten days.
>
> Ted

I would scream if I wasn't so terrified of waking Cherry while I'm still clearly drunk. She's going to have to neck one of the emergency bottles of formula in the cupboard when she next wakes up. Which could be in five minutes or two hours. Not enough time for my system to process the cider (delicious and cheap, though it was), and giving her a kind of milk-based Appletini tonight would not sit easily with me, after double abandonment and witnessing a mammoth row between Mummy and Daddy.

But, seriously, Ted?! You're so worried about me that you take a sodding sleeping pill and you're happy to disappear into another time zone again, to research a move that I just clearly lost my head over?! Does my voice count for anything any more?!

I munch through three digestives at the kitchen table. *I do count. I can earn my own money, my own way. I will show him. By the time he boards the plane back home and steals me another paltry blanket as a consolation prize, I will have that sample with Francesca and I'll have three more blogs out in the world. I'll get some advertising going and I'll SHOW HIM. Our life here can be really good – he can't just expect me to give it up.*

My fingers twitch to check my Facebook stats. This is the longest I've been away from the page since I started it and I'm clucking for a fix.

My heart rate slows as I see a reassuring number of Likes and Follows. I still have a voice that matters to these guys, then. Just the odd troll who I block instantly and satisfyingly.

There's also a message from Nelle: 'Can't get those tuuuuunes out of my head from today! Darren and I have been dancing around the kitchen to a Spotify Nineties playlist. ParentFest is going to rooooooock!'

I smile at the image, and because I really can picture in my head Nelle bouncing about to Blink 182 or Nirvana, her husband doing his best to keep up and not scatter the pile of school books on the edge of the counter. But how can I reply?

Woohoo! Well, my OH and I rowed like polecats in our kitchen tonight (or, to be more exact, I screeched at HIM) because he wants to move us to Asia and I would have to miss ParentFest. And never see you guys again. And be totally alone. Nighty night! Xxx

I'm not going to piss on Nelle's chips.

As I let myself scroll aimlessly through my phone, killing time that I should be using for sleeping and knowing I'll regret it in the morning, a familiar name catches my eye in my DMs: *@BBootsMum*.

@BBootsMum: Hey, how are things in the land of no sleep? I am now working my way through The Good Wife; one, because it's SO GOOD but two, because I hope it will teach me some more backbone in standing up to my husband. He's talking in really unsubtle terms about me going back to work sooner rather than later, now the kids are nearly all in primary school. But I'm not ready. Am I being a wuss?!

@First_Time_Mum: Hey, lovely! Agh, husbands. Spookily mine is also trying to push me into a big life change I don't want. But we're not Bugaboos! We can't be smoothly pushed and parked up where we don't want to be, right?!?!?! We need to tell them NO. We need to show them we can choose our own paths. Full disclosure: I am a bit drunk. It's the first time in a looooong time and I'm not handling it well. But I do mean it – if we are capable of growing a whole human life with just the tiniest of input from our other halves, then we should be trusted to make our own important decisions. And, you know, we do so much on our own anyway. In one hundred years they'll be extinct and we'll all live in very tidy houses with perfectly matched cushions. Or something. I'm going on, aren't I?! I'm going to hit the hay. But stay strong and do what feels right FOR YOU. You're awesome xxxx

I plug my phone into the charger that's permanently relegated to the kitchen and head to bed. Well, the sofa. I don't want to have to creep into the bedroom all silent and tip-toeing, like I'm the one who did something wrong. And I'll hear Cherry from down here. Then I'll figure everything out tomorrow. On my own.

Chapter 14

By the time I'm awoken by my plump alarm clock, sunlight is streaming through the living room windows. Huh? My watch says 6.15 but that can't be right. I don't remember feeding her in the night. Sweet Jesus, did she sleep all that time?

I bolt up the stairs to fetch her before she gets really loud and settle on the bed to feed, crossing my fingers that enough time has passed for all that very fine local cider to have worked through my system. Cherry doesn't seem to have a problem with what's on offer and gets into her rhythm. On the bedside table I can see two used baby bottles. She didn't sleep through, then: Ted fed her again. I can't believe he heard her and I didn't, when he was dosed up on sleeping tablets. Both guilt and a hangover are now rattling at my brain.

His side of the bed is almost made and his wardrobe door is hanging open, showing the empty shirt spaces. Oh, right. He's gone again.

'Well,' I say down to Cherry's sleep-sweaty head, 'we've got a lot to do, Chezza, while Daddy is off playing Mega Businessman. Mummy's got to write this book proposal – somehow – and we've got to help Nelle get ParentFest in full swing. So we can show him where home really is. And that Mummy is not just going to follow at his beck and call. You just fill your boots while Mum has a little blog.'

I awkwardly manage to lean over, Cherry still latched on, and grab my iPad from the side of the bed.

6.37am CHOOSE YOUR OWN FAMILY

There's something special about looking at a tiny baby and knowing it's yours. That you're going to love this kid for ever and wipe its nose and obsess over its teeth and help it sound out its first letters. It's a deep, heady, drunk love that makes everything else blur into the background and wait its turn.

But that doesn't feel any different if the baby isn't biologically yours. If the baby is adopted, or a stepchild, or a niece or nephew, or grandchild. We choose to pour out that love in just the same way. Because we choose who we love; we choose our own families.

And the beauty of our modern world is that we can choose our own networks of Important People: friends, family, colleagues. We can choose to surround ourselves with people who lift us up, champion us, maybe they even obsess about our teeth. Some of those people may be linked to you by blood, some not. In my life, I've been lucky enough to have a great family and make amazing friends for life, but in the last few months it's been brand-new friends who have really brought me back to myself. They've given me the jolt of electric courage I so sorely needed. They've reminded me of the magic, healing power of laughing at something stupid. They took me at face value and accepted the imperfect bits.

All hearts and flowers, yeah? Hmmm. Not quite. There's one big relationship in my life not going so well. Where I think that person has totally lost sight of who I am or who we are as a family. They've stopped listening to me, they've stopped laughing with me. I'm not sure I recognise them any more.

So, what can you do when one of your 'for ever' relationships starts going seriously wobbly? Well, I'm thinking you don't have to accept that that's the way it will be, and lower your expectations. I deserve better than that. And just as we can choose who we make our family, we can choose who doesn't quite make the grade. Who doesn't get a say in where we're going or how we get there. Sometimes things start off as 'for ever' but take a massive wrong turn. Do you blindly keep on down that path or do you risk it all on a U-ie?

Tell me, parent mates, have you ever changed the status of a 'for ever' relationship because it wasn't working out? Did you regret it? Or did it set you free? I know I've gone all Oprah on you this morning but I'd really like to hear what you think.

Love,

First-Time Mum x

We spent the day quietly shaking off my hangover with lots of toast and carpet time, Cherry gumming at toast strips while I danced her jangling toys over her tum. I studiously ignored my phone altogether in case Ted sent something that churned me up all over again. Then we had a reasonably unbroken night (well, up just the twice but I can't begrudge her anything after The Event at the Library Which We Will Never Speak of Again), and now I am ready to get stuck in. I'm ready for an entirely new, kick-ass day. I wrote for a few hours between the two feeds but it was so worth it – another thousand words in the can, another chapter taking shape. Francesca, baby, I'll do you proud! Ted – you ain't seen nothing yet. If, somehow, the stars align and I get to write a real, actual book, that will wipe the condescending, managerial smile off his face.

Nelle is cracking on with ParentFest plans, with Will and I as her very willing 'parental consultants'. Her family business pretty much has all the basic resources sorted out, but we are there to lend an eye or an idea any way we can. Next on the list, rather crucially, is food. Our part of the shires isn't trendy enough to get legitimate food vans just yet, but a half-hour drive towards London will take us to a very busy food market, which runs every first Thursday of the month behind a church in Borehamwood. We have the name of a few companies to specifically try out, ones who'd expressed some interest after a round of cold calls. And we are going well starved and hungry for ideas, ready to nibble on every dish going and chat up the owners if needs be. Knackered parents don't just need good food, they bloody well deserve it. If you can't get off your face on alcopops any more, the least you can do is be taken to a near food-coma with artisanal cheeses and Mexican street food. That's just basic human rights.

Cherry does not enjoy the car ride, failing to either drop off or be cheered by my 'Five Little Ducks' routine but I just keep thinking: *Dim sum. Fish tacos. Malaysian curry.* The foods from the kinds of establishments that I could have tripped over in my lunch break back in my working days, but which have now been elevated to mythical status in my new hometown, where a Thai is still viewed as pretty racy. Going without breakfast was perhaps not my best plan, especially on so little sleep but, man, I don't want anything to come between me and that fourth dish. And then churros for pudding…

As we park up by the church, good and early, my head spins slightly as I hook the pram out of the boot, unfold it and then start to withdraw Cherry from her seat. These are movements I could probably do with my eyes shut but even fully awake, I'm a bit slow and sluggish. Might be the day for a rare espresso…

'Hola!' I hear Will shout, a few rows of cars over. The twins are clipped into a double buggy and I find myself making a silent prayer of thanks that I wasn't blessed with two at once: there's no way my puny frame could take on that mutha of a pram and win, day in and day out. Will is definitely the man for the job. He rolls it over the bumpy grass without a flinch. 'Nelle said she might be a bit late and that we should start on the falafels without her. But if we hit the chorizo stall before she gets there, she'll disown us. She was quite serious about that.' He scratches the back of his head. 'Ready?'

'I think I was born for this, Will. I seriously do.'

We tramp off towards food heaven.

–

'So we're saying falafels seven out of ten, paella a solid eight. Beef burrito a big "oh yes" ten. We'll come back for the beer-battered fish and chips later if we have room. Feels a bit' – Will drops his voice politely – '*pedestrian* to me for the festival, but I could be overruled.'

Olive and Esme giggle at the way their dad says 'pedestrian', as if by his delicate delivery they can tell it's something a bit naughty. I wouldn't be surprised if someone at nursery gets called a 'pedestrian face' one day soon. Mind you, could be worse. If Cherry has been fully absorbing my rants at home over the last two days – while I've been unloading the washing machine and cursing Ted for being a knobbing knobhead, for example – I'm going to have to start worrying about her first word. But I'm not thinking about Ted now. I've got great snacks and great chat; I'm sitting on a fluffy picnic rug and my espresso did exactly the job. This is a good day. A day I have chosen for myself. A parenting family I have helped put together. This is me.

The location could not be more parent-friendly and conducive to a chilling day. As chilled as you can be when at any moment you might have to clean up faeces. But even if the bar has been moved for true relaxation these days, this is hopping right over it. The shadow of the church is giving us just the right amount of shade from the midday sun so that no one has to fret about sunstroke in tiny tots, and the stretch of garden where the food trucks are parked in a big circle is actually fenced off with a big, black, wrought-iron fence, so there's no need for holding toddlers by the hoods to stop them escaping at a leopard's pace. Will and I are stretched out, side by side, surrounded by a happy array of empty cardboard boxes. From a distance, we look like the jammiest couple on Earth.

His phone beeps. 'Oh, it's Nelle. She's here and by the brewery tent. Wants help loading a barrel into her car. Christ, hope her suspension can take it. Are you OK with the girls?' Esme and Olive have been taking turns to slap down Peppa Pig Top Trump cards onto one big, sprawling pile. They look up at him with doe eyes and batting lashes, as if all they have on their minds is starring in a Fairy Liquid ad.

'Sure. Go for it.'

As soon as Will's long strides have taken him out of earshot, the twins turn to me in a synchronised move. I'm trying not to feel intimidated. But I have seen *The Shining.* 'Can we do hair, Stevie?' Olive asks boldly.

Oh god, they want to glue things to my scalp again. 'Um, sorry, ladies. I haven't brought my mermaid wig today. But' – I think on my feet as Esme's lip begins to tremble – 'in my bag I have…'

My hand roots about in the bottom of the change bag, coming up against a furry cough drop and some pistachio shells. *Classy, Steve, really classy.* But in one of the million inside pockets I hit pay dirt: a super soft baby hair brush. Made of such unbelievably fine bristles that I doubt it can move even Cherry's fuzz in any direction, let alone be able to cause obvious damage to my do.

'You can brush Cherry's hair – very gently – then you can do mine, if you like. That's a different kind of playing hair.'

Esme looks to Olive and Olive nods. The game has been accepted.

I crouch behind the girls as they take quick turns running the brush down the sides of Cherry's perfectly round head. Don't want a wooden handle in the eye today, thanks very much. She gurgles happily and tries to twist around so the brush ends up in her pie hole, but Esme laughs. 'Don't eat it, baby!'

Olive is more of the disciplinarian of the two, a mini Robocop in turquoise dungarees. 'Babies don't eat brushes! You'll go in the corner.' She wags a tiny finger at my daughter and the seriousness of her action is, of course, hilarious. I cough to cover up my laughter.

'My turn then,' I sing-song.

The girls manoeuvre me so I'm sitting up straight, legs crossed, and they're standing behind me. When a minor squabble breaks out over whose turn is and isn't fair, I suggest they count five strokes each, then swap.

'Yes, we CAN do counting,' Esme replies happily, and this makes me instantly sure they can no more count to five than I could hold a plank position for the same stretch. But, on paper, it has the ring of 'fair' about it and that's all that seems to matter to twins.

'One, two, eight, five,' Olive says confidently.

After a shuffle, Esme takes over. 'A, B, C, D, E...'

This is actually not so bad. I'm not in physical pain. I won't end up with PVA residue this time. Cherry is content. This is not so bad.

'One, two, one, one... um, Esme?'

'One.'

'Oh, yes. One.'

It's almost like being at a spa, I suppose. That was the last time I think anyone other than me has touched my hair, at a spa. Ted paid for me to have an All-Over Mum-to-Be massage in my first week of maternity leave and it was such heaven. Ending with a delicious scalp massage where I came out smelling of lavender and citrus, mois-turised and zen and just sure that my baby would benefit from all this calm and come out in an easy, natural way.

Must have been such strong lavender that I was tripping off my head. Hah.

Where's that Ted gone? The one so thoughtful that he'd book and pay for me to totally indulge myself, when there was nothing whatsoever in it for him. Now he just wants to push his own agenda, his own career, with Cherry and me as the token family trophies. I want thoughtful Ted back. I want him to think about how much this move is sending me spinning out.

I want him to send me back to that spa as a sorry. That would be a great start. I could get in the Jacuzzi this time – the beautician stopped me en route with a warning frown as it was 'not advised for pregnant ladies'. As if I'd wanted to intentionally cook up the kicking thing in my stomach. I could get a facial. A manicure. Get my roots done and a lovely moisturising hair mask. Those ones that smell like... What do they smell like? It comes back to me suddenly. Avocado, maybe? Garlic?! No, that can't be right. But I'm definitely thinking of garlic and maybe just a bit of coriander...

'Stevie?!'

My eyes snap open and the avocado smell is suddenly right here, in the church garden, under my nose. And two wide-eyed toddlers stand before me, their fingers light green and dotted with chunks of tomato.

'GIRLS!' booms Will.

Nelle is next to him, both hands clamped over her mouth.

My fingers fly to my cheeks and hit something squishy. *Please, no.* But when I pull my fingertips back, I can see it's not a Code Brown. It's avocado.

Esme erupts into passionate sobs. 'We was... doing... hair, so we did Daddy's face... matt... too!'

At their feet are our two discarded burrito plates, with incriminating finger marks gouged into the leftover guacamole.

Will crouches down to their level, his face utterly calm. 'It's a face *mask* Daddy does. But did you ask Stevie if that was OK?'

'She was asleep,' Olive mutters, kicking the toe of her trainers through the patchy grass.

'I wasn't,' I blurt out, as if I'm next for a bollocking. But I must have been. One minute I was dreaming of spas, the next I've been given an exclusive organic 'dip' treatment. 'Or maybe I nodded off for just two seconds… but it doesn't matter, Will, honestly. I expect it's actually very moisturising. Nice, even. Once the smell of garlic fades.'

He purses his lips and looks between the three of us. 'They've seen Adrian do a homemade avocado, oat and honey one when his sister comes to stay – that's where they must have got the idea. Right: wet wipes, the lot of you. And a *sorry*, please, girls.'

Esme is still sobbing but manages to croak a little sorry. Olive barks hers to prove she really doesn't mean it. Fair enough. I was asleep on the job.

As I'm double-wiping around my nose and lips, eyebrows and chin line, I make my own apologies to Will. 'I'm so sorry, mate. I honestly didn't feel myself going. I suppose I knew we were in this enclosed space, maybe that's why I felt so relaxed… but that doesn't excuse it – I should have had my eyes *open* and on them at all times. You would think I'd learned my lesson after The Event—'

'Hey, hey,' Nelle cuts in, 'that's all in the past and Will gets it, don't you?' He nods. 'It's not something you did on purpose. So, how much real sleep did you get last night?'

She picks up a wipe and dabs at a spot I've missed on my forehead.

'Two stretches of three-ish hours. So that's pretty much six, which is what most people get, isn't it?'

'But in one go, not broken,' Will disagrees.

Nelle clambers down to sit next to me, Joe's head bobbing in his trusty sling. 'Was Cherry up all that much? She looks peachy this morning, the ragamuffin.'

'No, she was pretty good. I just needed to write in between. And I had a few extra ParentFest ideas for you. What do you think about classic, vintage-style carnival games? Those really classy ones, rather than the big, flashing, whirly-gig rides that blast out music? Something where you can shoot an air rifle, but instead of winning cuddly toys you get a free coffee voucher?'

'No. I mean, yes, I do like that idea, but, Stevie, you have got to stop spreading yourself so thin. Surely Ted has noticed by now that you're burning the candle at both ends?'

All I can muster in reply is a guffaw.

'Well, you're banned from coming to the keepsake event this weekend. You need to stay at home and blummin' well relax.' She nods her head with a very Don't Mess With Me mum-look of decision.

'Nooooo! I'm really looking forward to that, and not just for the carrot cake again. I *want* to help out. Please?'

'Nope.' Nelle picks at some grass. 'Stay at home, give Ted his Father's Day card, let him watch a whole rugby match on the telly, then cash in some favours for a break for yourself. You're going to end up ill. And I won't have it.'

'Oh. Yes. Father's Day is this Sunday, isn't it?' My voice is flat.

'Still plenty of time to get a card, and some socks,' Will says.

I pile the used wet wipes up unnecessarily tidily. 'Um, it's not that. He's away. Again. For ten days. Actually.'

'Again? So soon!' Will splutters. 'And over Father's Day?! Well, that is' – Nelle shoots him a stern look – 'that's unfortunate. For you. And him. Where is he this time?'

'Hong Kong again. They've offered him' – I fill my lungs with a steadying breath – 'a job there. He wants us to move. I do not.'

'Fu-fuddlysticks.' Nelle catches herself in time.

'Exactly. We fell out in a big way, and he went off to look at dream homes there, for his dream life and dream job. Uprooting Cherry and me doesn't seem to bother him.'

Will whistles softly. 'Christ.'

'We can't talk about this properly without more food and drink.' Nelle carefully stands up. 'I'll be back.'

After two varieties of chorizo sausages in buns, some slurpy pho and a huge paper cone of churros, we have a plan between us. A Modern Parenting Family Plan. This is why I have fallen for these guys so hard and so fast. They're not going to let me wallow; they're going to help me achieve!

Will can have Cherry for a morning while Ted's away, only if I *promise* to sleep as much as possible the night before. Then I can write like the wind. Nelle can meet me at the library or baby sensory class, where I can drop Chezza with her and grab another very useful hour's working.

'But I'm warning you.' She prods my wrist with her churro, which is still actually pretty hot and singes my arm hair a bit. 'I will randomly WhatsApp you at silly hours and, if you read it, if it goes all blue ticky, but you *don't* have a child attached to your boobs, I will be very, very cross.'

'Yes, miss.' I dip my head in deference. 'But I'm allowed to come to the keepsake day?'

Permission is granted, so at least I'll have something crafty and distracting this weekend to keep my mind off the long hours that stretch ahead, partnerless.

'I've thought of a new activity for the keepsake day, actually,' Will chimes in from his laid-back pose on the blanket, looking as comfortable as any person could with two toddlers sitting on his stomach. 'Edible homemade face masks. We could get some salsa, some sour cream and onion dip. Mix it up a bit. On Stevie's face, of course.'

'Ha ha,' I deadpan.

'You'd better write a blog post about that, by the way.' He ruffles the girls' hair simultaneously as he talks. 'I want that moment immortalised *for ever*. And it would maybe lift the spirits a bit after your last post.'

I feel a prickle of worry work its way up the back of my neck. 'That one was a bit heavy, wasn't it?'

He shrugs. 'But after what you've told us about Ted, it makes a lot of sense. And you should always say what's on your mind: the honesty is what people respond to. You can't be all "jolly, jolly, my kid puked on me today". That's not real life. And don't you dare become one of those perfect Insta mums. We don't need another one of those.'

I bite my lip. 'I haven't actually checked what the response has been like. Once I'd blurted it all out, I didn't want to look at my phone in case Ted had sent through his new salary details or something and I'd be forced to agree.'

'It had a *lot* of comments yesterday,' he tells me. 'A lot of debate.'

'Christ. Is that polite-speak for "trolls sharpening their pitchforks"?'

'No. Genuine debate. Have a read tonight. People have got a lot of thoughts, some agreeing, some disagreeing.'

So once Cherry is in bed, later in the day, I do just that. I charge up my iPad and make a giant cup of tea. Time to engage with the followers, as those YouTube tutorials tell me. Or time to face the music, as my reliable old gran would probably have put it.

There is a real mix of comments. Some positively 'For' choosing your own family, and moving on from unsatisfactory relationships:

> @ditzygirl78 Best thing I ever did, walking away from my first husband. He might have given me two gorgeous kids, but he took all my self-esteem as payment. Now I'm with someone who gets the real me and doesn't need to chip away at that.

> @Harryfan4Eva All you need is you, your babies and the occasional Wispa. Sod anyone who doesn't support you 200%.

> @BrixtonLady I'm all for the Urban Family – my little boy is looked after by his aunts, his grown-up nieces and nephews and a great nursery (his dad isn't on the scene, I don't see my parents). You could not meet a happier little guy! I don't buy into this idea that you have to have two parents. Just lots of love, from whatever source it comes from.

Some: not so much.

> @HannahandDave If you've had a kid with someone, you've made a lifelong commitment. You can't just change your mind because you had a bad day.

> @Winewinetime You owe it to your children to keep as much of your real family around you and them. My mum left my dad and wouldn't let us speak to his family afterwards. It's led to a lot of sadness in my life.

> @82Maddie How does your other half feel about you splashing your probs all over Facebook?!?!

And some just being a bit lovely and concerned for me:

> @WingingItSoftly First-Time Mum, what's up? This is not like you.

> @CarrieSparks What has First-Time Dad DONE? Do we need to come and smother him with a used nappy for you?!

In those hungover early hours when I wrote the post, I didn't think it would read so much like a divorce SOS – as everyone seems to be seeing it. I started off wanting to champion my amazing mates, but I ended up pushing Ted off a ledge. And he deserved it, just then. But I don't want to *leave* leave him. I just don't want to follow him at the moment. Is that the same thing?

Regret nibbles away at my heart. I should revise the post, tone down the anti-OH stuff which is now glaringly obvious, or just take it down altogether. Ted may not be completely innocent, but he's still my partner and Cherry's dad – he deserves a certain smidge of my loyalty, and not to be put to public execution like this. But then again it's had SUCH a big reaction. People are sharing so many of their important stories. To delete it and all their comments would feel like telling someone to just shut up in the middle of a deep-and-meaningful conversation between two best friends. And seeing it make such a splash is really good for my book proposal, selfishly: this way Francesca can see not just how many are connecting to my posts, but that I can tackle some heavier stuff, too.

My finger hovers over 'Edit'.

But I don't do it. Instead, I open up my working document and dive back into my 'Mum Mates Will Save Your Life' chapter:

Tips for finding some really cast-iron, honest-to-goodness mum mates who will never judge you for coming out with wet hair:

> 1) The first time you go to a toddler group, you probably won't come away with five phone numbers. This ain't an under-18s disco, Carol. You've got to go and loiter a few times, looking around the room cheerfully, sending out 'I'm here' signals. Yes, it's terrifying and awkward and you feel like no one will ever ask you to dance to 'Mambo No.5' at this rate, but eventually the magic will happen. You have to show up to be lucky, folks.

2) Weakness is good. You know when you manage to drop your precious bottle of expressed milk in the cereal aisle at Tesco and you just want to cry? Cry. It will let someone know you're in need of a chat. And when you see someone in a moment of weakness – having their own tears over spilled boob milk or otherwise – don't be scared of the emotion or feel British about stepping in. Try. These are the moments you need an ally. These are the moments you can show yourself to be a great mate.

3) Let it all hang out. If you tidy your house for two hours before a prospective friend comes round for a play date, what kind of message are you sending? That you are perfect, that you have everything under control, and that your potential mum mate can't possibly admit to her own disasters in front of you for fear of looking like a total imbecile. Yes, she might be saved from impaling herself on an abandoned plastic fork or Barbie shoes when she sits on an untidy sofa, but she might be left feeling too uptight to really talk to you honestly. Mess is human.

4) Men are parents, too. A bloke making conversation over his kids' heads at the soft play is not necessarily trying to crack on to you, you know. You won't be breaking any marriage/commitment vows yourself by passing the time moaning about the price of a cheese toastie with him. Don't overlook the

dads – they have had just the same disgusting, lovely, memorable experiences in parenting, so there's plenty of shared ground to cover.

5) Soul mates not necessary. Yes, we all want to find someone that just gets us instantly, knowing all the same Dirty Dancing quotes and preferring milk in their Earl Grey, but don't give up on a new mum mate if they aren't a 100 per cent compatibility match. It's always good for the soul to have a variety of people in your social world: those that get you, but also those that challenge you just a touch. Obviously if this person you meet is so your polar opposite that you feel unhappy hanging out with them, it's time to move on. But if they just don't know Dirty Dancing all that well, see it as an opportunity for an afternoon's DVD watching, with watermelon slices for good measure.

I slump back against the sofa cushions, giving my fingers a flex and a rest. Even when Cherry is asleep, I can't help but write in a speedy panic, as if a runaway train is about to smash into my iPad and drive a hole through all my hard-earned words. Time can be both so long and so short when you have a baby: the hours between 2am and 5am can seem like a full school term if you're pacing about with a sleepless bub. But then your 'break time' after 7pm and before the 10pm feed disappears as fast as canteen chips before you know it. I need to crack on while the going's good. Except my stomach is growling.

I suppose I should make myself a dinner that does not consist of McVitie's finest. I'll push myself. I'll heat up something Heinz instead. Without Ted here, there's no point going to the trouble of a stir fry or anything complicated. And I bet he's getting amazing Asian food right now. Dumplings. Aromatic duck. Singapore noodles. I wonder what he's eating. I wonder who he's with. The chair opposite mine at the dining table looks so empty.

Just as I'm googling 'Time difference with Hong Kong', a new email alert pings in on my Stevie account, not my blog one. Maybe I can distract myself with a good trawl through the White Stuff sale, then. I have done a bit of work already, after all. I'm positively Karen Brady.

> **From:** ted.cameron@syncedsolutions.co.uk
>
> **Subject:** FWD: Yay HK stuff!
>
> Dear Stevie,
>
> I'm sorry we didn't have time to talk before you left. Won't get into that all now, we should talk in person when I'm back. But I thought maybe some more info about life out here might help in the meantime? I'm having a great time with the team, solid bunch.
>
> Maddie will be a direct report of mine out here and she's been so helpful – see below.
>
> How's my girl?
>
> Ted

I have to admit my heart leapt at the sight of his name at the top of my inbox, but the email was less *Officer and a Gentleman* finale – some sort of gallant and noble gesture of total love – and more Office Warehouse missive about discounts on staplers: trying to sell me something I really didn't want in a pretty bland kind of way.

Maddie. Hmm. I scroll down to her original message to Ted.

> Hey Ted!
>
> So I've asked around the office (hope I'm not overstepping!!!) and got the name of some nanny agencies that seem really great and work a lot with expats: www.premiercare.hk, www.angelsinyourhome.hk, www.A1aupairs.hk.
>
> This was the agency that found my apartment and they were really, really good: www.trebonds.hk.
>
> Fingers crossed she says yes! I hope I can be the first one to have you guys round for dinner and cuddle that gorgeous Cherry in person. She is just really the cutest baby I have ever seen!!!
>
> Mads xxx

'Mads.' Hmm. Things I don't like about her email: that she *is* overstepping (trying too hard to 'help' someone through their relationship issue is usually a dead giveaway that you fancy them and just want a ringside seat for it all falling apart); that Ted has clearly told her *I'm* the one holding him back from his big Barbie Dream House future. I mean, yes, I am, but this makes me sound like some backwards-thinking bitch who doesn't want to see her husband succeed. I want good things for Ted – he works hard, he deserves it. But I want my life, too. What I especially don't like is that she has seen pictures of *my* baby and thinks she's actually going to touch her one day. Uh, no. Not happening, 'Mads'. With multiple kisses. Hmm.

Plus, she uses 'really' the most times I have ever seen a human use a word. And it is just really, really irritating. Really.

I can't believe Ted actually thought this would help! Some website links that he hasn't even found and tried out himself, just going on the word of some office flirt who probably wears gel nail polish. And the idea that I want Cherry looked after by a stranger in our home – where did that come from? Was it my storming out the other night that gave him the impression: 'Hey, I think she's on the ropes about this! The deal with my difficult wife is nearly sealed! Hong Kong, here we come…'

And what really stings is his sign off: 'How's my girl?' Not 'girls', just 'girl'. Obviously I love that he's thinking about Cherry. But couldn't he spare a thought for me, too? When my brain isn't whirring with ideas for chapters and themes, Ted, Cherry and our future are the only things I can think of. Where will we go from here?

Chapter 15

Darl,

I am just so in love with coconut oil. Have you tried it? I'm putting it on my shins, in my hair, frying my omelettes with it. It's so fabulous. Do you have it in the UK? I'll send you some.

Your father came by the store last week. He said that a shooting star over the Rockies reminded him of you. That's sweet. He said it represents great change and big movements. I said, I hope that's not in Cherry's nappy!!!! But he didn't get it. Sometimes divorce truly is for the best.

I'm thinking of replacing my futon. What's new with you?

Love,

Mum x

What's new with me? Well, not all that much I could actually tell you... I switch from Mum's email to the *Daily Britain* website.

Scrolling through the 'Showbiz' column is a dirty habit I've long been meaning to expunge from myself.

But today I cannot tear my eyes from the website, not for all the distasteful articles about Millie Bobby Brown 'blossoming' or Jennifer Lawrence 'flaunting' her size 10 'curves'. Because I'm in it. Rather, First-Time Mum is.

Thankfully it's not an upskirt shot, but it's an article all about my last post and the raging debate that's crazily sprung up around it. 'Slummy Mummy Blogger says: Mums are better off as single parents!' the headline shouts. Well, no, I didn't say that. I would never say that. I just had a low point in my life and wanted to talk to my followers about it. It wasn't a judgement on all dads; it was a tiny snapshot of my relationship right there and then. The Facebook comments have spiralled out of control for the last three days. Once I posted the blog and after reading some pretty nasty comments that called me an ungrateful, fat cow, I decided to step back and let it die away. Except it hasn't.

'First-Time Mum's Facebook post has been shared over 33,000 times in just seventy-two hours,' the piece states. And that is true. Mental, but true. My Facebook and Twitter followers have ballooned to such a level that it leaves me a bit breathless with the pressure. How can I post something when *all* these people will be waiting to love or hate or laugh or deride what I'm saying?! What could I ever write that would keep everyone happy? A few times I've started a draft of some idle mum-life observation and then deleted it instantly. The desperate toppings I've scrounged from the larder for my frozen jacket potato lunch (anchovy and sweetcorn, anyone?); the things Cherry prefers to her expensive wooden toys (empty cereal packets, labels on pillows, an orphaned Tupperware lid); none of this seems worthy or right or fitting. But neither do I want to start another debate on family models or parenting.

It's no surprise that this article has prompted just the kind of reaction from its readers it intended; they are spitting their tea out over their armrest covers all over the Home Counties, I should expect. Getting in a froth that if First-Time Mum had her way, all mums would be on benefits, or gay, or converting to Islam in a KFC while their kids drink Coke and shovel chips in their overweight mouths. But I *really* wasn't telling every mum to ditch their OH and do it alone, regardless. I was just saying that my OH had started to feel like someone else, someone I didn't know and, maybe, just maybe, that was not the best thing. Perhaps it should have been a conversation I poured out to Will and Nelle or even saved for Sarah coming the weekend after next.

But it's out there now. And it's growing like unstoppable green slime in a horror movie; sliding down the street and absorbing every man, woman and child in its path. So I'm choosing to close the curtains and pretend it's not there until it's slithered right past and straight into the stream at the bottom of the hill, where it can get washed away with all the traffic cones and duck poo. Good riddance.

Cherry nodded off post-afternoon-feed on my lap about twenty minutes ago and now her eyes gently flick open. I give her my best 'Everything is Fine and Mummy is Not a Social Media Pariah' smile. And she gives a sort of gassy half-smile back. My sweet little pudding. My gorgeous chubby delight. The rest of the world can fade away, they can all say what they like, but this girl knows the real me – the one that will always come running when she calls, the one that would fight a wild dog in the park to keep her safe (a scenario I have imagined in great detail, just to be ready). I am her mum: that is my number one job. How could you not feel fiercely loyal and stupidly besotted with such a peachy face?

I don't even really mind when the sick hits my leggings.

But a day later, at 6.45am, I do mind the sick. Because it's not just the normal bit of regurgitated milk feed from her reflux – it's everything coming up. Yesterday's lunch, yesterday's breakfast, some bits of banana. All her milk. And I couldn't give a Makka Pakka that I'm plastered with it and I now stink to the high heavens; the thing I care about is the floppy little baby in my arms.

OK, Cherry is sick pretty much every day but it's a few tablespoons of curdled milk. This is exorcist sick. This is stomach flu sick. And I've definitely not seen her so listless or red hot before. I feel sweat prickle at my own forehead. Is she OK? Will she be OK?! This has gone on for a full evening and a night now. She's hardly kept any kind of liquids down and turns her face away when I try and feed her. It was a long, scary night where Cherry passed into an uncharacteristic deep sleep and I paced the bedroom in my now very smelly dressing gown.

This is when having a mum in another time zone and a husband halfway round the world really sucks and sends you into an extra panicky spin. What should I do? Shall I try feeding her again to stop her getting dehydrated? Or will that start off more vomiting and just make things worse? I could do cooled boiled water again. Yes. Yes. I'll do that.

As I rush back and forth between the kitchen and the living room, keeping an eye on the steriliser and kettle and then also Cherry sitting upright but listless in her bouncing chair and surrounded by the oil cloth, having a purpose does nothing to shut up the screaming voice in my head.

What are you doing? Shouldn't you know how to fix this? You are her mother! You ARE her mother, right? Why don't you just innately know the solution? Do you call the GP or is that hysterical? She could be better in an hour's time and then your reputation would be torn of its last shred of sensibility at the clinic. You could call 111 but what if they decide it's really bad and take her away in an ambulance and then you can't park at the hospital and something's happening to her inside and…

The rumble of the kettle drowns out my crazy.

I pour water into a freshly sterilised bottle and will it with my whole being to Please Cool Down. Now. But the seconds drag out.

Settling myself down next to Cherry, I try my whole clownish act to perk her up: 'Five Little Ducks', monkey faces, blowing a raspberry into the crook of my elbow. She just blinks really slowly at me, as if she's starting to forget who I am. There's hardly any colour in her cheeks and when I touch her head it still feels boiling to my fingers.

Fuck it. Even if they send an ambulance and take her into care it'll be worth it, knowing she's being made better.

I snatch up my phone and dial 111.

The call handler is so helpful. He calmly, slowly (and yes, maybe robotically but it gets the job done) takes me through a series of questions about Cherry's last few days, her overall health, any allergies. He also prompts me to take her temperature properly and I feel like a right numpty for forgetting I have a baby thermometer in the bathroom cabinet – bought in my smug pregnancy days of ticking everything off a to-do list. She is at forty degrees – a few degrees into feverish, but he gently says he is going to arrange a GP appointment for me for the minute the surgery opens at 7.30am as with under-ones it doesn't hurt to check these things out.

You should have called the GP yesterday! You should have known that, if you were a natural mother!

I realise after hanging up that I didn't even ask the handler his name, so I could thank him properly. OK, no one can fully shut up my inner critic when the chips are down but he helped me out of a full-on flounder, and now Cherry will get some bloody lovely NHS attention. That 111 guy is a hero. I will always love him and his soft Liverpudlian accent.

So I have about half an hour left to get us ready for the GP appointment, and I set about digging out Cherry's red baby book and three changes of clothing, all the while running up and down the stairs to reassure her, 'Mummy's here and you're going to be fine and the doctor will be lovely and we'll be fine!' in an adrenaline-fuelled sing-song voice. I shove a change of top and toothbrush into the change bag, just in case we are rushed off to A&E and I have to stay away for a night by Cherry's bed. I mean, we won't, we'll BE FINE. But also, if we're not fine and everything is terrible I'll be prepared. I'm not going to take a shower and sort out my greasy hair with tinges of sick – Cherry might be ill again and I can't risk her choking on it. And I'm sure the GP will not judge me for my Guinness nightshirt and grey joggers in the midst of an actual emergency. Not that it is an emergency – it's FINE.

My phone is clutched in my sweaty palm. I should message Ted. Or should I? If it's a storm in a teacup, I will have seriously worried him all the way out in Hong Kong. And even though I may not be his greatest fan right now, I wouldn't wish this kind of anxiety on anyone, ever.

For his failings, I know he loves Cherry just as fiercely as me and thinking she's ill will make him want to drop everything and swim home. That mad, parental urge to protect is something we're both on the same page about. I can feel my nervous heart beat in my mouth, in my gums. But if it is more serious… and I haven't told him… he would never forgive me. *I* would never forgive me. I decide to wait until after we've seen the GP and I have more information. That's sensible. That's rational.

But I do text Nelle: 'Cherry poorly. Won't make the keepsake event tomorrow. Soz, love xxx'

And now it's time to go. I think I'm too shaky to drive, what with worrying and not sleeping at all last night. A brisk walk in the early morning breeze will do us good. In the hallway, I get Cherry gently clicked into her pram harness, the change bag and four different muslins packed away in the space underneath her seat.

'Time to get you better, pickle,' I coo with false confidence. 'Time for it *all* to feel better, you wait and see. Mummy's here.'

When I open my front door, something flashes in front of me like a blast of quick, sharp lightning. And the musty smell of cigarette smoke hits me.

'Stevie! Stevie! Is it true you're First-Time Mum?'

Two men stand on my doorstep, well within my personal space and one is snapping pictures on a huge camera. My first instinct is to leap back inside and slam the door: but I need to get to that doctor. I need to get Cherry better. So, in blind panic, I push the pram between them, narrowly missing the photographer's ankles.

'Stevie,' the other man continues to bark unnecessarily loudly, considering he's chasing me down the path two feet behind me, 'how do you think your readers would feel if they found out you were a kept woman, a wealthy housewife, but you're telling them to go it alone? Yeah?'

More flashes and Cherry starts to grizzle. I pull the pram hood right down so the bright light can't bother her and – it just dawns on me – they won't get a picture of her face. Whoever 'they' are, these aggressive morons.

My mouth goes dry as my brain foggily computes that they know who I am, who First-Time Mum really is. And where we live! Holy shit.

I must get to the GP now. This – whatever this is – can wait. It has to wait. It's about Cherry. It's always been about Cherry for me.

The photographer guy leaps in front of me, obviously trying to slow me down to get a better pic. But I will not have it.

I fling my hand, palm up, in front of the lens and snarl at them both, 'Get the fuck out of my way. My kid is sick. I have nothing to say to you. FUCK OFF!' I end with a yell. Both the men step away, out of my path. But they're smirking.

A few front doors open as I speed-walk away. I don't care. I don't care about any of it: Facebook Likes or neighbourhood disapproval or angry online commentators or book deals. Nothing matters right now but my girl.

Chapter 16

From: Sarah

To: Stevie

Hun, are you OK? I just saw something online – that's you, isn't it? Look, I'm here if you need me. Whenever. Just say and I'll be there. Obvs still want to see you for our lunch? xxx

From: Mum

To: Stevie

WHAT ON EARTH IS GOING ON?! Jeanie from our old street just sent me a link to this FailingMum thing?! Stevie?!

My hands are cold and numb as I lay the phone face-down on Will's kitchen table. Let one of the oilcloth mallards hold it for a while. I have no idea what to reply to anyone. I have no idea how they can write newspaper articles so quickly, either.

After I was promptly and kindly seen by the GP in twenty minutes, who told me Cherry had no other symptoms to cause real worry – no rash, no altered breathing – and it was a virus that I should keep treating with liquids and baby liquid paracetamol, I was left outside the double doors, my head spinning and no idea where to go. Those guys might still be there, at my door. With more shouted questions and long lenses. Did I open the curtains this morning? They might be papping my overflowing bin and leaning towers of cereal bowls by now. But I couldn't just shuffle about the streets with my sick baby – she needed to be somewhere clean and comforting, where I could change her nappy and her clothes the minute I needed to, even plunge her in a lovely bath if the sick got really bad again.

With no clue beyond the next fifteen minutes, I thought I might as well walk slowly to the pharmacy and pick up more supplies – wipes, Dettol, Calpol. The GP advised alternating Calpol and baby ibuprofen every few hours, to really get her temperature under control. That was one thing I could at least take charge of and achieve, if nothing else.

But after stepping out of the shop with two bulging plastic bags on my pram handles, I felt the dizzying spin of loneliness. I couldn't go home, not for sure. I felt too scared to call Ted, and it was probably 2am over there. And then I'd have to admit to this whole sorry mess of my own making, and how I'd been concealing it from him.

My eyes swam with tears as I looked up and down the high street, desperate for some open door, some beacon of sanctuary. Could I sit in the cafe and hope – just hope – Cherry would be OK and not catch something off a badly washed spoon while her immunity is low. The library?! Maybe not. If only it was the right day for a weigh-in. At least the health visitors could tell me what to do with my life.

But as I waited for the green man at the crossing, my watery eyes fell on a big tarpaulin sign strung up against some railings opposite – the Montessori would be having an open day soon.

I hadn't *completely* lost my mind: I wasn't going to take a Cherry full of sickness bug to a room full of toddlers – like a crazy terrorist with a deadly virus hidden up their sleeve in a deodorant can. But thinking of the Montessori – the twins were there. So Will wasn't with them. So if I was with Will, I wouldn't be cross-infecting any other kids.

I unlocked and hit the Contacts option on my phone. *Please be in, Will. Please.*

–

Three hours later, I am on my fourth cup of coffee in Will's kitchen and he's walking around with a pink Cherry high up on his shoulder, singing softly in her ear about The Grand Old Duke of York. She fell asleep an hour ago but I think he's enjoying the cuddle with a girl who can't yet run away or give a smart answer. And it's a good displacement activity while the updates come in.

When I turned up at his door, looking like an unwashed extra from *Les Misérables*, he ushered me in and listened to the whole sorry tale of the puking and the papping. He was quick to reassure me it was probably nothing, that it was a flash in the pan. 'And anyway,' he said calmly, 'I have a Google Alert set up for First-Time Mum – have done since you first confessed it was you, because I didn't want to miss a thing. So if something should pop up over the next day or two, we'll know about it. It'll do you good to have some time apart from your devices, maybe?'

He was right. I felt myself sink into his luxurious brown leather sofa, my limbs instantly going loose and heavy. It was probably nothing. *Who's going to be bothered about one little blog post? Who cares? Tomorrow a soap star will say something ill-advised on* Loose Women *and the news cycle will get its new fix. They probably didn't get any good pictures. And I didn't say anything they could quote. It's nothing. I'm just over-reacting because of the worry about Chezza. And now I know it's just a common or garden (though horrific to go through) vomiting bug that we have to wait out, I can grab hold of my marbles again.*

As I closed his front door, Will gently lifted Cherry out of her pram for me. He draped a big muslin expertly over his back and took her through to the kitchen. 'I'll get the kettle on,' he said reassuringly.

I *did* need a break from my phone. From blabbing out confessional blog posts and then obsessing over the outcome. From typing thousands of words with just my thumbs in the dead of night. From wondering when my husband would call me. I buried it deep inside the change bag, under a Tupperware box of raisins that might be some months old. It could sit there, have a time out. Think about what it'd done.

But when Will walked back into the living room a few minutes later, he wasn't holding a mug of warming, life-giving caffeine. He wasn't calm or reassuring. His face had fallen. And there wasn't even a trace of sick on his shirt.

'Stevie, there *is* something.'

It had taken them little shy of an hour to write up a lace-thin piece, chuck in the most unflattering pictures of a woman anyone's ever seen and slap it all over the *Daily Britain* website. 'EXCLUSIVE EXPOSE: First-Time Mum is wealthy housewife in the suburbs as she advises other mums to ditch their husbands!' I've got my hand up to the camera, an angry roll of my eyes making me look halfway batshit... but what takes me the other halfway there is my stained baggy T-shirt and greasy hair hanging in clumps. I couldn't bear to read it properly but as my eyes darted about the page, names and phrases leapt out at me:

> a PR executive, who we can safely assume is well versed in spin … husband Ted Cameron works a demanding job to support his wife while she vents her irritation at motherhood … relatively new to their town of High Wycombe … neighbours say they 'kept themselves to themselves, though the baby is often heard crying'.

Keep themselves to themselves?! That's what people always say about serial killers! And, yes, maybe Cherry does cry more than the average baby but that makes it sound like I pinch her fat folds for kicks.

So they found me. The real me. I just blinked and blinked at the glowing screen.

'How?' I muttered. 'But... I was so careful. I never used real names, or said where we live. How?'

Will sat down with Cherry in an armchair in the corner. 'Well, it can't have been anyone who leaked it, because there were just three of us in the know, right?'

I nodded.

'What would they do in the movies, Chezza? Trace the phone number, track a mobile signal, crack the IP...' His eyebrows shot up.

'Wait, what? What's an IP?'

Will rubbed a hand down his face, squashing his chis-elled features briefly. 'Your laptop has its own individual number, regardless of where you use it to log on. And it's hidden away when you send emails and post things online. But it's there if you want to track someone down.'

'I just didn't… I just didn't *think*.' My voice ended with a squeak. 'And now everyone knows. And it's all gone to shit.'

And sadly, to that, Will had no reassuring platitudes.

—

So much coffee in the following hours was probably not my greatest idea: I am jangling with caffeine and nerves and 'What ifs?' as we sit around his house and the responses come in.

I couldn't ignore my phone after the first hour – it vibrated against the old raisins in the Tupperware, sending out an angry rhythmic growl, calling at my soul like the Tell-Tale Heart.

Grrrr-grrrr. Here are your dirty secrets, it seemed to grumble. *Grrr-grrr. Come back to bite you in the arse.*

There was the message from Sarah, the email from my mum, a handful of uni friends I hadn't seen in years reaching out with 'U OK, hon?' My paranoid brain now had visions of them fishing for dramatic details they could flog to those two dicks on my doorstep.

Will is pretending not to be checking his own phone as he gets more and more Google alerts but I catch sight of his head dipped when he thinks I'm not looking. 'The good news,' he says carefully, over coffee number five now, 'is that a lot of First-Time Mum followers are behind you. Fighting your corner, in fact. Gin and Sippy Cups reposted as soon as she saw the article, with the heading: 'Why do they always come for the mums?' And everyone is re-sharing and giving you fistbumps. They know you weren't trying to tear down the convention of marriage; you were just saying what we all think in the black of night sometimes.'

His kind words can't break through the thick skin of self-loathing that has come to the surface in the last hours.

'Pssft.' I let out a long breath, looking around the room. 'I bet you've never thought that. You are nowhere near the mess I am.'

'Ha! Seriously?! I *also* stepped away from a job that I – too late – realised defined a lot of who I was. I'm used to being the parent everyone looks at, even when they're trying their best not to stare. Pretty much everyday I wonder whether I'm messing it up, messing the girls up, whether I'm still the man my husband fell in love with – while I'm scraping crusty cereal off bowls or inventing new ways to hide broccoli in toddler food. So... I've got a pretty good idea.'

'But you're so... so handsome!' I blurt. 'And your shirts are always pressed and your house is just... delicious!'

He counts off on his fingers, 'One: cleansing and toning. Two: laundry service. Changed my life. Three: Farrow and Ball. Literally no indication that I'm not just a hot mess underneath it all. Most of us are, if we're really honest. And you were being honest. It's just a kind of voice that some areas of the media don't want to hear, so they're going to try and make you look like a loony. Er, which, you're not. And you didn't look that way. Actually, when you look at it again, not at all. I wonder what's keeping Nelle?'

Nelle had been messaging at a rate of knots from home, only kept away by my insistence that passing on Cherry's sicky germs to Joe, and then possibly her others too, would only be the turd on top of my total shit-cake of a day. But she said the minute Darren came home, she would pass the parcel of the kids to him and be round to escort me back to mine, like my own personal mum security guard. That timing would suit Will's deadline to go and pick the girls up from Montessori.

But I was still bricking going home. What if those douche bags were still there? What if, like the amoebas they were, they had exponentially multiplied in the Petri dish of my drive?! My 'friendly' neighbours might be feeding them tea, sandwiches and more tasty fictions.

A knock at the door revealed what exactly had kept Nelle: she was standing there, a devious grin in place. And a step ladder at her shoulder.

'Chin up, kid. I have a plan. All thanks to my ill-spent youth.'

-

My knees jiggle up and down in the passenger seat as Nelle drives us home.

'Honestly,' she repeats for the third time, 'I *know* it will work. I mean, I'm still open to just running them down in my car to clear the path. I could even throw on my clown suit beforehand, to really scare the crap out of them once and for all. But if you're sure you don't want to dabble in a little GBH…'

I wave my hands. 'Let's just try and save the scraps of my reputation, if we can. Whatever is left of it. Don't get me wrong, I hate the fu—fiddle de dees. But all I really want is to get home, pull all the black-out blinds down, cuddle my girl and make her better, and not leave again until it's time to collect my pension at the Post Office.'

Nelle briefly takes her hand from the wheel to squeeze my knee. 'Don't be silly. By then Cherry will be old enough to claim it for you!' She winks and I feel a little warmth return to my skin.

But all Will's reassurances and Nelle's kind joking can't change the fact that my mug – my real face combined with my real name – is all over the internet. And they definitely have that in Hong Kong.

Instead of heading down our road, Nelle takes the turning just before, onto the street that runs parallel to ours.

'What exactly did you do with the apples you used to steal, then? Scrumping, I want to say?'

Nelle bites her lip and looks sheepish. 'We used to fill carrier bags with them, then leg it to the park on a dark summer's night and have a massive Apple War. I don't actually think the old boy who owned the garden would have minded if we'd just knocked on the door instead and asked to pick up the fallen apples. But climbing over the fence and trying not to wet ourselves with laughter was all kind of part of it. We thought we were *badasses*.'

'Badasses who battled with bruised fruit?'

'Hey!' She laughs. 'A cooking apple thrown over-arm blummin' well hurts, if it catches you in the wrong place. Those Apple Wars made a woman out of me.'

'I'll remember that, should the *Daily Britain* come back for round two. I've got some mouldy satsumas in the fruit bowl that aren't hard, but they would explode in a big squishy disaster, if I got some speed behind them out of the bathroom window.'

Nelle indicates and pulls over. 'Here we are. The apple orchard is now those three new houses up there.' She points further up the road. 'And this is the bottom of your place. I can't believe I am old enough to legitimately say, "I remember when this was all trees".' She shakes her head and sighs. 'But we're both still young enough for a little sneaky skulduggery.'

And that is how I fittingly end the day: with Nelle holding a stepladder with one hand and shoving me over the top of my garden fence, her other hand on my bum for the last push.

–

For the rest of the evening, I studiously ignore the rooms at the front of the house, just in case. Cherry and I have the most basic tea of scrambled eggs, with the lights off, and it's a huge relief that she will at least take a few mouthfuls and sip at some water. Her skin colour has now moved on from putty grey to a watery pink and I can see some of that characteristic Cherry brightness in her eyes returning too. I couldn't be more relieved. Let them crucify me, the red tops, I don't care, my baby is better. She's even more like herself at bedtime, only going down after her usual palaver of shushing and singing and jiggling. But for once I don't feel the tedium; it's like my head has floated off to somewhere else. It's been a surreal few days, to say the least. Eventually, I'm left in a dark house with just my laptop for company.

Before I dare go through my inbox, I send out an email that is the last thing I ever wanted to have to type but what I should have said in person, long long ago. I can't know for sure that Ted has seen the piece but with our names both in it and him being a full-on phone addict, it seems likely. And if my mum's seen it on Facebook already that feels like the ultimate litmus test of gossip wildfire.

To: ted.cameron@syncedsolutions.co.uk

From: Stevie **Subject:** …

Ted, I'm so sorry. I should have told you all about it but it was just this little thing I did in the dead of night. I never thought anyone would read it, let alone care.

But it snowballed, and as it did I got more and more scared to come clean to you.

The articles have taken it all out of context – I don't want to be on my own, it's just that sometimes I feel lonely as a mum. Really lonely. I have never said that to you before. But that's how I feel, a lot of the time.

God, I hope this doesn't get you in hot water at work. And I hope it doesn't embarrass you or your family.

Pretty much screwed things up, haven't I?

Let me know when you can talk. I can explain everything, honest. It's not the way it seems.

S x

PS Cherry's had a vomming bug but she's pulled through now. It was pretty scary for a while – I missed you.

With that sent and the blood roaring through my ears, I face the dreaded inbox. I could have tried calling Ted upfront, I know, but it's 3am over there right now and that's my convenient excuse for making a softly, softly first approach.

A real shocker is the top of the list.

> **From**: Jeremy@XpressPR
>
> **To:** Stevie
>
> **Subject:** Catch up?
>
> Hi Stevie,
>
> I'd like to firstly say that I'm aware it's outside the usual guidelines for your HR office to contact you before the ninth month of your maternity leave, but I want to make it clear that this is in no way related to your return to work.
>
> We just feel with today's media interest in you that you may want to talk, and we could offer some advice on handling your public image in our line of work, of course.
>
> If you'd like to come in, or just book a call, please let me know at your earliest convenience.
>
> Best wishes,
>
> Jeremy
>
> HR Executive

A prickle works its way down the tiny hairs on the back of my neck. Work want me to come in. They want to 'advise' me on how to handle this situation. My professional brain may be withered and shrunken from my time on maternity leave, but I still recognise the PR polite code for: 'Jesus, this is all super-embarrassing. Let's put a lid on it for you NOW, shall we? Before you do something else stupid, like come out of your house in full-on PJs and drop a C bomb to a hungry journo.'

The part of me that was bricking it about going back to work is suddenly gobbled up by the part of me that *absolutely* doesn't want to get fired. If I leave, I want it to be my choice, for our overall family-life balance, not booted out because I've become a liability. I had a vision of going out on a massive high, being able to tell all my old colleagues that I had a big blog now, a book deal in the works: I was going to leave them as a mumpreneur. I did not see myself carrying out my desk bits in a cardboard box with a pathetic shuffle, being eyed by the security guard like an intern busted stealing the copier paper.

God, if they sack me, that is just going to *feed* the news cycle. But they'd know that. Wouldn't they? Oh, Christ.

There's nothing in my inbox from Francesca and I'm too scared to reach out to her, in case I hear exactly what I know she would be sensible to say: your stock has fallen into the basement. Um, no thanks.

It's too much. It's all too much. My marriage is now a stony, silent wasteland. My career is screwed, even if I had known how the hell I would jump back into it. The internet trolls are probably out in force, ready to tear me apart. I'm too scared to actually look. Will kept reassuring me that loyal blog followers were coming to my aid, but I don't think my soul can handle sifting through the vile invective to find a few nuggets of loving gold.

My phone vibrates on the sofa armrest, shocking me out of my image of drowning in a sea of shitty website comments, the words 'disgusting', 'ungrateful', and 'lazy' swimming down my throat and up my nose as I thrash about for a little clean air. I snatch it up: Ted?

Sarah: *Hey chick, didn't hear back from you. I'm coming tomorrow, whether you like it or not. I just miss your face too much. And we can talk xxx*

I miss Sarah's face too, boy, do I. Someone who knew me before all this chaos. But the kitchen cupboards are empty and I don't want to risk a trip to the Co-op for lunch ingredients, being stared at like the village leper. And would she be able to bring her own stepladder to get over the back fence?

After a quick inbox refresh, there's still nothing from Ted. I mean, of course there wouldn't be at this time. But I wish there was. Tonight, I'm alone in this.

And maybe that's exactly what I deserve.

Chapter 17

'Fuck a duck!'

My throat is hoarse from info- and emotion-dumping on Sarah, and I just about manage a laugh at her response.

'Oops, sorry.' Sarah looks down at the beautiful lump on her lap that is Cherry and, slightly too late, puts her hands over Chezza's ears. Her nails are an amazing jade green and I feel a yearning in my heart for London nail salons. Those amazing, anonymous places where no one cares who you are, what you've blogged; they're just going to perform an excellent manicure and send you on your way.

I've covered the real experience of maternity leave I've been having (the shit sleep, the shitloads of washing, the actual shit under my fingernails, at times), the blog going viral, Ted's new job offer in Hong Kong, the book I've been speed-writing, my phobia of work and the scary HR email, plus the 24 hours recently when I thought Cherry was going to end up in intensive care.

'Blimey, Steve.' Sarah fills her cheeks full of air and then pushes it out in one huge exhale. 'That's enough for ten women to handle, let alone one. But why didn't you say? Why didn't you tell me that it's been so' – her hands cup Cherry's head again – 'crap? It always seemed like you were living this sweet, suburban life, all sunny walks around the park and scones for tea.'

'Ha!' I slump down onto the kitchen chair next to hers and dip a tortilla crisp into some salsa. I love Sarah so much for hitting the M&S at the train station before she got here. 'Walks around the park are not a jolly – they're a necessity to get this one to give up and go to sleep. After twenty minutes of wailing. Sometimes I'm doing that three times a day. And if I get to stuff a scone in my gob of an afternoon it would be a major treat. And maybe the first thing I've eaten that day.' I chuck my podgy angel under the chin. 'Maybe a different mum would handle it differently. Maybe a different baby would be, um, easier. But I do love her. And I didn't want to seem ungrateful. I know I'm lucky.'

Sarah rolls her eyes. 'To get puke in your hair and never sleep for more than four hours at a time? I do not count that as lucky, love. Though she is a total peach. Should have called you Peachy, shouldn't they, hunny-bunny?' she coos at Cherry, who waves her fists in delight. She had a crazy good night's sleep, for her: just one night feed. I wonder if she can pick up on my batshit vibes right now and has decided she doesn't want to risk me going fully nuts at 2am or leaving her behind more permanently in the library next time. Whatever it is, long may it last. Though it only makes me feel guiltier that I've ranted so much about sleeplessness and now here she is, defying all my moans.

'And I'm sorry, but where is Ted in all of this? He still hasn't called you, right?'

I shrug. As time and distance stretches between us, I'm regretting how I reacted to Ted's Hong Kong news. I don't regret saying it wasn't for me, but the emotional blow up and storming off to the pub like a reckless teen was unnecessary – if Ted ever just disappeared on me like that, without a phone or a wallet, I'd have helicopters out looking for him within the hour. And now after all that drama, he's dealing with the revelation that his wife is a secret blogger who slags him off the minute his back is turned. I can kind of see why he's not really in the mood to talk. Neither am I: I haven't posted or answered a single comment since the *Daily Britain* first picked up on the blog.

Sarah scrunches her lips up in the way I know means she's chewing back something critical she'd love to say, but which the PR in her knows is too harsh. 'So what *are* you going to do?' She dips a crisp in the tomato salsa and transfers it into her mouth. Dropping a blob on Cherry's head as she does so. When she freezes, I just wave away her concern.

'I've done worse – bit of a mint Cornetto the other week, while she was asleep on my lap. You get pretty good at pre-planning your snacks when you know you'll be hunkered down under a hefty infant for thirty minutes. It's harder to anticipate when you suddenly need to wee, though. Maybe I need a sort of space-suit that I could just relieve myself in...'

Sarah smiles but widens her eyes in a pointed fashion. 'Steve, don't change the subject. What's your next move?'

I run my fingers through my freshly washed hair, now feeling like it's been fluffed up with helium at the roots after so many days of being thick and heavy with grease. 'I don't know. Why are you asking me?' I laugh weakly.

'Tsk. You've forgotten so much of Magda's Magna Carta, haven't you? I'm going to have to remind you.'

Magda was a boss Sarah and I shared when we first started working together, years ago. She was a doyenne of old-school PR and had a strict set of rules by which PRs should live and die by. 1) Never look at your watch during a Lunch. 2) You must never tell a client you are 'busy'. Because nothing else in the world but them exists, so how could you possibly be? 3) Your hair says twenty per cent of your dialogue.

Magda made it her mission to impart every single gem of wisdom she had to us before she retired; we used to have a Word Document with them all written down, in fact. It started off as a joke but we quickly realised we were taking ourselves much more seriously after absorbing her words and, as a result, other people then took us more seriously.

Sarah wags her finger at me in a very Magda way. 'There are no disasters, darling, only stories. And if you're telling the story, you're writing the ending. If it's someone else doing the telling, who knows how the last page will read?'

'I just don't know… I remember it all, somewhere deep down. And I know it all makes sense. But that Stevie from the office – she feels like a distant memory. I don't know if I can do what she does. I can't talk the way she used to talk: making it up on the spot, faking confidence until she found it. In that way she's just like First-Time Mum – able to say all the things I'm not.' I break a tortilla into little crumby pieces on the table.

Sarah shifts Cherry around on her lap. She may be losing sensation in her thighs at this rate.

'You can lay her down on her play mat, if she's getting a bit weighty. It's that shiny bit of Cath Kidston fabric.'

Sarah takes Cherry over and lays her down, fat legs kicking. As she stands back up, her eyebrows knit together. 'Do you know, when you talk about the "old"

Stevie and First-Time Mum, you talk about them like they're separate people. You talk about them like they aren't you. But they are. It *is* your voice, Steve. It was back when you rescued that Myers' new homes cock-up. It's there in all the blog posts that people have loved and shared and felt… connected to. Those were you, you great numpty. Did you think the words just fell out of the sky and onto your keyboard?'

I bite down a wonky smile. 'Um, yes. At times. God, Myers Development. I haven't thought about them in years.'

Sarah gets up to open the second bottle of fizz, fishing it out of the fridge. 'We ran that huge campaign all about their brand-spanking-new housing development in Epping for weeks: *actual* affordable London living was the whole line. Quality houses to last your family a life-time. And then just before the big launch day, with the press visiting in forty-eight hours, their shoddy plumbing floods the communal gardens smack-bang in the middle of twenty houses. And you…'

She swivels to face me, rotating her hand in the air to get me to fill in the rest.

'…I told the journos it was the beginning of a wilder-ness pond, to bring back local wildlife and get the kids reconnecting to nature. God, that was cheesy.'

'Cheesy?! It was bloody genius! You got that envir-onmental team in double-quick to advise, and you made Myers promise to actually follow through. You saved them loads of house sales *and* the local kids got somewhere to watch frog spawn and beetles and all that gross stuff. That came out of your head, lady. No amount of hormones, no rough patch, is ever going to change that in you. Listen, I only had time to read a few of your posts before I came today and it makes my boobs feel strange to read so much about cracked nipples when I haven't done any of that stuff yet, but that's you. That's your voice. First-Time Mum is *you*. So let's spitball this, two of Magda's finest pupils: what's your next step, Steve? Who's telling the last page of this story?'

There're a few wet grunts from the floor, and then silence. That worrying reflux-baby silence. I grab the kitchen roll.

But instead of seeing a few white puddles and a cross Cherry, I find her blinking at herself in the glass of the kitchen door, her hands pushing her arms and shoulders up, her portly tum meaning she is so far off the floor that her toes barely graze it.

She rolled over!

'You did it! Oh, my clever chicken, you did it!' I scoop her up into my arms and she just keeps on calmly blinking, as if to say, *Well, yes, it was a piece of cake, actually. Now, can I pull your earrings out of your ears, please?*

'What did she do?!' Sarah rushes over.

I try to blink back the soppy tears in my eyes and pull myself together a bit. 'She rolled over. For the very first time. Roly-poly baby!' I start to sing and jig about with Cherry, and Sarah quickly joins in. Within five minutes we have a very short conga line making a circuit of the kitchen, and on into the living room: 'Roly-poly baby, roly-poly baby!'

All the shame and guilt and worry is falling off me with every bouncy step I take and Cherry swings her hands together, only missing a clap by three inches or so. That will be the next milestone! And before I know it, she'll be collecting her PhD!

I can't stop the happy weep that now takes over – my clever girl is growing up.

-

Three days after Sarah's visit and things seem to have died down on the online front. Without any comment or activity from me, the trolls have nothing to feast on and the online papers have moved on, too. For now. I'm sure they've still got half a beady eye on my page, to make sure I don't say anything – gasp – honest about motherhood ever again.

I still can't get over how miraculous it is that Cherry can now just roll herself over whenever she pleases. Fine, it might be the most basic of gross motor skills but suddenly I start imagining her taking her first steps, skipping along a playground, doing cartwheels… It's just so mind-bending that something that started out as two microscopic cells can grow and develop to such a magical extent that one day you're eating M&S nibbles and suddenly they flip themselves over without any help from you.

Sarah left me with a big page of scrawled ideas that we pooled, over more M&S tortillas and dolmas and falafel, and she braved the front door for me. No one was there – no fag butts discarded to show they had been there recently, either.

Seeing as it had been Father's Day that Sunday, I sent Ted another email, with an attached photo of Cherry happily covered in carrot purée, from chins to forehead.

To: ted.cameron@syncedsolutions.co.uk

From: Stevie

Subject: Happy Father's Day!

She rolled over! Can you believe it?! This gorgeous lump is missing her dad. So am I. Can we talk?

S x

And I got a response the next morning, but not exactly the one I'd hoped for.

To: Stevie

From: Ted

Re: Happy Father's Day

Thanks for the pic. Clever girl! Love her and miss her so much.

Not ready to talk just yet. Soon.

T

At least I knew he was OK. And if he was still using his work email, he wasn't fired. I wish he'd said he was missing me, too, though. I wish there was a kiss at the end of the email. A ray of light. Some hope. Maybe I don't deserve it, but it would help me push through this hard bit alone before he's back in the flesh.

Spending that time with Sarah had been like an incredible shot of one of those cleansing wheatgrass juices: not something that went down easily at first but after it had, I was pumped up, clear-headed and full of energy. I really *had* been seeing First-Time Mum as her own person, rather than my creation. I hadn't even been giving myself credit for that. And so one media outlet had put their spin on what I do – was I going to let them write my story for me? A former PR raised by the elegant hand of Magda?!

No. I still had something to say, even if some familiar old wobbles keep niggling away at me.

The blog is no longer a place for me to hear my own voice echoing back to me, just to prove I still exist, like a dark cave where I could only bother the bats. Now it's a Sydney Opera House, a Wembley Arena where I'm on stage amongst thousands of spectators. And that doesn't feel all that relaxing. But I can't just stand under the burning lights and say nothing.

Sarah and I decided on my plan, just for the next week. 'No need to think beyond that,' she said calmly, underlining 'Stevie's One-Week Plan' with a wiggly line. 'Crack this week. Then you can think about the next.' They were wise words we used to reassure any freaked-out client, and they were sensible ones. So I put out a statement, thanking my supporters and asking for a bit of space. And then I stopped logging on, and I'm not going to for the rest of the week. A good long while in First-Time Mum land. As proud as I am of First-Time Mum, as much as she's woken me up to the fact I do still have a brain and there are other hopeless parents like me out there, just doing their best to keep afloat and keep a smile on their chops, she's not more important than working out what's best for Cherry, Ted and me. That's what this week is all about. Some day-to-day happiness, in tiny ways, before I tackle, 'Where is my life going? What's left of my career?' kind of stuff. Grains of sand before standing stones. That's the way forward.

I took Cherry to the park on Monday. There were a few knowing stares from other playground mums, but no one approached me. I decided just to look at my girl. Gentle pushes in the swing, back and forth, back and forth. Now June is fully fledged it was warm enough to come out in summery clothes and let my baby feel the breeze on her toes as she swung in a slow rhythm. Her gurgles were heaven. If life was just this and nothing more, for the rest of time, it would be more than enough.

We had a bath together. We played 700 games of peek-aboo. I made her an industrial quantity of mashed-up swede for the freezer. I found out she doesn't really like swede. I savoured all these tiny little moments of happiness and calm and reminded myself that I was damn lucky to have this kid. Cherry's amazing run of sleep continued: sure, she was still giving me hell in fighting the need to sleep at bedtime but, once down, she would go through till 3am, wake up for another feed then sleep again until 6am. Not my dream sleep pattern as a none-too-springy-chicken but definitely an improvement. I even dared stay up till 10.30pm on Tuesday night. Rock and roll!

And tonight I have the mental energy to dig out an old cuttings file. It started as a sort of ironic thing I did in my twenties, starting to place my first few pieces in news-papers, but really under the guise of being ironic, I just wanted tangible proof of what my days were spent doing. It's important when you basically rotate between your phone, the post bag and the photocopier as a PR. Your stock in trade is how you talk to people, how you make yourself and your client really memorable. But sometimes that can feel a bit insubstantial and you want to see proof of where all your smooth talking goes. Reminiscing about some of the hairier, last-minute saves of our work life with Sarah had made me nostalgic for those ripped-out pages of glossy magazine paper Sellotaped into a craft book. Proof, actual proof, of my fast-talking, spin-cycle skills. Of what my brain used to do without that much conscious effort.

There is a box in the home office that contains things I couldn't bear to part with in the move from London – just too unbelievably important – but that aren't all that important enough to have been unpacked over the year we've lived here. And my purple cuttings book is right on top. I sit crossed-legged on the floor and try not to pay attention to the lingering smell of Ted's aftershave in here. Hugo Boss. It makes me think of our early dates in dark bars.

I'm not sure many people would feel a tingle of pride looking at a picture of a cow dressed in a satin sash and wearing a crown of flowers, but the *Psychologies* article on Miss Heifer UK was the last thing I stuck in, not long before going on leave, and it still makes me smile. We were working with the Dairy Council who were getting a bit nervously sweaty under the collars of their farming overalls about what the huge surge in veganism was doing to their business. So we set up a beauty pageant weird enough to be worthy of Louise Theroux – organic farmers brought their finest, rarest breeds to compete for who had the best-tasting milk, who had the strongest muscle definition from their free-range lifestyle, and who was just (we had to play the kitsch card) the cutest cow. The oddities made it a great filler piece for glossies and local newspapers but we also managed to slip in the stats about how the farmers were suffering economically, risking the end of a Great British tradition, and how beneficial just the right amount of dairy can be in your diet. Plus, I fell in love with one long-lashed beauty called Maureen. So I made sure she got Miss Congeniality.

'We told the story,' I whisper to myself, remembering how Sarah, some colleagues and I fleshed the whole madcap idea out in a fancy gelato place near the office, surging ahead on the dairy power of a really good chocolate and hazelnut ice cream. We had a brilliant idea and we made it happen. It was risky, it was bold, it was creative. I can do those things. I have and I can.

How did I leave myself so far behind for so long? The woman who dreamt up a cow beauty pageant was somehow the same one sobbing on the floor of a boarding school toilet. She went from proudly putting her ideas out into the ether to blogging in a furtive darkness, ashamed of how she really felt and definitely too scared to admit it to anyone.

Was it at the delivery suite? Did I push and pant and scream so hard that some core part of Stevie took fright and legged it down the stairwell before I had time to realise? Or was all my vim and vigour slowly drained from me over the countless hours of feeding and soothing and singing during Cherry's little lifespan? Can there be all that much left for yourself when you give *so much* to keep another person happy and healthy?

As I place the cuttings book back on top of the Important Junk box, something is dislodged and slides out onto the carpet. A glossy white photo book, from our wedding. I pick it up and place it in my lap. We have a formal leather-bound affair, somewhere safely tucked away, but this is one that a group of our friends got together and made from all their phone pics of that day, and it's by far my favourite version of events.

Here I am crossing my eyes as the grumpy hairdresser sticks the forty-third bobby pin into my up-do and also my scalp. I mean, I did warn her my hair is crazy fine and slippy. She ended up using so much hairspray that even with the pins removed the next morning, the do held its own, like an organic motorcycle helmet, at breakfast.

Here is Ted and his best man, Phil, conferring in the corner before the ceremony starts. They have no idea they've been snapped, and it looks like some deep and meaningful chat about commitment and love and responsibility. In actuality, Ted told me, the first time we leafed through this book with tears in our eyes, Phil was running past Ted the fact that he might include in his speech the story about That Time in Bristol when they were students and tried to barter services in a strip club. And Ted was telling him Absolutely Not.

And here we are, clumsily dancing in a black and white snap, Ted trying to dip me back and me squeezing my eyes shut in half-fear, half-delight, a huge smile filling my face and possibly dislodging all my lipstick. I remember that moment being just like the schmaltz from romantic movies — everyone faded away. I knew there was a ring of all our nearest and dearest watching, cooing, filming the moment, but for the length of 'A Million Love Songs' they were just wallpaper. It was Ted and me. It was us.

How did I come so far from that moment? I promised on that day to always love and care for Ted, my best friend, my challenger and protector, and as the vows slipped easily from my lips they seemed so obvious as to be a bit laughable. *Of course* I was going to worship this guy for ever — he was my world! Plus, he was a total fox! How could I envision doing anything but?! It was a no-brainer. Simple.

And maybe because it felt so simple was why it was so easy to lose sight of. I'm not saying he hasn't had his part to play in things going pretty wrong recently, and it's definitely not my job to be ready for him in heels and a pinny when he gets in from work, steak and kidney pie cooling on the windowsill, but why didn't I talk to him about my blogger side? My best friend, my challenger and protector. Why didn't I let him in? That is definitely on me, just me. If I'd been honest about how I was really feeling he might never have suggested the Hong Kong thing at all. He might have known what was in my heart if I hadn't been hiding it so deep down.

Tears are falling on the glossy white cardboard cover of the photo book and I wipe them away quickly with the hem of my PJs. The photo that our mates chose for the front cover, a small little square of an image but pretty powerful nonetheless, is us at the cake cutting. Ted must have been preparing for the day by watching one too many US reality TV shows about weddings, because just as soon as we'd made the ceremonial cut into the top layer of our gigantic lemon drizzle cake, he dabbed a finger into the icing on the top layer and then playfully wiped it onto the end of my nose. Someone captured the exact moment that my eyes widened in shock and laughter and I turned to him, the knife suddenly looking very threatening in my hands, my lips pursed in mock-anger.

That was the Stevie he married. Ballsy, in the moment, happy to laugh at herself but also happy to give as good as she got. The Stevie who put cows in pageants. The Stevie who could walk into any room and be on first-name terms with complete strangers within ten minutes.

But the Stevie who left the hospital with a filled baby seat and a whole lot of stitches was nowhere near that woman. She was someone else. And if I admitted that to Ted, would he still want the new Stevie? She wasn't exactly a bundle of laughs – neurotic, zombie-tired, a virtual hermit who at times didn't even have anything interesting to say about the weather. I so wanted to be the old me again, but I didn't quite know how to get back to her. I had no map. I had no petrol in the tank. I had no seat belt to hold everything together.

Through First-Time Mum, I had my first road trip back towards Happiness. I was getting there. But it wasn't so much a well-planned journey as a hairy hitchhike.

My fingers start to tingle. This would make such a great blog post – this breakthrough in how I'm feeling. It's honest, it's something maybe someone else out there is struggling with. It could really reach people.

I know who I have to write it for.

Chapter 18

It's funny, Sarah has never met Nelle and yet they are totally in sync as great, great mates of mine. Within about twenty minutes of each other, they have messaged me this morning saying, 'Are you really sure you're OK with this?' And I've reassured them that, yes, I am. I really am.

Three days on, and still no word from Ted. Technically, he's due back in two days and then I hope he will be ready to talk, to hear me out. But just in case he isn't, I'm going to try another tack. One that can't be ignored. Because I really owe it to him to be honest, and to set the record straight for both of us. Thousands of people out there have the wrong idea about us and maybe that shouldn't matter but, in reality, it does.

Apparently the keepsake craft day went really well and turned in not a bad profit for Nelle's business – she's thinking of another one ahead of the last day of the summer term for kids to make things for their teachers. She did sheepishly admit that lots of people were none-too-subtly asking about me and was it true that she knew me, all that bumpf, but the PR Stevie kicked in and I replied that there's no such thing as bad publicity. And I really meant it. If my major gaffes can help boost Nelle's customer base, then that's something good to come out of all this mess. That's something to focus on.

Life feels a bit less like a Bourne movie now – no looking over my shoulder as I leave the house, no worrying my phone has been tapped. I think because I've been so quiet and not posted on social media or the blog, the press have got a bit bored and moved on to the next 'scandal': Mitzy, the back-flipping feline who won *Britain's Got Talent* last year, has been exposed as three separate cats, two of which have their white patches turned Midnight Noir with the help of Just For Men every week. The animal rights organisations are angry, the sponsors are angry, and – worst of all, in the nation's hearts – Ant and Dec are angry. I feel momentarily sorry for the trainer whose doorstep is now getting as crowded as mine temporarily was, but then I remember he puts hair dye on animals and he can have all that bashing if it teaches him not to do it again.

Cherry and I have done our usual supermarket shop without being accosted – just maybe a few whispers down the refrigerator aisle. I even braved the library sing-along session again with Nelle and Will in tow as my 'heavies'. I managed to come away *with* the child I arrived with and the little demon librarian even gave me a sympathetic nod as he replenished True Crime.

Life has levelled out in lots of little ways, but of course there's a big, gaping Ted-shaped hole smack bang in the middle of everything. And every time I notice his absence around the house I'm reminded of how badly I screwed things up between us. I've been showing Cherry pictures of him, pictures of us as a couple and of us as a family. Mostly to remind her that he's her dad and he loves her, but also to remind myself why I'm about to do the crazy thing that I'm about to do. The kind of thing that six weeks ago would have reduced me to a wobbling wreck in a bathroom stall. But it must be done. And I can do it. I can.

It's 3.50pm and I'm due to kick off at 4pm. I've managed to fashion myself an elevated stand for my iPad at the kitchen table out of hardback books and cereal packets. This way I can see myself back in the screen at the right level without bending down awkwardly or getting any unfortunate chin angles. Let's just say Cherry doesn't get her multiple chin layers from her father. She's in the bouncing chair at my feet, with the forbidden remote control to drool over for entertainment, and if she gets fussy I can jiggle her with my foot. I'm not sure this is how the legion of mummy vloggers do it – it's doubtful, and it's very much proof why I didn't gravitate towards YouTube as my blogging method of choice. Too much tidying up of the background shot, too much angling of lamps so you get some form of lighting that doesn't make you look like the re-animated corpse of a toad. With the only image associated with me out in the world looking like an *EastEnders* extra from a heroin den scene, I'm happy to put a bit of effort in today to cancel that out – but I won't be a vlogger any time soon. OK, I've got some primer and foundation on (the lid of the foundation was caked shut from old age, but I soldiered on), a swipe of eyeliner and some lip balm. I feel like I'm as scrubbed up as it's possible to be. My face is quite literally ready to meet the world. More specifically, the Gin and Sippy Cups Facebook page.

Sarah helped me polish an email approach to my fellow blogger while we finished off the last of the M&S nibbles – an exclusive Facebook Live moment with First-Time Mum, the only interview she's willing to give: she's throwing it open to the parenting public to ask her whatever they want about *that* blog post, about her real life, about getting sick stains out of a car seat.

Bloody luckily for me, she said yes.

So I'm syncing up with her at 4pm. The beans are ready to be spilled. The loose ends will be snipped. First-Time Mum will pop her video cherry. *Maybe there's just enough time to pour a glass of wine to keep out of shot, just in case it gets bad...*

The screen flashes into life just as a text pops up on my phone, from Stephanie, the real name of the blogger who's given me so much great support. I mean, she really broke me out. So if Ted is angry with anyone, maybe I should quietly share her number with him...

> Steph: Looks like we're good to go – if you're ready.

> Stevie: As I'll ever be! X

As the seconds tick down to 3.57, I slug back some wine, clear my throat and fiddle with my hair one last time. *Tell your story, Stevie. Tell it your way.*

'Hey, guys! Yes, it's me, First-Time Mum, not all that long ago outed as Stevie, really average mum from High Wycombe. Average but capable of causing some serious chaos, it seems. So my lovely friend at Gin and Sippy Cups has let me jump onto her Facebook account today to talk to you, clear some stuff up and then let you send in your questions, which should appear down here.' I point down towards the table top, and already on my screen I can see some comments appear:

OMG, is that really you?!?!

Love those cabinet doors, are they IKEA?

I try to keep the cracks out of my voice and rally on. 'Ha, oooh, I feel like a *Going Live* presenter. Anyway, I've got a bit of a thing to say first, if that's OK. I figured if I could say it with the mighty reach of Sippy Cups I'd *definitely* reach all the switched-on parents of the UK. Because, to be honest, I've been freaking out as to what you guys think of me.' I shuffle the handwritten notes on the table a little.

'OK. This last week I've been accused of lots of things – being ungrateful, being lazy, being a hypocrite. You might think those things, you might have made up your mind about me and that's that.' I shrug. 'But I hope – if you've started a family of your own already, especially – that you can appreciate things are never so black and white. Parenting is all about shades of grey.'

I can hear my pulse thumping in my ears. 'I am grateful every day that I have a beautiful baby, a family, a roof over my head, food in my cupboards. Each of these things is a sign of the universe being crazily kind to me. I never once meant to insinuate these things were burdens, or encourage anyone to throw them off and be pig-headedly selfish. What I meant to say was that you can have all this, all these wonderful luxuries in life, and it can still *feel hard*. And just because something is hard, that doesn't mean you are weak.' My voice catches on the last word and I briefly lean out of shot to take a drink. 'Pretend you didn't see that,' I mutter.

Ha ha, it's wine o'clock round our way too!

Explains why she's such a state, glug glug glug...

'If you read any of my posts, you'll know that I did find it hard, in a million small ways that somehow wore me down from the confident woman I'd been to the shell of a mum I felt like. Maybe I had hidden strengths I wasn't seeing, maybe you guys have always felt strong as parents, but I didn't feel strong. At all. I felt scared to talk to people – and I used to be a PR! I felt lonely, even though I had a husband living right here with me. I felt like such a terrible mum because I have a baby that rarely stops crying long enough for me to butter a piece of toast, even though all babies cry, in different ways. I felt like I was falling behind as a mum, in a way I never had in my adult life. Before, I could set myself a goal and follow it through. In motherhood, I could hardly follow through on one load of washing, let alone match up to the cosy Insta images of perfectly neat babies and glowing mothers. I felt like I was failing, lagging behind.'

We've all been there, FTM. Chin up, love.

Behind you?!

'I felt like a let-down as a mum. Was my baby so sad, so sicky, because I was just intrinsically crap at motherhood? And if I admitted that I was so sad, so bored, so lost, would that mark me out as a heartless old moaner? It's not exactly a great conversation starter at a playgroup, is it? "Hey, I think parenthood has drained my life force, how about you?" Or, worse, to your partner: "Yeah, thanks for bringing home all the bacon and that, but let me just recite to you the top ten things I hate about newborn nappy changes: the peanut-poo smell, when it gets under your nails, when it somehow gets on the skirting board…'

I rub my hand over my temples. 'I have been a pretty rubbish person to live with. I don't think I could have helped most of it, the way I was feeling, and not sleeping a full night's sleep will make even a saint lose their shit over an unloaded dishwasher. But I shouldn't have said the things I needed to say to a blog, when I couldn't even say them to my husband first. Yup, guys, that is the sad truth of First-Time Mum. In all her righteous ranting, she couldn't just look over the rim of her Special K bowl and say "I'm struggling. I feel like crap. Help me."'

My throat is crying out for more vino, as is my courage. The comments rolling at the bottom of my screen are whizzing through at a bonkers speed; I can hardly read them before they are replaced with the next. My phone buzzes on the table.

> Steph: Did you set this up?

What's she on about? Of course we set this up. She knows that! Maybe she thinks what I'm saying is too rehearsed, but I needed to have some notes or I would have blurted tears and snot all over the place and never got to the core of what I really wanted to say.

'I owed my other half so much more than complaining about him behind his back. He's a great dad, he loves us both so much. Now that I've had time to think things through at a distance, he's only giving it his best First-Time Dad shot, just as I'm bungling my way through being a First-Time Mum. I can't expect him to read my mind. I need to tell him what's going on with me.

'He works really hard for our family. In fact, he's away working now. He definitely didn't need to be dragged into a public shaming. And, for the record, in case you are still in any doubt: I don't think single parents have it "easier"; I would never advise anyone on their relationship status until I actually knew them really, really well. And then possibly only after four gins.

'The only truth is: no one has it easy. Single, married, straight, gay, rich, poor, one kid or twelve. If it feels hard to you, it's *not* because you are weak. It's because it's bloody hard! I might get that put on book bags, you know, because we'd have a lot more fun as parents if we remembered it and didn't beat ourselves up so much. No one has a manual for being a parent. No one has the right to look down their nose at anyone else's family style or setup. We just need to stick together and get our heads down. And firstly that starts with the people you love most.'

He's right there for you, girl!

Um, HELLOOOOOOO, FTM? LOL you are clueless!

'So, I don't know what the future of the blog will be right now. I might be coming back, I might not. A lot of that will come down to what's best for my family, and that's a group decision. But the one thing I will stick with is a brilliant thing called ParentFest, which is taking place not far from me, at the end of the summer. It's a festival but for *us*. Where kids come second, and there is a gastro grub, places to sit, craft beers to knock back. Oh, yes! The link is, again, somewhere down here.' I waggle my fingers below my bust line, hoping that I'm hitting roughly the right area. 'That looked a bit rude, didn't it? Good job, too, to balance out that whole *Oprah* spiel. Just wish me luck with saying it all again to my husband, yeah?

'Right then, who's got a question that isn't about the best nipple creams because I never cracked that and you don't want to know what mine look like these days. Do you remember the ads with those singing Californian raisins? Well...'

'I have a question.'

My mouth freezes in the perfect position to catch blue-bottles and I whip around. 'Ted?'

He's leaning against the kitchen counter, briefcase in hand, crumpled-up coat over one arm. His face is blank except for his slightly narrowed eyes. 'Are you talking to someone real there?'

I feel my throat ping red with heat. 'Um, it's a Facebook Live thingy but...' I look back at the screen and the twirling carousel of comments. If there was ever a moment to sum up the crossroads I was at, this is it. My audience or my husband. 'Sorry, guys, I'll have to pick this up another time. Husband's home!' I hope the whites of my eyes will tell them just how excited/petrified I am right now.

Don't cut us off now!!!!!

First-Time Dad is hot. FILTF.

Seriously, girl, you'd better let us know what happens... in due course. ;)

The screen goes dark and it's just the three of us, as it should be. Cherry has barely made a gurgle through my whole speech, saliva dripping off the Sky remote and onto her purple onesie. And now she smiles up at us both, her legs turning circles in the air at the sight of Mum and Dad back in the same time zone.

'How long have you been listening?' I swallow the lump in my throat. The wine is sadly all gone.

Ted looks down at his shoes for a beat. 'Not long enough, Steve. But I came in somewhere around you being desperately lonely, even with a husband right next to you.'

'That sounds bad out of context. It's not that I'm not happy with *you*, it's just—'

Ted lets his bag drop to the floor with a gentle thud and throws his coat on top. For the first time this stirs up no irritation in me whatsoever. In a weird way, I have missed his little baggage hurdles. He reaches his long frame down and picks up Cherry. She makes an instant grab for his ears.

'Nothing beats that slightly off-milk mixed with custard smell, right?' His eyes light up as he takes her in. 'My girl.'

I feel a hollow coldness in my heart. I have thrown so much away. I have hurt such a great man, such a loving dad. His name has been dragged through the mud behind mine, maybe dirtying his career permanently. He didn't ask for any of this. Definitely not an emotionally constipated wife.

'I need to tell you it was never *you*, Ted. All the things that I was feeling, they came out of me. Not because you did or didn't do anything. But because motherhood hit me like a truck and I've been... flat ever since. And I didn't know how to tell you. Because that wasn't the Stevie you met. When I was—'

'Full-bodied?'

The slight smile on his face catches me completely off guard. I hop out of my chair. 'What?'

Ted shakes his head. 'I'm not going to say this has been my *favourite* week, Steve. You walking out that night was... a shocker. And then suddenly we're internet news? Yeah, pretty full-on. I should have called you but I needed a bit of time.'

I bite my bottom lip. 'Understandable.'

'And I thought you'd have your mates rallying round you, your parent mates.'

'They've been amazing. Yeah.'

He hitches Cherry further up on his side and scratches the back of his neck with his free hand. 'I've been feeling a bit boring in comparison to them, actually. They're all you ever talk about.'

'*You've* felt boring? Mr International Man of Travel? Mr Entertaining Clients at The Ivy? And I wouldn't say they're all—'

A rapid knock at the door interrupts me.

With a sigh, Ted goes out to open it – to find Will panting and leaning on our doorframe.

'Came. Soon. As I saw.'

I look between the two men. 'Um, hey, Will. This is Ted. Ted, this is Will.'

Will swats my introductions away. 'Yes, obviously. But you…' He lets out a light wheeze.

'We need to talk,' Ted says flatly. 'It's what we *are* doing, mate, thanks.'

Will nods furiously. 'Yes, *mate*. That's why. I came. Take Chez. You guys go out. Talk like this needs. A real drink.' He holds out slightly wobbly arms and after a reassuring nod from me, Ted hands the baby over.

Will plonks himself down at our kitchen table with Cherry. She has never had such a teatime drama unfold in her midst, so many comings and goings, and she is positively a fountain of excited drool as she watches it all keenly, her natural nosiness at its peak.

After a few deep lungfuls of air Will recovers himself and smiles broadly.

'Why did you run here?' I ask in a low voice, not wanting to seem ungrateful for a chance to escape the house.

Will blinks. 'I don't know. I was watching the Face-book Live, saw Ted arrive in the background and thought you'd need some proper grown-up time. So I made

Adrian come down from the home office once his conference call ended. Then I sprinted over.' He looks genuinely baffled by himself. 'It seemed the Richard Curtis thing to do, in the heat of the moment.'

We're shrugging on our jackets awkwardly, not really knowing how to behave when someone turfs you out of your own house, when Will continues: 'And Nelle wanted me to say that ParentFest tickets are now fifty-five per cent sold, from thirty per cent this morning. Looks like that mention worked wonders!'

'Aiiieee!' Forgetting the seriousness of the situation otherwise, I jump on the spot and clap my hands. 'Amazing! Oh god, I am so pleased.'

Ted stands by the door, holding it open for me. 'There's a lot to catch up on, it seems.'

–

The Fox and Gherkin shushed just briefly when we walked in. Local celebs are a bit thin on the ground round High Wycombe so I suppose a flash-in-the-pan online type will have to do. Just to get away from the bar and to a secluded table as quickly as possible, I ordered two pints of the special offer cider. Ted followed me to two red velvet-covered stools.

We've been sipping now for ten very long, quiet minutes.

I catch his eye and give a cheesy grimace, the kind that hopefully says, 'Well, this is so awkward you'd better forgive me quick so we can get on with things, huh?'

In reply he curls his lips in on themselves a little, in a kind-of smile.

He takes a deep breath. I can't let him make any sort of final statement before I apologise again. 'I'm sorry!' I almost shout, just as he says, 'I'm sorry, Stevie.'

I laugh, with relief and disbelief in equal measure. 'Why are you sorry? Or have you been secretly writing a blog about your hidden life that I don't know about? Desperate Dad, Pissed-off Parent...'

Ted snorts through his nose. 'No. But I'm sorry I wasn't paying proper attention. For quite a while now, it seems. It's funny, though, to hear you talk about loneliness into that iPad back there. Because I think, maybe... at times I've felt lonely, since we've had Cherry.'

'Really?' I ask in a small voice.

He waves his hands over his pint. 'I love her. I never want to go back to a time before she came. She is almost everything to me. But the two of you, you have this crazy-close bond. Right from day one. She only wants you to soothe her to sleep. Only you to feed her, give her a bath. Sometimes I feel like the spare part. I suggest stuff to mix it up, but then feel like I'm just making it worse. For the first few months I felt like' – he looks up at the ceiling – 'a bit of a sham of a dad. And... I don't know, I can't put this stuff into words that easily... so I think I get why you didn't tell me how you were feeling.'

A mouthful of cider almost goes down the wrong way. 'You felt like a sham, too?'

'All the time. And you just seemed so in sync with Cherry, to know exactly what she needed and have this amazing patience and skill in being her mum. So I figured, if I couldn't help you with the parenting bit so much, I should be...' He shrugs. 'The provider. A few times you sort of said you weren't sure about going back to work full time. So I set myself this goal.' He takes a drink. 'To earn enough, and fast, where you could stay home full time, if you wanted. So…'

'You started working more, and harder, to get promoted?'

He nods.

'And I felt you were getting further away by obsessing about work, when really you were doing it to be closer to us.'

Ted looks right into my eyes, creases forming above his cheeks. 'Yes. But it was a bit of a dickish move, in hindsight. I can't expect a better bond with the chunk if I'm just not there.'

I cover his hand with mine. 'Hey. Come on. We've *both* been a couple of dicks.'

A relaxed smile spreads over his whole face.

I swallow. 'So, what do we do about Hong Kong?'

'It's clearly off the table.'

I slap my palm to my forehead. 'The press stuff ruined it, didn't it? I knew it! Oh god, I'm sorry. I mean, I really didn't want to go but I didn't want you to get fired!' My voice squeaks at the end.

'Hey, hey! I didn't get fired. Actually, they kind of loved the attention. Digital Asset Management doesn't often make the headlines and they got some good website traffic out of it. I think it gave me' – he cringes as he does the air quotes with his fingers – '"cool points". But right from when we fell out about the job, it hit me like a punch to the guts that I'd gone in the wrong direction. So I went out there really to see how I could politely turn it down and still work at the company. And maybe speak to HR about a better work–life balance. Reading all your blog posts from my hotel room only made me realise more and more how much had been going on under my nose that

302

I'd missed through living for my emails. So I needed time to sort a few things.'

'Oh.' I gulp some more cider.

'They've said they don't want to lose me. And they're happy for us to have a trial run at four days a week. I'll drop some direct reports, which is more than fine by me. But...' He rips the corner off a beer mat.

'But?'

'It obviously means a fifth less money, at the end of the day. So it has to be something we're both cool about. Holidays won't be as fancy. You wouldn't have the option of giving up work completely—'

'I don't want that!' I blurt the words before I've even thought them.

Ted frowns. 'You don't?'

'No. No, God, no! I think I said that because I was absolutely bricking it about going back to my old role with my confidence like a damp doily. But I want to work. Some kind of work, at least. I'm not one hundred per cent what kind, but I need to use my brain again and I want to get paid.'

'Well, that's a fucking relief.' Ted puts both hands behind his head.

'I nearly had a First-Time Mum book deal.'

'You did?'

'Well, I had the chance at trying for one, maybe. If I was lucky. Not sure how that will go now.' I rip an edge off my own beer mat and add it to Ted's, making a tiny pile. 'But Sarah came to see me, last Sunday, and just talking about the spin we used to pull made me really miss that part of my life. That part of my brain. I don't know if going back to the office is the answer, though.'

Ted shuffles his stool round to my side of the table so we're next to each other. 'I don't think we have to sort that now. Shall we just park ourselves here and promise to actually talk like grown-ups from now on, yeah?' His arm slots easily around my shoulders as he pulls me in. Hugo Boss. Oh, I have missed this.

I shut my eyes and just breathe.

'Oh, hey, it's YOU!' A slightly too-loud voice startles me from what was the best moment of my year.

When my eyes flick open, I see Long Haired Ginger teen, from the pub quiz.

'Oh, hey,' I force, as I can feel Ted's muscles tightening beneath me. As if braced for some other bonkers revelation in the Stevie experience. Had I joined a cult with this guy? Made him Cherry's legal guardian?

The teen nods, his waterfall of red hair echoing the action. 'Mummy Pig and the workhouse, yeah?'

Ted mutters, 'Oh, come on.'

I decide to dredge up a little more of old-school Stevie. I plaster on a mega-watt smile. 'Great to see you again! But we're kind of in the middle of something here, so if you could—'

Social niceties, however obvious, do not hold water with an eighteen year old. Ginger Guy pulls up a spare stool without asking and joins us. 'Saw you online. Man! Look, I shouldn't ask this but I have this blog – about anime – and I really want to get it off the ground. Do you do any consulting work?'

Just as I'm working up a direct response to close down this extra strand of crazy, Ted clears his throat and chimes in, 'Maybe. But you couldn't afford her, mate. She's national news. She's *First-Time Mum*.'

Epilogue

The British weather has given ParentFest a dose of its finest: a morning of elephant-grey skies and showers, so that we all felt crap and like giving up as gazebos and hog roasts were erected in the drizzly damp. But, just as we were on the ropes, a needle of sunshine poked through, followed by another and another until – bam! – we had a warm day perfect for mooching and drinking and relaxing, albeit with a few wet bums from the hay bales and a little bit of mud splattered up the ankles. But that, as Nelle kept reminding us as we took tickets at the entrance gate, only 'added to the authenticity'.

Ted's new four-day week gave me the focus and head-space I needed to really help Nelle properly as the festival came together. I even took baby steps in setting up phone interviews with local newspapers as the event's official PR spokesperson, and thinking more outside the box about getting in touch with food magazines and music ones too, plus some parenting glossies, whose readers would totally get why we were launching a new kind of festival. With some of the PR hitting home, some clever ad placements by Nelle's company, Will forcing the mum-mums to get on board as local 'influencers' at the school gates, we were sold out. And it felt awesome.

I'm not sure 'awesome' is quite how Ted would describe his new Cherry Fridays. Possibly 'awesome' with a caveat of 'knackering but also' or 'bedtime is'. But he is loving it. He has decided she's just going to have to get used to him putting her to bed and doing the bath more and more, and he's going to dig deep and find more patience for her loud protests when she voices her opinion. Opinionated: that's my girl. He might not always do this less-than-full-time week but for now it has really brought them closer together, and it has loosened the tight feeling around my ribcage that I sometimes felt when he'd go off to work on a Monday morning. I am not in this domestic lark entirely alone any more.

And he's loved getting behind ParentFest in his own way too, putting Nelle in touch with someone to maximise her search engine optimisation and doing some serious manly bonding with Will over which retail part-ners to invite to show their wares. Will had called all his favourite suppliers of cookware, artisanal produce and needlessly lush, personalised stationary from his time at Selfridges. Just the kind of thing that slightly sloshed parents happily treat themselves to. The two men also almost bought a time-share in the world's most overpriced indoor barbecue together, before I shut that nonsense down. And today, on the big day, Ted's ripping tickets and fixing wristbands alongside me. Cherry is in her 'eagle's nest' as we like to call it – a second-hand baby carrier that gets worn in the backpack position, so she can peer out from over Ted's shoulder like the imperious overlord she is. She is inspecting every face that passes by our table and is in busybody heaven. She has only been the tiniest bit sick twice down Ted's back. (I've now ripped up a spare muslin to tie around his neck. We are the MacGyvers of parenting.)

When our shift on entrance duty is over, we can start to enjoy the day proper. Ted insisted he didn't want to drop Cherry in the kids' enclosure, as safe and secure as it was, because he didn't want her to miss out, and my chest went fluttery at the words. 'But,' he added, 'next year, when she'll be walking? I'm shoving her in there with ankle weights.' It's so rewarding that our parenting styles are now completely in tune with each other.

I'm looking forward to cutting loose today – there's been a lot of intense graft from Nelle's clan to get the day together in such a short time, with Will and I doing our bit to be useful and hopefully not just get in the way. I want to raise a glass with my mates and my family to all that's got us here. I've had a handful of hard stares as families pass through the ticket checkpoint – some people are just never going to change their perception of me as First-Time Mum from what the newspaper put out there. And I have to live with that. The exposure helped make this day a big financial boost for Nelle's family company and – weirdly, ever so weirdly – it helped Ted and me sort ourselves out. And my mum is apparently dining out on the story over in San Jose. Cheers, Mum. With just 45 minutes left to go before we can venture in towards fancy bratwurst and fruity-smelling beers and a neck rub from the Massage Angels. I can deal with whatever grumps pass my table before then.

Grumps, yes. Perfect blow dries and Von Trap children? Eh, not so much. Chloe and her poster-family are marching towards us. She's got a half-smile ready to go, so I'm not sure if she's going to choose blanking me or some snide little dig to make her mark. That's fine. The acceptance of the mum–mums is no longer an issue. I'm winging it and I'm proud.

Her beefy and equally blond husband stalks past, the children obediently following in his Italian loafer foot-prints, but Chloe is slower to hand over her batch of tickets. In fact, as I go to take them off her with a poo-eating smile, she doesn't release them to me.

'Tickets?' I say brightly.

'I just want to say…' she mumbles, so I have to lean forward, catching a whiff of her expensive botanical shampoo. God, it smells impossibly good. 'I've wanted to say' – she breaks off eye contact and instead stares at her fancy wellies – 'I love your blog. It means so much to me. And I should have said that, when all the stuff was going on in the papers, but I didn't want to meddle…'

My eyes are aching slightly, they are so wide. What?! Empress Queen of the mum-mums read my blog?!

'You actually…' she continues, 'messaged me a few times? BBootsMum? My bluebell boots, you see.' She lifts one dainty foot and I find myself gawping.

'But – but – you always seemed like you couldn't stand me!' I say, before the PR in me has time to swallow the words back down and smooth everything along.

Her face gives a wince of what looks like genuine pain. 'Oh god, Terry is always saying I can be such a cold fish. But I get so shy, I never know *what* to say with new people. I tried talking to you a few times, out and about, and always bottled it. Like at that lovely craft thing, I just got all tongue-tied. At the café, too. And the school mums are always expecting me to turn up looking smart and the kids all matching and sometimes the exhaustion of getting us out of the house all neat and pressed just *kills* my social energies, you know?'

I can't help my laugh. But at us both. 'I do know. I do. Well, BBootsMum, it is so lovely to finally meet you.

"IRL." Come and find me later and we can really talk, yes?'

She smiles sweetly and almost bounds away. I guess Will was right. Not all mum-mums are intrinsically bad.

Man, this would make a good blog post – we're all for embracing the chaos in our parenting lives but that shouldn't mean we should judge the glossy, either. They could be having just as crap a day as us, and they have to work in a thirty-minute blow dry in the midst of it. Maybe I'll draft something next Friday, from my working spot in the local Costa. I'm not posting anything new right now, because I'm actually in talks with a big parenting forum about doing a regular blog through them. The advantage is they manage all the back-end stuff – how the advertising works, plus any troll-like comments – so I can get a steady payment and just let my opinions fly. Sounds good right now. There's still time for me to think through if or how I'd go back to my day job and I'm not putting myself under pressure to make any huge decisions too soon – rushing into things has not exactly played out well for me in the past. Officially, I need to talk to my bosses when Cherry is about nine months old, so just taking things a few weeks at a time for now is working for us. Any new steps forward are going to be family ones. Maybe we won't get where we're going all that fast or efficiently, but we'll get there together.

Someone squeezes me round the waist. 'Alright, Stew, I'm letting you off early for good behaviour.'

Nelle's face is slightly shiny with sun cream and perspiration but happiness is glowing from every pore. She's actually without her customary sling and wee Joe today – his grandparents have taken him into the kids' enclosure and are happy sitting in there with a cup of tea, far from 'the noise', as they have termed our music selection.

'Really? Are you sure?'

She folds her arms. 'Don't you have a hot date to meet?'

Ted holds up his hand but she pokes him in the ribs so he's forced to cave. 'No, *actually hot*. Like "literary agent hot".'

'Mean.' Ted sticks out his lower lip. It's actually rather adorable.

I check my phone for the hundredth time this morning. Francesca had said she'd be arriving around about now and I suppose me ripping her ticket like an amateur usherette might not be the most professional image to project. Plus, I could do with quickly sorting my hair in the Portaloos first.

She was brilliant when I got in touch the week after Ted returned, explaining that I needed more time than I originally projected to get the material to her (I had been ever so slightly manically overzealous in promising just a few weeks) because I needed some family time. And I also said I completely understood if the recent coverage had put her off. I think her instant reply was something like, 'Are you mad?!' Apparently her publisher mate had been hounding her for any news of my sample since the paper coverage broke and my 'five minutes of fame' kicked into gear.

Since then, I have worked on some chapters I'm really happy with – scrap that, I'm *damn proud* of them – and she's sent some notes back that all make sense. So she's coming today so we can meet in person (while her kid goes nuts on the bouncy castle and her other half dives deep into some paella), and make sure we're the right fit to work together. It feels like a teenage first date and a job interview all in one. So, yes, my palms are like wet wipes right now. But not as hygienic.

Nelle gently shoves me towards the field. 'Go. Be free, get a book deal. Just dedicate the whole thing to me, yeah?'

I pull her into a massive hug. 'I do owe it to you,' I say right in her ear. 'And Will. And the creep who tracked down my IP address. But he's not going in the acknowledgments. And Ted and Cherry, too, of course.' I pull back and tickle the toes of my hefty love as they dangle out of the carrier. Ted smiles down at me. 'We're all in this together. That's the one thing I know for certain.'

Acknowledgements

Thank-you to all at Canelo for supporting me in writing another book that's very close to my heart. You guys are THE BEST. And biggest thanks to my editor, Louise: attentive, intuitive, wise. I hope I haven't spoilt anything for you...

I have been so lucky in my life to know and love and learn from some extraordinary mums. Firstly and most importantly, my own. She makes Mary Poppins look like a trainee babysitter. She is all things kind, patient, giving, fun and creative and I only aspire to be the kind of mother she has been to me. (FYI my dad is also a smasher.)

To the very special mum mates who've helped me find and keep my sanity again in a post-baby world: Emma D, Sarah, Vicki, Emma S and Vanessa. Thank you for listening to every mad panic and whine, and for reminding me that things look better if you just stop, breathe and laugh about them.

To the bloggers whose honesty gave me strength in my most weepy, self-doubting times with a newborn: The Unmumsy Mum and Like Real Life. You do good work. Please never stop.

The health visitors in this book are very much modelled on the lovely ones I've met during my time as a mum and I'll never forget the time one patient lady really did give me a Penguin biscuit and a safe space to cry without judgement. That meant so much to me then, and still does now.

To the Whisky Soc.: thanks for the memories, and the owls. But, seriously, no more owls. Please.

Thanks to my other half for the child-free weekend hours to write and for being the best dad I could imagine. The biggest stretch for my imagination in writing this book was inventing a husband who didn't pick up on feelings and talk them through in that moment. Also one who never cooked the dinner or set off the dishwasher. Though Ted's dumping of shoes and bags and coats is ALL you.

And big, squashy, juicy thanks to all the readers and bloggers and Tweeters who come along for the ride! It means so much that you've picked up this book.

Author's note

If you've just read this book and thought, 'What a load of silly moaning about babies. Mountain out of a molehill or what! It's not rocket science. Be grateful for nature's finest miracle, etc, etc,' then I am SO, SO, SO glad for you that you have had or only ever known lovely, easy babies, who sleep and smile and sit quietly. But that's not been my experience to date, and so I've drawn on what I know.

I don't think it's mutually exclusive to love the bones of someone and also admit that they can test your patience sometimes. To the point of mouthing swear words behind a cupboard door. We all have very different parenting paths and I wish you the very best on yours, as I trip and trudge and skip and dance along mine, in my own way.

Thanks ever so.

Poppy x